Claudine Giovannoni was born shortly before Christmas, in 1959 in Locarno – Switzerland. Since youth, she was enthralled by learning foreign languages and cultures. She lived and studied in the USA and in the Dominican Republic, she fluently speaks 7 languages and her commitment is to help children and animals in need.

She is, as well, deeply interested in philosophy and theology. All these topics mixed together brought her to travel around the world. She takes inspiration from real life experiences and subconscious ones, transcribing her happenings into novels or poems.

"Annwyn's Secret" (Il segreto degli Annwyn) is her fourth novel, now translated into English, and soon into Portuguese.

There were agreements with the Torino Film Lab for transposition of the novel into a movie.

Previously she published the novels: "The Sun's Kumihimo" (Il Kumihimo del sole), "The Crystal of peace" (Il Cristallo della Pace), "Mist on the moor" (Nebbie nella Brughiera) and as well the poetry anthology "Traces". She published as well several short stories in Italian anthologies.

Her next novel "Taiga's Dream" (Piccoli passi nella Taiga) will soon be published, first in Italian and after in English.

But most important, the adventure of Chrysalis and her brother Joshua, will continue with the second volume entitled "The vibrational matrix".

THE ANNWYN'S SECRET

Year 2222: humans have to rebuild on the ruins of a world ravaged by natural disasters. The young Chrysalis finds a strange object, which is not of human nature. She is an *"annwyn"* provided with great capabilities, which not even the Experimental Team of the new born Unified Power can oppose.

Focus is given to REM, the paradoxical sleep. Dreams are the key to opening the *"Mystical Gate"* which allows entry to other Dimensions. But there are obscure forces working, and the Unified Power is aware that only an *"annwyn"* can operate a *"Vibratory Matrix"*.

Chrysalis may discover more mysteries related to the people living next to her since some of them are hiding further secrets.

Chrysalis' past lives and the search of the Collective Memory play a determinant role. She must choose between accepting herself as she is becoming an instrument of power which may also damage other human beings.

But actually the *"Vibratory Matrix"* could be, in the wrong hands, another terrible instrument of destruction.

About the Author

As a citizen of the world, she travelled by land, sea and air always looking for new emotions and learning about other cultures.

She is very sensitive and looks at the world "with the eyes of the heart." In all her novels, the respect of the Fauna and Flora is the issue dealt with extreme rigor.

She is convinced that "our life is as a pentagram: day after day we insert our actions, our thought, our dreams and these *notes* from a *melody* which changes as the events involve us."
She feels like a composer who desire to leave a sign over the pentagram of the existence... to defend this wonderful planet Earth.

Dedication

The Annwyn's Secret is dedicated to the dreamer, especially to Chrysalis that appeared to me in a dream and asked me to write her story.

Claudine Giovannoni

THE ANNWYN'S SECRET

AUSTIN MACAULEY
PUBLISHERS LTD.

A CIP catalogue record for this title is available from the British Library.

ISBN 9781785544637 (Paperback)
ISBN 9781785544644 (Hardback)
ISBN 9781785544651 (E-Book)

www.austinmacauley.com

Published in English (2016)
Austin Macauley Publishers Ltd.
25 Canada Square
Canary Wharf
London
E14 5LQ

First published (2013)
Edizioni Ulivo – Balena (Switzerland)
ISBN 978 88 98018 07 9

Acknowledgments

While writing the text I got a lot of information from the website of the Stazione Celeste and from several other written philosophy and theology scripts.

If every experience is an apprenticeship, my life's experience can be summarised in this work rich of vibrational emotions. Maybe it's concerned with my other lives remembrance, where every fact is recorded in the karmic memory of each sentient being.

But in order to take advantage of these experiences, I had to open the view that thus enabled me to perceive reality not only as a reaction to some facts, but as a relevance of awareness of my Mind/Soul's consciousness.

But what is the dichotomy between the real and the unreal? And what if both were co-existing? I don't deny that the ancient Celtic legends have always intrigued me in a special manner: those dealing with the Human and the Divine!

Embroidered like drops of dew on blades of grass stirred by the northern wind, these Legends and Rites became the fulcrum around which the novel develops. It is a sort of fabric, into which I then braided and weaved my experiences, many myths and a good portion of fantasy.

For those who know me, I am eternally wandering aimlessly, desperately searching for our true human identity where the bipolarity of the Divine breaks into that one of the Evil being. Always ephemeral in the flesh, but immortal in the essence of our soul!

Thus to all the people who have, although in an indirect way, helped to intrigue my mind, I extend my deep gratitude and appreciation.

I tell you that I made several changes by transposing real facts into imagination. The text should be read and intended as a novel and not scientific material or similar. The mental processes are my personal suggestions without any actual paramedical or parapsychological importance.

If I describe events that will happen in the year 2022, it is for superstition, if I may so call it, because I'm sure something is bound to happen, but won't necessarily lead to the annihilation of 3 billion people.

After all, the subject matter is about the eternal war of good against evil, of what is considered right or wrong, of the conflict between the divine and the diabolical, as well as of human selfishness in relations with his fellows and with the Nature, flora and fauna.

Although it is a text of a marked chimerical character, I tried to use names and terminology in order to allow a pleasant, easy reading, albeit an addictive one.

Here I take as well the opportunity to express my gratitude to my husband Massimo and to my children, Emanuele Giosuè and Sara Luna. They too are real dreamers who have contributed to the evolution and provided very valuable inspirations to this written adventure, which has taken more than three years!

A very special and heartfelt thanks to Professor Alberto Jelmini and again to my husband, who have given me their patience in the difficult task of reading the "first outline" and by giving me valuable suggestions for the final draft of the novel.

My genuine thanks also to Guido Monte, who helped me to translate the titles into Latin, a language that I love but unfortunately [in this life] I still haven't learned!

Introduction by Prof. PhD A. Jelmini

Claudine Giovannoni never ceases to amaze with this astonishing new Novel!

After the escapes and pursuits in the Pacific Islands (The Sun's Kumihimo - Il Kumihimo del Sole), which later became a perilous journey through the doors that separates the possible dimensions of the human mind (The crystal of Peace - Il Cristallo della Pace), everything always filled and pervaded with a deep love for our Planet and the desire to save it from the implicit dangers of the disordered and selfish progress; after the romantic succession, always fraught with danger and marked by unexpected twists, from the blur of a distant past existences right into the present lives (Fog on the Moor - Nebbie nella Brughiera), here in this new Novel, she propels us into the realm of Norse mythology. And she does it, as always, with blindly cuts, combined with a sure hand, which gives the text a scent of a strong psychological eerie.

At the centre of the story is a mysterious and magical object (the *Vibrational matrix*), around which as mentioned about the Kumihimo, rotates the whole story. But if in the first novel the events gave rise to a small epic poem (also because the protagonists are children), with run-up and chases that make us discover beautiful and not well known corners of our globe, thus these events develop first along a horizontal line (although the awareness of some of the characters show us a depth-self inner search). In this compelling and gripping new novel, the vertical line is dominant, while attending a triangle of movements between Ascona, Paris and Ireland.

But the verticality is presented on every page, along two directions: first through Time, by the Druids to the residents of the 23rd century (when the story takes place), and secondly in the growth, in parallel, of the ability of the Mind, skills that are manifested in the search for past lives and the capacity to pass through the doors that separate the different reality-sizes. Here we can see all Claudine's skill, who knows various ways to differentiate these "discoveries" concerning the strength of mind among people who seek to acquire, with selfishness, personal benefit, and people who want to put their knowledge and resources for the benefit of mankind's life and the Planet that hosts them. But not only this: the story is steeped in mystery due to the fact that in addition to the characters of which we understand very well, we find others that deliberately, just as in a detective story worthy of respect, some of them hide their true intentions. Even the characters that turn around the protagonist, a young *Annwyn* (person able to separate Mind from body and move into Time-Space), projects over her a shadow of doubt by casting in her soul deep, even painful, conscience's fears.

The most significant, with a superb choice of time and space (an extremely old yew tied to the oldest age of Irish Legends) is about the love that is subtly to differentiate between the most sensual one, linked to beauty and physical strength, and the other one which instead leans towards the bliss of the soul and the power of sacrifice. All wrapped in a scenario full of light and shade, mysterious dungeons and wild nature, makes us think of Botticelli's Primavera, which, although in a calmer and more classic atmosphere, paints this dualism, leading to the answer given by the victory of the noblest.

Chapter 1

The Vibratory Matrix

The rain pours over the rooftops of the city still enveloped in darkness. The silvery flashes of lightning, ripped through the night sky, illuminate the steps of the woman who runs at breakneck speed along the bike path that extends beside the lake. The long flowered skirt is glued to her body, highlighting her thin figure. With an angry gesture of her hands, she raises the fabric just enough to clear the knees to facilitate her movements. The long amber hair, collected over the nape, wriggles to the rhythm of her quick steps.

The smell of the water penetrates everything, with arrogance, creeping into the nostrils of the woman. There are sparkling rivulets along the edges of the sidewalks carrying a few leaves torn from the branches of the nearby trees by the force of the wind. Everything is enveloped in darkness, every form seems to come to life whenever a flash profanes the sky. The trees rise like ghosts of other worlds, driven by the fury of the elements. Are those the moments where the human is related to the divine, those moments of profound atavistic fear in which man realizes the tremendous force of Nature?

Apparently everyone is asleep, living dreams representing a kind of parallel life in which each one finds themselves unconditionally. It's the frustration that sometimes generates anxiety that becomes nightmares in those who, dropping all barriers, finds themselves in a dream-like sketch which involves them in the daily life.

But it is not like that for everyone: there are people who consciously know how to teleport from one dimension to another, psychically forcing entry into the paranormal world, where they can manipulate their very existence. These faculties are believed to be reserved only for the followers of esoteric occult practices, but later were revealed as innate qualities of the "dreamers".

These "dreamers", commonly called *Annwyn*, although their molecular structure is exactly equal to ours to protect them by disguising their presence among us, have immeasurable powers of the mind.

The *Annwyn* began to arrive in large numbers on planet Earth around the end of the second millennium. Initially, beginning in the Seventies, they were treated as anomalous cases, sometimes subjected to real psychological torture, confined in hospitals and sedated through the administration of psychotropic drugs. They were always restless and peevish children who made life a living hell for their parents. Then, growing up, they had become hyperactive students and always at the centre of conflicts and disputes. There have been a myriad of theses written about them, each one crazier than the last. Only later, at the discovery of ancient *codes*, was the real reason for their presence on planet Earth recognised: to help human beings to grow spiritually and then escape from the imminent global catastrophe predicted since ancient times.

The woman who pursues her destiny is in fact one of them: an *Annwyn* and her name is Chrysalis, Chrisa to her friends.

Chrisa stops for a few seconds, looking at her back. She's breathless and she feels *his* presence. She's aware that the pursuer will not give her a break until her exit from the REM phase.[1]

She loses her balance for a split second, stepping on something slippery and, full of surprise, she bent toward the ground, seeing a strange, relatively small artefact. Despite the danger of losing the advantage that separated her from the pursuer, with the typical curiosity of the *Annwyn*, Chrysalis collects the object from the ground without even verifying its nature, hurriedly put it in the bag that she carries on the shoulder.

Cascades of water flooded the strip of asphalt that was the cycling path, painted green which, like a poisonous snake, streaked further east, towards the port. There was no living soul around at that inappropriate hour; soon the dawn will start to illuminate the sky from the East and erase the fears of the night.

*** Matrix Motus ***

On the boat, definitely still blissfully asleep and completely unaware of what's happening inside the dream world of an *Annwyn*, is Chrysalis' brother, Joshua.

---

[1] Rapid eye movement is indicated most frequently by the acronym REM, is the "rapid eye movement" that occurs during a phase of sleep accompanied by other bodily physiological alterations. REM sleep is also called paradoxical sleep and is accompanied by dreams.

Chrisa jumps over the barrier of the dock and launches herself in a last effort along the boards that look like the keyboard of an old piano, so much they shine in the scary glow of lightning.

But the curiosity, which most of the time the young woman can't handle, is always stronger than the immense wisdom that should be inherent in her being. For her, it is a real dilemma of not being able to refrain from the uncertainty of most often risky decisions.

"I must stop, once and for all! But why can't I lead a normal life, like him?"

Chrisa bent and kiss on the forehead her brother asleep.

"Damn those who have bequeathed us this M*ission*: is it possible that humans should be forced to require *our presence* in order to progress in their spiritual evolution?"

The woman is nearing her physical shell, which is lying helplessly curled in a foetal position; she slips her bag from over her shoulder and throws it on the ground. The vibration in the surrounding air is altered, assuming a very intense golden colour: the energies of the two camps - the astral and the material - gathering together while the *Annwyn* falls into her physical structure.

At dawn Joshua wakes up in a good mood. He goes on the deck of the sailboat, checks the ropes that moor the boat, then, running, he reaches the shore.

"Hi, Marius! Are you ready for tomorrow's race? Look, this time my sister and I will give you a hard time!"

Joshua watches the old man with eyes that sparkle with cunning, while he grabs the handlebars of the electric bicycle. Along the lake there are already a lot of people, tourists and inhabitants of the village, taking a relaxing morning walk.

A day seemingly like any other: the air is charged with the perfume of flowers, a gentle breeze rattles the iron rigging of the moored sailboats, as the first rays of sunshine caress the landscape with tingling heat.

Some men of the Experimental Team, accompanied by their enormous cats resembling a genetic mongrel between a jaguar and a bobcat, do not go unnoticed because of their blue and silver uniforms. They stop a few individuals and are about to verify the identity papers before carrying out a body search.

Marius glares with a significant look in the direction of Joshua; his face scorched by the sun doesn't betray his disapproval, but he makes no comment on the newcomers. He pretends to be too busy to curl up a rope and, approached the boy.

"Watch out, small fresh-water wolf," he whispers, "I don't believe that you and Chrisa are capable of beating me, I'm far too smart! The proof is that instead of sleeping or wandering far and wide with the bicycle, I sail to train a bit. And remember the old saying, 'laughs best who laughs last'. Come on up, run to get fresh bread at Fabrizio's shop before all the chocolate croissants are sold. Wolverine that you are! See you for a bit of *pasta and potatoes* at noon? Ask your sister to get busy in the kitchen, she's a good cook, and I'll take the sweet goody!"

Joshua readjusts his slightly wavy black hair, his eyes, bright as a pool of sunlit river water, rests upon the figure of his friend. Then he returns back an amused grimace to the elderly gentleman, who makes a sign with his head, laying a finger over his lips, in the direction of the agents. It had not escaped the boy that those of the security force had loaded the arrested people onto the armoured SUV.

"Brrr... We won't see those guys again."

Then, he continues turning to Marius with an excited look:

21

"Well? For lunch will you bring some more of that wondrous concoction? Holy God, I still haven't digested the sort of potion whose recipe claims to be the work of the ancient Druids. Anything except apricot's cream! Okay. Let's go for the *pasta and potatoes*. We'll see each other at 1:00 PM on the Avalon's Mist."

The young man jumps on the saddle of his bike and moves away quickly, pedalling at a good pace as if to prove to his elderly friend that he actually trains for the race as well!

Chapter 2

Divining Force

Chrisa, after waking up in a murky mood, quickly begins to write the details of the past night's travels in her Moleskin notebook. Her soaked clothes drained onto the floor, leaving a conspicuous patch of water: the colourful flowered skirt looks like a spring flowerbed, soaked by the sudden downpour.

The young woman is aware that these records are important for her present existence for the purpose of leaving a lasting impression if something unexpected happens. How long had she lived with these strange premonitions? They were like the swallows foreseeing a sudden weather change. It's a kind of oscillation in the solar plexus, a contraction that induced her to be prudent. For this reason, transcribing everything had become a habit, a ritual.

*** Vis Divinationis ***

The young woman was able to read, write and speak eight languages perfectly from the age of three. She was considered a prodigy child by several doctors who had visited her, in short, a kind of *paranormal creature* as indeed were all the *Annwyn* children considered.

These singularities have forced the *Annwyn children*, at least initially, to lead strange, segregated lives because they didn't need to attend schools. Their ancestral memory has a potential that other sentient beings don't have: Chrisa remembered many previous lives, and much more... maybe too much! The young woman cursed this power which, several times, had caused her big problems.

During the first years of life, Chrisa's parents were very protective towards her; only after her eighth birthday did she learn of the existence of other young people with similar psychic qualities.

Through the intercession of the Unified Power, these young people obtained a special treatment by the authorities and they received some sort of unparalleled protection. They were given the opportunity to participate at the Supreme Congress, where only the key figures in the conduction of the Planet Earth had access. Chrisa had by then already crossed the *"Al-Hillah"* of Ishtar, home of the Unified Power during a couple of her *dream trips*, although this was highly prohibited.

After the year 2200, each *Annwyn* was regarded by ordinary mortals a sort of ascetic or sage. They were given the onerous task of aiding the human race in the ascent towards the perfection of Mind, enlightenment, or even simply *in the reunion with the Essence*. The harsh living conditions, even aggravated by a kind of repression by the Unified Power, had brought most wisdom to the humans.

But to err is still always human and unfortunately many of the errors that occurred after 1900s did not serve as a warning. There was something intrinsic, which was thought to be inherent in human DNA: the presence of *evil*. Hence the eternal struggle of Good vs. Evil! Throughout the ages, man progressed and then fell into the limbo of his own irresponsibility and continued to wander and generate horror and destruction around him.

The Unified Power, even awakening great opposition between free thinkers and scientists, allowed only the select few to conceive. When a man and a woman joined together in marriage they had the opportunity to seek permission to procreate, but not without first being subjected to a severe examination related to morality and ethics. The Unified Power had the conviction that only couples capable of managing in full consciousness the birth of a child, could raise the offspring in the dignity and morality.

But they concentrated only on the genetic effects; in fact, few theosophists in the ranks of the Unified Power welcomed the definition of karmic Mind/Soul and its itinerary linked to karmic-imprints generated during previous existences. And this was an unforgivable mistake, a mistake that unfortunately would again affect humanity!

Being an *Annwyn*, Chrisa could choose her genetic parents and the environment in which she wanted to live; to be reincarnated as soon as the *shell* that housed her needed to be abandoned. But an *Annwyn* is long-lived, and time does not mark her body as it would an ordinary human being's. The passage through death and rebirth is a sort of metamorphosis, painless and self-imposed, that the members of the Unified Power had tried, unsuccessfully, to decode.

But this is a kind of secret that every *Annwyn* guards jealously and carefully. Chrisa, some years before, as a result of the immense pain felt at the disappearance of her parents and overcome by a profound need to share, had confided to her brother a few details, but without ever going into the information about the obscure symbols that concealed the true identity of the *Annwyn*.

The bond between Joshua and his sister was very deep, even if sometimes the unsociable character of both siblings ended up creating some bickering and dissension. Joshua feels deference to what he can't explain in simple words. All the magic that hovers around the *Annwyn* are not matters on which the young man loved to talk or quibble about.

Chrysalis sensed that there was something else that brought them together, something that she has not yet been able to discover. And, perhaps for this reason, the girl began to introduce her brother to the enigmas of the *Annwyn,* in small steps, to avoid unnecessary fear and anxiety in his mind. The girl kept to herself the legend of the *Codes* and the *Sacred Mirror*, which would make it possible to exit from the cycle of life, death and rebirth.

Their mother and father had died some years before, in strange circumstances; even the agents of the Experimental Team were not able to examine the reasons or motives. But Chrisa thought she knew. She is sure to know the truth, because in many of her dream-travels she meets the only *Presence* that she thinks could upset the existence of mankind: Hathor.

With these thoughts swirling in her mind like butterflies gone mad between stormy whirlwinds, Chrisa slips into the small shower so that the hot water could awaken her from the slumber of her nocturnal raids.

"Brrrr… Damn, Joshua has used all the hot water in the tank; I don't want to wait an hour for it to warm up. Let us have courage, I shall hurry up and not waste time as usual."

From the shores of the lake up to the oldest part of the town, miraculously restored a century after the cataclysm, you need just a few pedal strokes. Joshua could cover the stretch of road on foot, but he felt the same reverence for his electric bike as he did for Avalon's Mist, their sailboat.

The bike was a gift from their father; who always had a deep respect for nature and tried to preserve its charm in every way. He was a man of science, very wise and respected. He was a careful and strict father, but full of feeling towards his two children.

Both Chrisa and Joshua had been accustomed since they were very small to nourish respect of the flora and fauna. Their parents were always mobilized whenever emergency situations required the direct involvement of citizens.

The rise in global temperature over the centuries had contributed to a succession of terrible ecological disasters. This had changed the geology of the planet in an irreversible way, forcing the residents to reach safety zones. As time passed, new environmental groups took critical positions in the matter of saving the planet, since the events at the beginning of the third millennium had upset the ecological balance.

There were very strict laws enacted which punished offenders by forcing them into segregation in hospitals or even into hibernation. There were many strange voices that reported what really happened in these hospitals. Centuries before, it was said, in the heart of the Amazonian rainforest, one of the great lungs of the planet, was discovered a tiny parasitic fungus, the *Cordyceps Unilateralis.*

This fungus was accidentally found by looking at insects that had changed their behaviour in an unusual way. The tiny spores of the fungus had entered the bodies of the insects through the respiratory tract, changing their perceptions and instincts. These were then used as a breeding ground and an incubator for fungal proliferation.

Offenders confined in hospitals and laboratories owned by the Unified Power were exposed to direct contact with the *Cordyceps Unilateralis.* The fungus proceeded to destroy the individual, condemning them to progressive physiological destruction and bringing death in a few weeks. Nothing illegal, apparently; Nature rebelled against those creatures that didn't deserve to live.

Thanks to these drastic repression measures, the Unified Power was finally been able to control the rampant plague that had been deliberately ignored for too many centuries. Perhaps even, thanks to authorized procreation, crime was now under control.

The new generations of the third millennium had gradually begun to bring the Order and the Knowledge; much had been permanently changed after the terrible events that took place in the year 2022. With the arrival of the *Annwyn* on the planet, the visionary dreams pursued by various so called 'New Age' movements, had finally become reality: the Vibration of human beings and therefore the elevation of the planet Earth itself into other Spheres, was about to be implemented.

But for centuries, always lurking, very influential and powerful people, unscrupulous individuals who seek hegemony only for their personal interests, existed. These people, from the beginning, strongly opposed the Unified Power.

The Unified Power had to take drastic measures: the Experimental Team was created shortly after introducing Martial Law, and despite its unbreakable power, sometimes evil could still get away unpunished.

Some of them relied on pseudo-scientists trying to find the elixir of immortality, or that passage which would open a path through the grid of Time. Those who refused to cooperate and worked against the Unified Power were eliminated.

But the assassins of Chrisa and Joshua's parents were able to disappear without a trace; unfortunately such events continued to happen every day, despite the *vigilantes* who were attempting to protect their fellow citizens. They helped each other, working together to prevent acts of vandalism and crime; everyone could intervene directly to protect human rights. In more complicated cases, they called the Experimental Team, who immediately interposed to restore order.

The new pedagogical model used since about hundred years ago had allowed the use of a new kind of teaching. The new model emphasized Respect and Cohesion. Unfortunately, it was centuries before fate would bring the Unified Power to finally make the decisive step, by which time Nature had suffered irreversible damage and thousands of species were extinct.

Two hundred years of history had so substantially transformed the political economy and the financial world. Furthermore, due to the presence of these unique creatures, the opening to 'other Spheres' was facilitated and the exchange could take place over several vibrations' levels, although this practice was only granted to the *Annwyn*. This last was then treated with special respect and reverence, albeit with a certain circumspection.

The fragrant smell of the bread tickles Joshua's nose, and he looks around with the voracious enthusiasm of someone who would gladly have gobbled down pastries and sandwiches. Joshua walks into the shop and Fabrizio, pulling the last four chocolate fudge croissants out from under the counter, give them to him.

"Get these, skipper," Fabrizio said. "I kept them for you! Because of you I will probably lose some other customer. I will have to bake a dozen more of these calories bombs! They sell really well! But tell me, is the old Marius already out with his catamaran? Apparently they all are in fervour for tomorrow's race. Uhh, you're blessed. Honestly I don't understand a damn thing about boats, sails and wind... What are the organizers offering as a prize?"

Joshua smiled at the baker, glancing in the direction of the vertical refrigerator where Fabrizio enshrines some sweets with honey, a rare and expensive delicacy because of the shortage of raw material.

"Look, Fabrizio, how about *'one of those cakes'* that usually you give me as a birthday present in exchange for information to satisfy your curiosity?"

The little man, always covered from head to toe in flour, had an infectious laugh. Fabrizio rubs flour from his hands on to his long white coat, before placing both hands on his hips.

The young man was already delighted at the prospect of biting the wonderful little mounds that dissolve on the tongue before releasing a heavenly taste. Joshua has several weaknesses; in addition to his passion for sailing, he loved desserts, which would certainly cause him weight problems in the long run. He hadn't yet managed to find out if the flour and the other ingredients used by Fabrizio were really provided by the Unified Power. He suspected that the good man was not using *an approved supplier*.

There were so many stories, which would soon become legends, in regard to 'illegal' biological products that could not be bought freely on the market. Unfortunately, the situation on the planet had worsened over the decades. At a certain moment, because of the deteriorating climate and the several atomic disasters, many plantations were destroyed while the soil and the water had been contaminated by radiation. Governments had to fall back exclusively on genetic manipulation and in-vitro culture in the hope of being able to cope with the tragedy and feed the already decimated population.

Then, little by little, the proponents of the so-called 'biological products' were dropped in number and placed under greater control. A law forbids the sale of other products that did not bear the mark of the Unified Power.

Joshua never had dared to ask Fabrizio how, considering the near extinction of bees, he managed to get the honey that was almost considered outlawed and therefore forbidden.

Fabrizio casts around a furtive glance, raising himself on his toes to peek out the window toward the alley, and then he approached Joshua and whispers in his ear.

"Well, I agree. I'll give you two of them. I feel generous today. Your birthday is in a few weeks, isn't it? These are worth a fortune, my friend! But not a word, otherwise they will make me close the store. This isn't a joke!"

The baker smiled and winked at Joshua.

"Sit down over there on that big bag of flour and spit it out. I want the details. Who knows, maybe I will be able to sell some nice cakes to the organizers of the race... or those tasty snacks?"

Chapter 3

The Truth of the Mind

The boat of the two young people is anchored in the harbour of a town that, like other places on the lakeside, recovered after the flood, and for three quarters of the year is full of animosity and fervour linked to the tourism that comes there from all over the world.

The small town of Ascona in the southern part of the Alps, which had remained nearly unchanged over the past two centuries, is located on the shores of Lake Verbano. It had not suffered major damage, except the sudden rise of the sea level. In summer, the town came alive with colour and music into the early morning hours. This kept a hint of nostalgia, and was broadcast several times on *Unynetweb*, the global news channel.

There are countless villas and holiday apartments that were mainly owned by members of the Institutions of Power or Control who visited during the good season. All this contributes to the prosperity of the town which has flowerbeds in every corner and well-maintained luxuriant parks.

The twenty-third century had led humans to deal with drastic and sometimes terrible changes. Though two centuries before one third of the planet was effectively destroyed and the dead numbered more than 3 billion, the strength of the survival instinct implicit in the genes and DNA allowed humanity to re-establish a sort of *community bond* in the span time of about 120 years.

The Unified Power was supported by a group of philosophers, philanthropists and scientists. The *Annwyn* were trying to give their contributions even though many of them didn't approve of the methods used by the Experimental Team to maintain order and control at all.

Many people, in an attempt to live in peace, had adopted a fake optimism and avoided dealing with ethical or political problems. That's a kind of 'no-see-no-hear-no-speak'. This is also, paradoxically, a situation that recurred during the crucial moments of human evolution and therefore marking the History.

The young Chrisa, like every *Annwyn*, is aware of the reasons for her presence on the planet. Not surprisingly, since nothing was left to chance, then there was even a reason for the existence of her brother, Joshua.

*** Veritas Mentis ***

After the premature death of their parents, Joshua and Chrisa had decided to skip the hassles of property management of the house they had inherited. Helped by a lawyer, they had sold the property and deposited the proceeds of the sale into the Citizens-Fund, which had replaced the banking institutions of the second millennium. It was a handsome sum of money, which also allowed them to live comfortably and with the innocence of those who makes passion their primary reason for living.

Their sailing boat *Sphynx*, named Avalon's Mist, of the Bénéteau shipyard, was the dream cherished since a young age. Their mother had loved the sea and it always had been her desire, one day, to leave and turn it round and venture into the immensity of the oceans in search of the lost continent of Atlantis.

The woman was always, up to last, a dreamer, an idealist who found comfort in stories of utopias. But many had considered her a lunatic. Yet, in her recklessness, she succeeded in emotionally engaging both children. When mom spoke, there was a respectful silence; her words were like balm to the soul of both kids. The stories she told had a deep meaning tied up with the thread of love and respect. They found themselves, she and her husband, two eccentric and rather special personalities.

The kid's father had a unique personality; he was a professor with several academic degrees, and he taught in many universities across the globe. But none of his family, in truth, had ever known exactly what he was teaching.

Chrisa had adored her mother; she believed she was an exceptional woman who had filled her with tenderness, giving her that significant support which, after all, every child needs. She remembered her sweet, reassuring smile, her eyes caught by a bird swing or by the flickering of the leaves in the summer breeze.

Yes, mum had always played a predominant role, and *hers* was the essence of love. Chrisa perceived her, sometimes, right next to her side and, in times of great distress, even coming to speak to her as if she was a tangible presence.

Chrisa physically looks a lot like her mother: long, brown hair highlighting the beauty of her face, always very pale, in which, like two pieces of amber, shines her big eyes. The young woman measures five feet and six inches in height with a lean and inconspicuous body, but her real beauty is in the look that seems to reflect each beam of light.

Chrisa wished more than anything else in the world that her mother had been an *Annwyn*… but Chrisa is aware that *Annwyn* can't procreate, in the material sense of the word. This is a story related to the *mysteries* of their origins, their real metaphysical structure, connected to the reason of their presence on planet Earth.

After the death of her parents, during her dream-journeys, Chrisa had wandered in the night and between dimensions in search of her mother several times. She knew that if her mother had already been reincarnated, she would later be able to give birth to other *Annwyn*, other Souls of Light.

But her searches had been unsuccessful. Chrisa questioned her fellows numerous times about the quest for the *codes* and was always met with disappointment. She realized that this lifetime wouldn't be sufficient to find the location of the *Sacred Mirror*.

However, the young woman had understood that the choice of her mother had a very deep meaning, since it was not the first time that the Mind/Soul of her mother had allowed to incarnate other *Annwyn*. The *Annwyn* defined these women *'diviners'* because from the first moment of conception they were aware that they bear a special being gifted with supernatural powers.

But the young woman understood that something would happen: Hathor was convincing in his brief statements; Chrisa thinks she knows why she shouldn't trust him, and for this reason she escapes from him.

For a long time, she had tried to talk to Joshua, believing that he deserves a more accurate and detailed explanation, but at the same time she didn't want to anguish him. Joshua wasn't at all fascinated by esoteric practices, nor was he intrigued by what he didn't know. He jokingly calls all of Marius' stories about strange events 'hocus-pocus.'

Chrisa adored her brother; she liked to watch him in secret, especially when he's asleep in his bunk, curled up in a blanket. His black hair was shiny and glistened in the sun or at the glare of the moon over the water's surface. Joshua is a handsome boy who had made several girls lose their minds. His physique is tempered by the sailing, making it look even more attractive and desirable. Yet at the bottom of his heart, he was a coward: he's afraid even of his own shadow!

Chrisa had become protective towards Joshua over time. After the death of their parents, even if she was two years younger, Chrisa immediately felt the weight of responsibility as her brother seemed to live in a world of his own and was oblivious of hazards. Joshua is also stubborn and grumpy when he persists: like that day when all of a sudden he decided to sell everything and go to live on the boat. The sailboat was a gift from their mother who had dreamed of going on a long journey across the oceans: but unfortunately, her dream of circumnavigating the globe was never fulfilled.

A flash of anger veiled the gaze of the young woman. Chrisa has always tried to trust in fate, tried to see something positive in every small opportunity. But now she sows only regret on the fertile soil of her anguish!

"Damn bastards," she muttered, "I hate you with all the force of your own limbo. One day, I'll find out the codes and go out from the projection and will destroy the *Sacred Mirror*."

Hot tears flowed down her face, and with a sudden gesture she brushes rebellious hairs away from her face. One day she'll find out who murdered her parents, since she is sure: it hadn't been a trivial incident.

But now she has to finish writing her notes in the notebook, no detail can be missed. Everything has to be faithfully transcribed, every little detail contains symbols that would, sooner or later, reveal the right move and this would mean destroying Hathor, bend him to her will, once and for all!

After she finished recording her journeys, Chrisa's eyes settled upon her bag, lying on the floor near the bed.

"Gosh," she whispers, and as she lifts it, the strange object found during her night's run in the rain, falls to the floor.

A glow in the blackness brings back to her a flash of arcane memory. She sees herself running down a grassy slope, feel the damp and fragrant moss under her bare feet, hear the laughter of other children in a circle, following the flutter of colourful birds that soar in the sky. Then she sees, silhouetted against the sky, the shape of an enormous millennial yew with a gnarled trunk and big branches that seemed to embrace the entire heavens. As the vision came, it blurs up to leave a strange feeling in the pit of her stomach.

Chrisa kneels and with some caution touches the object, first with one finger because something within her called for prudence. She perceived the oscillation of the particles that made up the artefact.

"It's not terrestrial. It isn't man-made, but it isn't an *Annwyn* object, either, of this I'm sure!"

All of a sudden she feels thrown back in Time, enveloped in a peculiar sense. These are images that cross her mind with the fury of a storm: she now sees faces that belong to other ages, feelings become pungent and Chrisa feels her stomach constrict. Then all of a sudden, everything became quiet. The scene changes and the seconds appear to assume a frequency similar to the beat of her heart. These are déjà-vu: remembrances or clairvoyance.

"What the hell? Perhaps it is this strange object recalling my archaic memory in this manner?"

But the curiosity of the young lady is too big to be long hampered by the wisdom.

Chrisa collects the object, protecting her fingers with a kitchen-towel, keeping it as far away as possible from her body. She lays it on the shelf, where there are board instruments and a halogen lamp.

"Well, now let's take a closer look," she whispers through her teeth.

Suddenly, a familiar voice from the bridge frightens her:

"Hey little sister? Are you still in the arms of Morpheus? Where are you Chisa? The early bird catches the worm!"

The arrival of the brother sent her into a rage because she was so preoccupied and alarmed by the object she had found that Joshua's screams quite scared her.

"Hey, don't be arrogant!" She shouted back to him, "is it possible that the only thing you can do that well is to scream? There isn't a wind force 12, so no reason to yell to be heard and, small irrelevant detail, I'm not deaf."

Chrisa takes a breath, panting nervously, while Joshua with two steps jumps down the stairs ending up a couple of inches from his sister, who moved away from the console, in a dash.

"You frightened me!" Chrisa complained. "You know I hate it when you fall below deck in this way... like a ferocious beast. Good morning to you! And thanks for using all the hot water in the heater. I recommend you to think of me, if by chance you can remember that your sister even lives on this boat... but usually you remember that I exist only when you need my help!"

It's always like that, between them, a sort of love and hate, which alternates at regular intervals. They quarrel and then embrace each other passionately, their grudges never last more than a couple of hours, then either one or the other apologises. At the bottom of their heart they know it, they couldn't live apart.

Now Chrisa's face took on a saddened expression, something that Joshua cannot stand.

"Please excuse me, little sister," he told her in a sweet and sincere tone while approaching her. "I'm sorry. You are absolutely right. I'll write a memo to be stuck on the bathroom mirror. I'm always in a hurry and forget other important things. I understand that you haven't had a peaceful *sleep*; do you want to talk about it? Or before that we get a nice cup of coffee with Fabrizio's wonderful croissants? The usual, the ones stuffed with chocolate!"

Chrisa furtively glances at the towel, which, fortunately, hides the strange object.

Chapter 4

Fear of the Unknown

On board another vessel, moored at 300 feet as a crow flies from the Avalon's Mist, a person holds a pair of binoculars in his big sweaty hands. Apparently he's interested in the preparations that fervently occupy the marshals and several other people: they are placing buoys and rafts which will be used the next day for the race. Annoyed, the man wipes his forehead and behind his neck with his arm, covered with a beige linen shirt with gaudy purple lines. His small, bloodshot eyes and crew-cut hair gives him an unreassuringly look.

"Damn!" He growled, "I didn't need this situation. Too many people, too many witnesses: call *him*, we can't implement what we have been commissioned to do. Ask the Chief if there is an alternative plan, otherwise we must wait."

The man arrogantly throws the binoculars to another enormous guy with a face that would scare the bravest dockworker. He catches the binoculars and places it on the counter as he blurts out a couple of curses before answering:

"Okay. But there are no problems for me. A sharp blow to the neck and..."

The voice is harsh, with a strange, indefinable accent. He brings both hands on the collar and makes a very significant gesture.

The one dressed with the beige linen shirt with gaudy purple lines, which appears to be the more intelligent of the two, answers:

"Asshole, but where do you have your brain, you moron? I remind you that we aren't here to impress any females in search of adventure, idiot. You do think with what you have between your legs. You do what I say and try not to use that too little brain of yours, it's better for both of us!"

The first moved away, cursing and shut himself under the deck, slamming the little cabin door. The eight-foot tall man remains dazed on the bridge, then he shoves a finger up his nostril and next he sucks it with a delighted expression. He takes the binoculars from the counter to watch the catamaran which was about to dock next to the moored sailing boat of the two young people.

"Just what we needed was that geezer with his catamaran to derail the whole plan we had so carefully devised," he mused to himself.

He picks up the phone and typed a number from memory:

"Hallo, Dr Sella? It's Paolo. There are some drawbacks…"

The brute shuts up, poking a finger in the ear to scrape it while listening to the phone.

"Yes, that is, no... Perhaps, but there are too many people, because of tomorrow's race. Dammit! We have thought of this... Augusto is skilled in these things, and he believes that we have to wait. I know that there's hustle,

41

but... fuck, it is not about money, believe me. Even if you add another hundred bucks... that's your problem, Dr Sella. We don't move from here until there are fewer witnesses around on inflatable boats and various ships. We wouldn't want us bitten by those bastards creatures unleashed by the Experimental Team. Okay, I'll talk to you later."

He puts the illegal phone, shielded from *Unynetweb*, in his trouser pockets.

"Go to hell, you piece of jerk, you can clean your ass with your money; I don't really want to end up back behind bars. Christ, I've already risked hibernation more than once!"

The henchman went down below deck to inform Augusto, and finds him in his cabin in front of the laptop, intently browsing details of the area surrounding the town of Ascona on *earth-frame*, and of a piece of the creek divided in two by the riverbed Maggia, already drained hundreds of years ago.

"What is the exact location of tomorrow's race? From what little I understand of this map, it seems to me it starts here, then moves to about half a mile from the shore, here, perhaps to take advantage of some favourable current... then go down to the islands and then fall back on this side. I think Borgo Novo, no no, Roncolocarnese to be exact, then again turns and return to port. Bloody hell, this fucking program operates at stinking intervals. Look... you fucking pervert, and don't stand there staring at me like a debauched."

Augusto looked pissed off and not happy with his assessment, but since he was scarcely a nautical expert, obviously he didn't expect more from his skills.

"Look Augusto, Dr Sella wasn't very happy with the message. He says he can't wait until tomorrow; the Experimental Team have carried out checks at the Trust company that holds the records for his 'business'. He doesn't know how reliable the tip he received from London is, and says that he needs the girl right now. Immediately! I don't understand any of this... he was babbling nonsense about the *Annwyn*... Jeez, what can it mean? The boss is haunted by this story; he never behaved like that in the past. And what if we *delegate* the work to someone else? Christ, there are 200 bucks up for grabs, but only if it all ends by midnight."

Augusto rose angrily:

"And who the hell can we take? That pair of lunatics who you usually dump of the illegal business on? They would piss in their pants as soon as we explain *what* they would have to deal with. Do you realize that this woman is too dangerous? You wouldn't have time to breathe before she reads your mind. Holly shit! She isn't human; she's one of those strange creatures that have helped the Unified Power rehabilitate the planet. But you know what I mean? We can't get close to her more than necessary because she can pick up our brain's vibrations... perhaps her extrasensory gifts have already revealed to her that something is about to happen to her, and only Satan knows what she could do to us. You can't deal with it at night because *that thing* doesn't even sleep!"

*** Ignoti Metus ***

Paolo's hands trembled, and the muscles of his jaw visibly contracted.

"But, but... and who has told you this crap? Holy cow! Why didn't you let me know that before we entered this stinking contract? I don't like vampires, or paranormal stuff, and these things bother me to the bowels. What does it mean that the woman 'has extrasensory powers'? Explain, before I wet my pants..."

43

Paolo is livid, all of a sudden his stature has become wobbly and unstable, making the sign of the cross, being a believer, and left himself fall heavily on the bench, adding:

"That woman is an *Annwyn,* you fool!"

Chapter 5

The Power of Thoughts

Suddenly Joshua's eyes perched above the object partly concealed under the towel. It was visible only at an angle, and glistened under the intense light. Curiosity is an issue inherent in the DNA, certainly very evident in young children but that sometimes remain latent in adulthood.

"Hey, what is this thing?" He asked. "Where the hell did you find it? Don't tell me you were fishing last night and that *thing* hooked instead of those chub that inhabit the waters around the boat…"

Chrisa bites her lower lip while considering the words to use. She could feel static in the air like there is before a big storm. She looks at the tip of her shoes, searching for a futile pretext, and breathed the smell of agitation that gradually condenses onto her brother's body. Consequently, even the aura of her brother had changed, switching intensity and colour.

"Well, I... but maybe it's better to have breakfast first," Chrisa said, "otherwise we will lose our appetites. I don't know what this thing can be, though somehow it looks strangely familiar. However, I'm certain that this isn't a *human* artefact. Last night... I tripped over it; I didn't see it because of the heavy rain. Yes Joshua, I made a *journey to find the codes* again. I would have told you, on the right occasion, but don't worry, nothing can happen to me."

But her brother's face became stern, that typical grimace which to Chrisa means 'apprehension'. With a gesture of annoyance, the young man removes a long tuft of hair from his forehead. Yet Chrisa knows perfectly how her brother is worried about her. Since their parents are deceased, he has become even more protective.

His mother had told him several things about the peculiar faculties of his younger sister, about the need to listen to her intuition because her extrasensory powers were extraordinary. If they were to continue to have a harmonious relationship, they could both benefit from each other. Joshua hadn't forgotten a single word of his mother's teachings: for him these were the absolute Verb.

"Chrisa, I would like to share this *task* with you, but I realize the big difference that sets us apart. Our mother explained it to me... but I feel I don't know every detail. Damn, I would just like to help you, after all! I'm so terrified one day something could happen to you, and that you get stuck in another dimension, and not be able to come back to me! I cannot think of the idea of living without you, sis. I would rather die!"

Joshua's heart swells, the beat is loud in his breast, while the young man pushes back the burning tears which impetuously want to fall. He feels like a river that is about to break its banks.

"I know you want that," answered the young woman with a trembling voice, while her index finger approaches the edge of the object, "but I don't want something bad happen to you. I don't want you involved. I'm barely controlling *his* movements, those of Hathor, I've already mentioned him. But it is not only him who spies on me…

there are other presences, maybe not all of them are *Annwyn*, but these aren't good appearances. I feel so much malice in them. It is a strange world, brother. It's a kind of 'parallel dimension', if you can perceive it better that way. The Unified Power hides the existence of other worlds from everyone, more or less like this…"

She stops, her voice cut off by a thought that suddenly took shape in her mind. She takes the other edge of the kitchen's towel and also covers the exposed portion of the object, and suddenly it seems that in the cabin even the light has dimmed.

"Chrisa, don't tell me anything, I don't want you to violate the prohibitions of the Unified Power, I know there are many secrets, and to be frank, I'd rather not get into these stories of hocus-pocus. I would just like to protect you, as surely mum and dad would have wanted me to."

Joshua comes close to his sister and throws his arms around her, hugging her hard. Rivulets of tears are stinging his cheeks while sobs tear his chest.

"It is as if mom and dad were still here with us. I feel their presence; everything reminds me of them," Chrisa whispers, drying the tears from her brother's cheeks.

But Joshua's eyes do not move from the towel that hides Chrisa's mysterious object. A strange glow in the eyes of the young man indicates that soon, very soon, he would have some brilliant idea about how to analyse the artefact. He doesn't like magical or paranormal things, but curiosity is inherent deep in his nature. This is the big problem. And the girl knows it, used to interacting with her brother at a subliminal level. Reading his thinking, she understood that he wouldn't do anything reckless. Joshua feels the 'burden of responsibility' on his shoulders since they were orphaned, when he became even more apprehensive and protective. Evidently, the young woman knows that everything is dictated by the love he felt for her and from his innate desire to protect her from the evils of the word.

In Chrisa's mind swirl the dreamlike visions that merge and combine, creating a complete picture. She knows by instinct that her job on this planet is very important; she understands that it isn't only helping to advance those people with whom she shares her daily life. Chrisa possesses sensory abilities which seem to transcend the ordinary limits of space and time. Each *Annwyn* possesses these characteristics, which are sometimes terrible because of the inhuman strength that is given to its possessors.

*** Vis Mentis ***

Chrisa's mother had repeatedly experienced the *altered state of consciousness* which is acquired during meditation. She had always spoken about it to her daughter with absolute frankness, also pointing out some extraordinary events that had upset her life when she was a teenager. Chrisa knew that her mother had been in contact with appearances from other Spheres, beings of Light, who had very different purposes depending on their psychic development. In her past four incarnations, Chrisa's mother gave birth to *Annwyn* children: Joshua was an exception, but his presence would allow Chrisa to achieve her tasks.

This had led the woman to understand that the nature of Man is not unique: it is even true that not all people are of benign nature, since each Mind/Soul that settles in a material body has a distinct karmic path.

The Buddhist philosophy has encountered increasing interest from scientists over the centuries. In the last two hundred years, there has been tangible evidence supporting Buddhist ideas, especially thanks to quantum physics. As a matter of fact, the actions of our lifetime directly affect the karmic memory of every living thing, and then resolve into 'reactions' at the time of ripening, in this or other future lives, and will lead to commensurate effects. Again, thanks to quantum physics, we also recognized that the power of thought, both positive and negative, had its vibration which gave a boost to the entire collective human evolution.

In short, the creed 'you reap what you sow' was validated... although the harvest may not necessarily take place during this lifetime, but will happen in future reincarnations. It was important, however, to reincarnate into a new human body... then *where and in to what* a living being was reincarnated is at the very foundation of spiritual advancement. By means of quantum physics and the implementation of specific genetic mutations and other studies, the scientists were finally able to isolate the 'God Particle'. The rest was like a game, first at the genetics lab and then to perform the 'implants' on unsuspecting 'mice'. Unfortunately, not all the Unified Power's goals were noble!

Even the theosophical discoveries had led to terrible friction within theological institutions that sought to achieve hegemony and consolidate their control of mankind through dark movements.

They were then found in opposition: on one hand there was the manipulative pseudo-science, on the other the ecclesiastical Dogma that lived as the Absolute Principle. Then everything was shattered. The leaders of different churches and religious movements had been killed or rendered powerless and after this the Unified Power had seized control and responsibility of restoring order among the nations hardest hit by environmental and natural catastrophes.

Chrisa spoke little with Joshua about these things because the young man was apparently more interested in his sailboat and regattas than investigating philosophical or scientific issues. More than once the young woman had

49

asked her brother to keep track of his dreams, but Joshua claimed not to remember what he saw and heard during his dream's journey. Chrisa however, was not sure about the power of her brother, she didn't know whether he could perform extracorporeal travel. The girl had never had the courage to see if his astral body clung to the physical one or whether, perhaps with her help, he could 'split' from it and maybe follow her in her dreamlike journeys!

Chrisa suddenly realizes that her brother's curiosity about the object was uncontainable; she reproaches him with a pleading yet authoritative voice:

"Please, Joshua! I read your thoughts, you know it, you're well aware that you can't hide anything from me... leave aside your curiosity for a little while!"

Joshua wrinkles his nose and tries to take on a detached demeanour.

"Come on, little sister," he pouted, "don't act like that, I'm only teasing you. I would just like to give it another quick peek, and then I'll help in the kitchen. I forgot to tell you that our 'competitor' Marius wants to eat some pasta and potatoes, your famous recipe! He will bring us some Irish sweet delights, you bet!"

With great delicacy, as if she were lifting the veil that hides the features of a sage of ancient Greece, Chrisa exposes the object. Both of them look at it, wide-eyed, the object's surface reflects the halogen light, sending around unusual reverberations.

"It's definitely not man-made," Chrisa explained, "I'm more than certain, but it is not an *Annwyn's* artefact. It looks like a three-dimensional mechanism, but why this unusual shape? Then there are these segments..."

Chrisa's finger approaches the object. The finger produces a spark like the ones you see now only in museum collections, inside the old light-bulbs used since the beginning of the twentieth century.

The young woman withdraws her hand with a jerk.

"Ahhh, I got an electric shock!"

She throws the towel back over the object with an angry gesture. Her face is contorted by a grimace of pain while she rubs her aching arm vigorously.

"Joshua, forget it," she snaps, "I'm not ready to confront this *thing*. Not now."

Chrisa feels a long, icy shiver down her spine. The feeling of inadequacy is even more marked. She senses that something isn't right: she tries to pretend that it is because of the object, but there are other images that look like holograms in her rational mind. Something is happening, something that even she can't control!

Chapter 6

Legends and Truth

Fortunately Marius arrives with a tin box painted with sunny and bright colours.

"Hey, I don't smell the aroma of spaghetti sauce! Chrisa, Joshua... 'The early bird catches the worm'. I've gone around the islands to double check the locations. There was a flat wind that forced me to work on the arms. Bloody, bloody hell, I hope that Aeolus is on our side tomorrow! Come on, I'll give you a hand; I brought some biscuits and soda scones. The recipe is my grandmother's, which she used to tell me she received from an old Irish lady named *Wynne*, which means 'Joy' in English! This woman was well known for reciting legends and myths of the ancient Celtic civilizations."

The siblings shared an exhausted look, but they don't breathe a word, they knew the old sea dog too well to underestimate his narrative flair.

"Hallo Marius, we are below deck. We had... a little unexpected problem. Nothing harmful, well, at least we believe not. Came down, we'll all go to the kitchen, and we'll tell you a couple of things that will pique your curiosity."

Marius lays the intriguing tin box on the shelf then he looks around with a smile.

"Well, well," he beamed, "everything shines down here; you've treated your houseboat well! You don't seem to miss the very ground beneath your feet. I dare say, I have a job for you, Chrisa; a guy who occasionally has been around here in the harbour. He needs a couple of translations from other languages. Pays very well, but is in a terrible hurry. He's that guy who sometimes spends his weekends at his villa near the golf course. Remember him? Tall, in his fifties, dark hair that is greying a bit at the temples, quite attractive... and he doesn't go unnoticed because of his very old Bentley Continental! I remember you didn't like him. A few weeks ago he made some questionable joke at your expense."

The old man looks at the young woman making a funny grimace with his mouth. Then he takes off his sweater, wrapping the arms around his neck and sits, stretching his legs.

"If you accept the job, he would pay you 5,000 crowns. But I don't know, Chrisa, I don't trust that guy at all!"

Joshua freezes with his hands in the air, as he was about to put the potatoes to peel and onions on the table.

"What? Are you kidding? I think that your brain has been fried by too much sun. Gosh, but my little sister certainly agrees... Hey Marius, you don't spit on five thousand crowns!"

Chrisa whirls and fixed her brother's eyes with a look of angry agitation. She can't stand people making decisions on her behalf, even if that someone was her beloved brother. The challenge hangs in the air while Joshua's smile disappears, he has overstepped and as usual failed to notice until the mess was already done. The atmosphere gets heavy and the tension feels like static electricity in the air just before a thunderstorm. A strange cramp clenches on his insides, while with one hand he wipes away the usual tuft of intrusive hair that hangs over his face.

"Excuse me. That just slipped out! It wasn't my intention, I'm sorry... really sorry... I know how you can get greatly irritated by my attitude... Chrisa, it's always the same problem. I'm spontaneous, terribly spontaneous, and I always forget that I have no right to manipulate your will."

Chrisa's gaze softened. She always appreciated when the hot-headed bungler noticed that he had gone overboard. This means that, at least in part, he listens and takes her advice seriously.

"Well, guys," bumbled Marius, "okay, scratch that, let's pretend I hadn't arrived yet. We'll repeat the scene from Act I, when I was still on the deck."

Chrisa bursts into laughter and playfully punches Marius on his forearm, made muscular by pulling the shrouds and ropes of his catamaran from morning to night.

"Come on, everything is okay Marius! What's in that attractive, colourful box?"

"It's a secret of the ancients," Marius whispered, suddenly becoming serious. "It opens the mind to visions of the past and the future."

Then, mysteriously, he begins to hum a lullaby in a strange language that even the young girl can't immediately classify, although, by coincidence of emotions, she remembers.

While the old man is carried away by the rhythm, the boy sits opposite with peeler and a small cutter, chopping the onions. Fascinated by the melody, which is a little bit throaty, Chrisa and Joshua are seduced by the unfamiliar words that undoubtedly are telling of the prowess of some mysterious character out of the mists of the past.

After the sumptuous meal, they reorder the small kitchen before Joshua prepares the coffee.

"The turn of events has deep meaning in the memory of Humanity, my friends," Marius tells them. "I learned from the many stories of *Wynne*. Many years ago in my country we celebrated Wicca in honour of the Divinity, and later on the pretext of the monotheistic religions, no longer we did remember the power of these Gods. Nature was outraged: the good Gods of the backwash waters have been forgotten... man became selfish and an ambassador of hate. Don't let your heart be tainted, my friends! You should always worship the Great Mother because it all stems from the bowels of the Earth, and her womb was disfigured, violated, offended... A couple of centuries are gone and we have been able to recover so little of the civilization of the twenty-first century. Everything has been destroyed and rebuilt; now we, the survivors of the Great Alignment, struggle to continue the vibration ascent... Or rather, those that we had been and what our karma has agreed for us to become, today... here and now."

*** Fabulosa et Vera ***

The gaze of the old man has become sad, immensely melancholic. A shadow had fallen like a veil over his eyes, and Chrisa, without imposing herself, reads his thoughts. Marius loved the siblings very much, from the bottom of his heart. He was aware that *something* extraordinary binds him to them. Since their parents had died, Marius had been the only one to get their intimacy and the only one to be able to appease the terrible pain that had hardened them. But there was something that eluded even the young *Annwyn*: Chrisa was convinced that Marius concealed a secret!

Marius had taken the decision to try to help them in the best way, without becoming overwhelming and without imposing specific choices. He knew the children since they were 9 and 6 years old, and had learned to appreciate their unusual talents. He knew that Chrisa was not only a prodigy child but belonged to a mysterious race... legends told by *Wynne* had taken shape and had paradoxically become reality. And Chrisa knew that he knew.

The cookies were of an Irish recipe and were really worthy of being considered magically delicious! Not even the crumbs were left on the bottom of the box, which now shone like gold.

"And for tomorrow's race?" Joshua asks Marius, winking at Chrisa. "You have already been analysing the path, I assume. You'll also have checked the weather; I saw on *Unynetweb* there will be rain from the north in the morning and then the wind should rise from the west, so with the wind in its sails should be a piece of cake... provided that the wind doesn't change direction, otherwise you, alone on your catamaran, will have to work hard!"

Joshua knew how to tease his friend. He was enjoying himself a lot, since discussing winds and boats is the passion he shares with Marius. Chrisa became silent, her eyes occasionally ending up on the checkered cloth which conceals that mysterious and dangerous object. The object made Chrisa uncomfortable, but she was unsure whether or not it would be wise to share her findings with their old friend, so she preferred to remain silent.

"Marius," Joshua blurts, "about the work for that guy, do you know when he wants the translations done by?"

Joshua's gaze moves to cross the eyes of his sister, then both looked towards Marius.

"Well, I don't know. I saw him this morning in the harbour when I was getting a cup of coffee. He was been rather vague, he asked if you were still in Ascona and if I saw you regularly. He just said he has several translations to do, I think for a site on *Unynetweb*, but if you would agree you both should meet to define the details. Chrisa, I don't know what to tell you... I don't like the guy, but you can use some additional crowns."

"Well, yes. After all, even though we are living from the annuity, a bit of extra money comes in handy. We need a new computer with some updated programs, which would not leave us much to live on. Then there is Mom's project!"

Her voice chokes in her throat, while she sees her mother's smiling face when she announced that she had bought a sailboat and it was her desire to take a sabbatical year to go round the world with her family.

Marius takes her by the shoulders and squeezes her in his arms.

"Come on baby," he comforts, "don't worry. I know how you feel... one day your mother's dream will come true. Chrisa, if you desire it enough, all dreams become real. These things have been proven for a couple of centuries now: the Law of Attraction, quantum physics... remember? Always keep in mind that everything is simply a projection of yours, my child!"

The young woman smiles; Marius knows the peculiarities of the *Annwyn*... and prefers to pretend that nothing has happened.

"Listen, Marius, if you see again that guy, tell him that I agree. But I don't want to meet him, and I don't want to confer with him, categorically. I'm not going to allow him in my presence. Whether he's a slippery and sneaky type, he can be very dangerous... if he wants, he can give you the material with a written explanation and then I'll give it a look. But do you at least know his name? I don't think he presented himself with his surname, did he?"

The girl immediately regretted having used those adjectives; however she understood from Marius' reaction that he felt the same way.

"I heard someone calling him 'doctor' but I missed the name. Never mind, I know where he lives, if I don't see him here around, I'll pass by at his villa and leave him a message. What do you plan to do this afternoon? Maybe an inspection tour as well, or do you want to come up to Canobbio? I promised an old friend I would go see him a while ago. In times like these, considering that everything is under the control of the Unified Power, Giacomo is one of the few people I really trust. Then we can go shopping at his little store, in the old town, where he sells all these delicious cheeses and a selection of amazing prohibited bio vegetables and fruits! Nowadays it's so hard to find fruits and vegetables grown in the earth rather than from the hydroponics-culture."

"Come on, you're right," smiles Chrisa. "Let's have the afternoon free to roam down the lake. We can stop at the pizzeria on the way home, where they serve the best pizza on the north shore of Lake Verbano."

Joshua is happy not having to think about anything else, the next day would be a battle to the death! Chrisa remain below deck for a while under the pretext of having to change her jeans. After getting back on the deck, she helps her brother to lock the door of the boat and check that the anchor ropes are securely attached to the dock.

"Hey, Alessandro," calls Chrisa to the man who stands nearby, "keep an eye on our boat for us, could you? The three of us are taking a jaunt down to Canobbio."

Alessandro, who takes care of the security and is always to be found in the harbour area, responds with a hand wave. It didn't occur to Joshua and Marius that other eyes were watching their movements with curiosity, but

Chrisa noticed an increasingly pronounced strange feeling in her stomach.

"There is someone watching us," she informs the others. "Someone who spies on our every movement... Marius, who owns that big outboard moored at the second right mark, the orange and green one?"

Marius turns around slowly, trying not to attract attention.

"It has been anchored here in Ascona for a couple of days. Take no notice, don't look in that direction. Are you sure about your claims? Come on, let us go quickly back on my catamaran to look for a couple of things. From below, we can see without being seen, I also have a binoculars."

The old man is alarmed by Chrisa's apprehension.

"I immediately noticed that big boat, I think they are two people aboard. I admit that I found their presence a little strange because they don't fit in with the lakeside scenery... In short, they doesn't seem to be Soviets looking for some pretty girl to be woo and they not even look like the usual tourists who sometimes dock for supplies. Yesterday, one of them must have had a spat with Alessandro because of the drinking water pump. I heard swearing and shouting in such an absurd manner, a redneck attitude and certainly not suitable for an educated person. That boat is worth half a million crowns... What's a slob doing on it?"

Unfortunately, even with the aid of the binoculars, Marius couldn't manage to unravel the mystery. Apparently, the yacht is deserted. Yet Chrisa is certain that there is someone on board. Joshua knows that his sister is never wrong, but prefers to remain silent, avoiding further argument.

Resigned, the three re-emerge with a fridge bag and a couple of woven raffia baskets and with purposeful strides they go towards the public space where Marius had parked his small electric car.

After leaving behind the town, climbing the hill towards the Monte Verità road, Marius seems quieter.

"Of course I do have some weird adventures, because of you two jokers," he sighs. "I'm too old to immerse myself into the stories of spies. The tension of the race is already sufficiently wearing."

The elderly man, however, appears restless. Something deep inside makes him taut. He can't explain to his two young friends about the concerns stirring in his spirit. It was not yet the right moment to reveal the whole truth to them! This was a solemn promise made to their parents many years ago. There were secrets that needed to be protected, even at the cost of their lives. Chrisa and Joshua's mother was especially clear and determined that everything must be done in relation to the Great Legend.

Marius tries to drive out the nagging thoughts, then he laughs heartily and nudges Joshua who been sitting in silence, lost in thought. He was watching the image of his sister reflected in the rear-view mirror. Suddenly the girl squeals.

"Brakes! Marius, pull over, I beg you, fast! I need to check something, I'll be right back."

As soon as the car stops, Chrisa jumped out and ran towards Parsifal's Park, immediately followed by her worried brother.

"Hey, wait a second! Where are you going? Why have you got the devil on your tail? Chrisa please stop! What is Marius thinking?"

The young woman slows down and looks back towards the car. She beckons to Marius to join them. Marius grabs his binoculars without hesitating and heads in the direction of the waiting siblings.

"Listen! From up there we can take a peek at the harbour," Chrisa explains, "I'm sure that someone was watching, and if they were waiting for the right moment, it's possible that they will try to get on board the Avalon's Mist."

The young woman betrays herself by taking hold of her bag with both hands. The gesture didn't escape Joshua's notice.

"Ahhh, I would bet," he snapped vehemently. "You bought along that weird object! How are you going to explain it to the Experimental Team, who are always checking people's belongings? You know that the Unified Power doesn't tolerate transgressions! What would you say if they would stop us along the road and demand to know what it is, and worse, why do we have it?"

Marius tries to ignore the quarrel, but he's too smart not to guess that there is something that his young friends are trying to keep hidden from him.

"So what? Are you going to give me some clue in this 'treasure hunt' or do you want to participate by yourselves?"

Chrisa ignores Marius' request and lengthens her step, following the Via Gottardo Madonna. She takes an overgrown path that faces south, towards the lake below. Fortunately the mountain area was now protected and virtually unchanged over the past 200 years. The wood is luxuriant again after being repeatedly decontaminated and cleaned by alluvial material. The breeze caresses the leaves which release their fragrance while some bird chirps happily, hidden in the foliage. Here and there are large, flowering bushes at ground level which filled the unused path with agate and purple, while at some point the rocks are so sharp that might pierce the soles of their shoes.

Once in an open clearing, the girl is hesitant and with a frown, turned to her friend as he approaches.

"Come on Marius, be kind, hand me the binoculars. Then I'll explain the rest to you. I won't keep anything hidden, I only fear to involve you into a damn strange and risky story!"

Chrisa looks for a spot where the branches of the trees were less dense and the light could penetrate, the chestnut leaves shining like emeralds. She examines the surface of the lake before looking to the area close to the shore. The boats are anchored about 700 feet below the hill. With the binoculars Chrisa could see Alessandro sitting in his red and white striped deck chair. Everything looked calm, a few tourists wandering around, but on board the suspect yacht there was no trace of a living soul.

"Holy Grace. Yet... I was convinced... I'm not usually mistaken..."

With an annoyed grimace, Chrisa returns the binoculars to Marius and sits on the first big rock she sees.

"Well, promise is a promise Marius," Chrisa sighs. "I want to show you something special, an object that we haven't yet been able to understand. We don't know what it might be nor where it may have come from."

With extreme care, the girl pulled the kitchen towel from her purse and hands it to the old friend.

"Who knows, maybe because of your experience you might have an idea... although I doubt that this is an easy question to answer."

Marius's eyes lower. With one hand, he adjusts his glasses while the other takes the object from the hands of the young woman. In turn, he crouches to the ground and carefully lays bare the artefact. Stunned and incredulous, the old sailor blurts out a curse in Gaelic, evidently not believing what he is holding in his hands.

"It's simply amazing!" Marius stared in wonder.

"Oh goodness of the Gods... but... it's... it is impossible!"

Chapter 7

Abnormal Presences

The powerful car roared down along the ancient Via Borgo, ignoring access bans and creating problems for the surprised pedestrians that had to jump to the sides of the road.

"Hey, you lunatic!" One local resident hollered. "Who do you think you are? Can't you read the signs? Access is forbidden even to your hubris on four wheels!"

The driver either did not notice or did not deign to respond.

"Step aside, you herd of inept morons!"

And to emphasize the wrath of its owner, the car expands a thunderous roar from the 800 horse power engine. The roar bounces off the walls of the buildings which encircle this meandering passage that leads to the lake. A couple of tourists shake their heads in disbelief; there is no need to argue about the insolence of some transgressors.

Arriving at the end of the street where the lake begins, the driver leaves the car, an authentic ancient relic, just outside the town hall, slamming the door. He looks angrily around as he throws his beige linen jacket around his shoulders.

He takes off with a fast pace, taking the left road that leads directly to the Piazzetta San Pietro, where, near the wall of the church, a very flashy woman is waiting for him.

Sella passes his sweaty hand through his hair, trying to feign a smile which turns out to be terribly forced.

"Veronika, darling," he pants, "sorry I'm a bit late... I had an unforeseen delay."

The blonde, swaying on the thin heels, takes a few steps, trying not to lose her dignity by wedging her heels between the pebbles. She's barely covered by a woven silk chiffon, a mix of medieval and Hawaiian shirt certainly of 'French Couture'.

Her voluptuous form was kept within a tight corset, which buttons threaten to give way with every breath. A cross split accentuates the precariousness of the creation, perhaps more appropriate to an anorexic model than to a wealthy and prosperous woman from Moscow. Looking fleetingly at her, one might imagine an Orthodox icon of a Madonna, but for the glaring make-up and the provocative aspect, which was a striking show of poor refinement and anything but chaste. Veronika just smiles, baring white teeth too perfect as to be the work of Mother Nature, as indeed, aren't many of her 'curves'.

In fact, Dr. Sella needed this appetizing *bait* that always makes some greedy hoarder bite. This is 'his' world, where only the strongest survive, filling his pockets out of all proportion and even mocking the controls of the Unified Power. These are the 'Dominants', a society defined by their illegal business and have made theirs the Seven Capital Sins. Whatever it costs, Sella wages a kind of war to last drop of blood. He jeers about the Unified Power and the felines of the Experimental Team; he would kill them and use them as bedside rug.

Veronika is good at her profession. As a prostitute, she is accurate and very skilful in the arts of lust, almost as good as the Babylonian goddess Ishtar, the Mother of All.

But the woman, who seduces and is seduced, doesn't know the Scriptures, and therefore can't understand that deception comes from the erroneous doctrine, hegemony and corruption of the systems of the world. For her, as for her usurer, what counts is the money and pleasure. Everything else, including ethics and morality, can wait for Charon and his boat across the river Acheron.

The sun casts long shadows of coolness that creep through the narrow alleyways, past the colourful paintings of the shop windows that were filled with a multitude of luxury goods, where gold and precious stones are set like infinitesimally small eyes that merely know how to observe.

Everything apparently remained as it was a couple of centuries ago, perhaps only the plaster of the old patrician houses are a little ruined because of the acid rain. But the Unified Power invested a lot of money to try to preserve history and its artefacts. What was left after the terrible floods had been carefully restored and is periodically repaired. It was almost as if history and its sad events deserved to be preserved forever for future generations. Perhaps to serve as a warning, so past mistakes do not recur?

The buzz of people is a suffused and flushed echo, accentuated at times by a loud laugh or cry of some happy child. One afternoon like many others, for thousands of tourists poured into the squares following the afternoon siesta: the shops stay open until after 10:00PM and many others even beyond established municipal edict.

Sella is nervous; he should also find time to meet with Augusto and Paolo, those other idiots. After all, he can't just blindly trust the men with whom he deals with for this type of business: it isn't like with the stock broker or economics specialists, hired to make more of his already substantial wealth. These debauched idiots are big and strong brutes but with tiny brains; they follows orders without thinking, they are like a panzer that crushes everything on command.

*** Hospites Novi ***

The problem of the girl begins to weigh on him, why hasn't she contacted him yet? He had asked the old Irish sailor to offer her a handsome sum in exchange for some minor translation. Blimey, it was a tempting offer and any young person would be interested in making a lot of money without much effort. But perhaps she suspects something?!

"Of course she does. It must be so..." he mutters, "she's a psychic and she senses that there's more... she will feel threatened... well then, after the horrible end gave her parents... holy shit... that's why!"

Veronika tactfully pretends not to notice Sella whispering to himself. The woman is wise enough to know how to keep her mouth closed when not being asked to open it for some reason.

The businessman, however, is very restless, continues to brooding while his steps lead him through the narrow streets, followed by the woman balancing on her heels.

"No way! They will not succeed to take her. *Those things* don't sleep at night... and those two idiots might risk ending up in some other catch. The Experimental Team is still investigating the events that occurred some years ago, and they actually came very close... but apparently they haven't yet found the killers hired to do the dirty job. At that time, the affair had cost the lives of her parents. Christ! It's worse than at the time of the first Crusades when the fanatics sought the Holy Grail!"

"Move!" Sella suddenly snaps at his traipsing companion. "Damn you and those high-heels! Remove them, if you can't even walk, Veronika! Better that you walk barefoot."

The grim look of the woman is disguised as an ironic smile, and then with an out of place hysterical giggle, she complains:

"I'm sorry... but you're running! If you slow down, I can keep up with you!"

Everything looks like a poor quality theatrical scene, in which the actors try to adjust to their stage set, but under the skin the weight of each one's character emerges clearly. Something is out of place, terribly in conflict with the expectations of Dr. Sella. And he doesn't tolerate smears, as everything must be tuned like in a Wagner concert, his favourite composer.

Turning yet another corner, they find themselves in the Via delle Cappelle. A few more steps and then Dr. Sella opens a heavy walnut door, with solid brass knobs that is distinguished from the others in the area by its fine workmanship. Even the marks left by the water that had flooded the town, had disappeared under insistent polishing using oils favoured by the most famous carpenters. What you couldn't get through substantial cash payments!

In the bourgeois home, Sella has a meeting with a famous lawyer who already awaits him at the top of the travertine stairs. A big bouquet of cut flowers, with an intense fragrance adorns the atrium with the ceiling of carved wood, painted with gaudy trappings of indigo blue, gold and brick red. Two large Victorian paintings adorn the east and west sides of the hall: *The Magic Circle* and *The Pandora* by John William Waterhouse. The story about the two paintings is a mystery shrouded by dubious provenance, and Sella knows this because the paintings are the original works and not imitations.

"Welcome to my studio... always perturbing, these two Ladies of our friend Waterhouse, aren't they? This is the right place to stay in the complacent gracefulness, so the goal is reached and the myth has become reality... and reality is bound to the *Dream*. Hiero-Gamos."

The lawyer is dressed in a lead coloured two piece suit. A purple silk shirt and a Hermes tie complete the picture of elegant simplicity. Veronika watches him through long bushy eyelashes from too much mascara, with a strange grin from under the hot pink Chanel lip gloss.

"Madame Veronika. Enchanted by your presence... as always!"

He reaches out his arm and takes her hand in his and, with a well-studied movement, brings her hand to his lips to kiss it with a gentle sensuality. The man remains in that position for several seconds, while with his eyes brushes the contour of the arabesque around her breasts and then up along the neck to rest languidly on her swollen lips. Veronika, in total embarrassment, blushed markedly and then looks to Sella, who has moved to the side for a closer look at Waterhouse's beautiful Pandora.

Veronika is struck by an icy chill down her spine, and she smoothes her dress on her thigh, a gesture that still doesn't escape Sella's acute eye. The bastard smiles while in his head ideas are emerging that were anything but chaste. She senses that something is out of place, the malaise is strong and she reels backwards to find herself against the wall. Sella pretends not to notice and reaches for the linen handkerchief in his pants which he passes on his forehead; he was beaded with sweat, though in the hall is cool.

"Well, well... my dear lawyer! Shall I remind you the reason for our meeting? For the rest, I would dismiss the story quickly, if you don't mind. I'm as dutiful as ethics dictates... at least when it suits me."

His interlocutor opens the great doorway to the study, hissing between his lips while still feigning a smile:

"Your reasons," answers the lawyer, "if you will allow me, Dr. Sella, are certainly *not* my own... that's already clear! My time is priceless... perishing. I'm the one giving you the courtesy to take advantage of my service; I have the honour to point out!"

Chapter 8

Divine Artefacts

Marius tosses and turns the object found by Chrisa, his hands trembling.

"It looks like a damn *Vibratory Matrix*. It's an artefact that helps people to remember and reconnect with their place in the Universe. A sort of activator, if you prefer; with it you can open the different doors that allow access to other dimensions!" The old man sighs deeply and shakes his head. "It was used by my ancestors, long before the coming of Christ. Centuries ago, when the Gods were worshiped, the vibrational matrix was also used by Druid priests."

"How do you know all these things? I've never heard about it at school... and of course these rumours may not be available on *Unynetweb*, are they?" Joshua's voice was quiet. "The Unified Power banned and destroyed all material that could transform human minds, I remember that was a source of heated discussion in those groups that Mom and Dad attended."

Joshua stared at the old man with wide-eyed curiosity.

"He knows all this because he has studied, dear brother!" Chrisa urged with marked seriousness. "Marius isn't just the person we believe he is, or am I wrong... you old sea dog?"

The young woman addressed him with a big smile without adding another word. Marius remains in silent contemplation. It is certainly not yet the time to reveal everything to the two young siblings; he had promised their parents that he would wait for the right moment.

The mysterious object gleams sinisterly in the afternoon light, Joshua refrains from touching it. Something in his deepest, at the same time, strikes between fear and respect.

"Maybe you also know why it was abandoned along the route of the cycle track? I didn't have time to snoop on *Unynetweb* to see if there was some more detailed information." Chrisa asked before taking back from the hands of Marius the object wrapped in the squared towel.

"Ah, but I don't think you'll find something, my friends. It isn't a known artefact and it is catalogued even less! I already checked ten years ago, to be frank with you. I received a lot of confidential information from an acquaintance in Ireland; he showed me some pictures that depicted a piece of Matrix in poor condition and obviously unusable. Apparently, it had been found during an archaeological excavation in a small town about forty miles from Paris. But when I tried to discover the name of the excavations' Office and the person responsible, I found nothing. Nobody knew anything, nothing had been notified to the superintendence of the French museums, and there wasn't even a recording of the finds, which dated back to 2000-3000 BC. At the height of the mystery, there is also the disappearance of Steven, that Irish friend of mine. He disappeared from circulation and no one has heard anything about him. For years I have sought him in various ways, through a network of friends and relatives in Ireland and in

72

all those places with which I thought he would keep some sort of contact. To avoid problems of another kind, we have refused to reveal the disappearance to the Experimental Team. If he escaped, he wanted to erase all traces of himself, but if it's as I think happened... someone killed him! Or maybe he managed to use the Matrix, and if he did, who knows where he went!"

*** Divina Artificia ***

Joshua swallowed with difficulty, looking warily at his sister and that *thing* which she holds in her hands.

"Then what are we supposed to do with it? Marius... aren't you about to say that you are able to use it... that stuff, isn't it? And if that friend of yours has really made it work... where does it take you? Do you dare believe that, through it you can fly?"

The hoarse tone of voice, distressed and measured, pointed to the state of mind of the boy, while his sister looked only thoughtful.

Marius passes both hands through his hair, perhaps unconsciously attempting to brush away with that gesture his foreboding. He gets up very slowly looking at the lake.

"Oh, God only knows how much I want to be able to use it," he mumbled. "I think that is one of those things that could have the same function as the Holy Grail or the Covenant's Ark... Do you know what I mean? No kids, your old sea dog is not able to use the *Vibratory Matrix*. But I think it's not a coincidence that Chrisa was the one to have found it, was it, my dear?"

The inquisitive glance of Marius pierces the young woman, who looks away and begins to contemplate a large bush of gorse with some gaunt yellow flowers. The emotions follow one another very quickly in the woman's mind, step by step she revises the previous night's race. Again she sees the scowling face of Hathor, her pursuer. And still she feels the rain that scratches her face like glass splinters; and suddenly she feels a violent pain in her heart.

She relives the moment in which she had collected the damn thing from the ground... was there something escaping her? Is there any other form or shadow that lurked from her eyes? Perhaps there was a clue, a trace that could help to figure out why that thing was right there at that precise moment? Chrisa retraces her steps, and confronts the brother and the old man with piercing and inquisitive eyes.

"No, actually I don't think it's a coincidence. Someone put it there hoping that I would find it. No doubt that person is aware of my extrasensory abilities... because that's what you alluded to, Marius, isn't it? This thing can't be used by just anyone. Maybe only an *Annwyn* would be able to make it work! And maybe your friend Steven received help from someone of my kin."

Marius became thoughtful, his gaze fixed towards the blue lace of the lake through the trees. Some clouds drew dark shadows on the water's surface, creating greenish patches shadows chasing each other and then back over the coastal shores up to reach the woodland's area.

"You know what my true nature is?" Chrisa accused. "Marius, what did you tell my mom before she was killed? What else do you know about the *Sacred Mirror*?"

Chrisa, by uttering the question, felt released of a constraint.

The air is mild and smells of moss and leaves; a suffused buzz of insects distracted Marius's gaze, which moved away from the young woman to a flood of small flowers bursting with busy, industrious beetles.

In Marius's mind he sees bright glimpses of his past when, as a teenager, he found himself among the green pastures near Clonmacnoise. Ah! His beloved Ireland! He saw the ruins of the 'Seven Churches', as the monastery was often called in the past, with the cemetery and herds of fleecy sheep.

The memory, through vivid images, hurts him. But since everything has a meaning, everything falls into a perfect blueprint, Marius is aware that his mind is recreating a kind of *map* that will help the two young siblings. So, without paying attention to Joshua's complaints about wanting to leave, Marius kneels in front of a large boulder resting in the middle of the clearing, free of trees and undergrowth.

"Be quiet Joshua," Chrisa stops her brother with one arm, whispering, "I feel his thoughts, and Marius is trying to retrieve information on the Matrix from the collective memory. Come, now sit quietly and try to send your energy to him... you know how to do it, brother, you just need to be aware. As we did with mom and dad, especially when something serious had happened or someone was hurt. These were our *prayers*... before they departed. You remember it?"

As in front of an ancient Dolmen, the two young people squat on the ground and closed their eyes. Joshua, even if a little impetuous, never underestimated the power of meditation. Indeed, when their mom and dad were still alive he joined in whenever they meditated. In truth, he always drew a big benefit. So, with a strong awareness, both young people began to relax their breathing and concentrated on the figure of the old sea dog.

Gradually Marius also perceived the energy that the two young people were sending him. In his mind an image assumed blurred outlines, then, suddenly, the vision becomes clear. *The Cross of the Scriptures* shines in majestic glory.

"Ach saor sinn ón olc..." he exclaimed, "mar is leat-sa a ríocht, a chumhacht agus a ghlóir!" [2]

Long minutes elapse, in which every material perception faded from their consciousness. There was no longer the wood, the smell of living and penetrating Nature, the whirl of small insects. Everything is still in the moment, while the energy seems to flow like liquid amber from the bodies of those present. Finally, very slowly, Marius gets up and reaches towards the two young people.

"Not coincidentally I saw another symbol: *'As above, so below'* and this was the paradigm of Hermes Trismegistus. Guys, I saw one of the most famous Celtic Crosses, still certainly the most visible representation of the microcosm in relation to the macrocosm. The Man, the Centre, through the cross that is oriented towards the four cardinal points, the four elements, to arrive at the rim of the seasons marked by the solstices and equinoxes. Do you follow my thoughts?"

Although slightly confused, both young people are hanging on his words.

"So it isn't a static relationship but rather highly dynamic, determined by a centrifugal movement that carries from the microcosm to macrocosm, from the macrocosm to the microcosm. All this suggests to us the symbol of the cross. So the *Matrix* is forcedly a spatial and temporal symbol, which property allows her to express the mystery of the universe in which our planet Earth is inserted."

Beads of sweat decorate Marius' head. The man smiles at the young people, and then with a hand he ruffled Joshua's hair. He seems invigorated; the contours of his face took an almost charming opalescence.

---

[2] Translation from Gaelic: "But free we from evil... that is because is with you the kingdom, the power and the glory".

"Hey, have you both swallowed your tongues?"

Joshua punched the old sailor on the shoulder. "Wow... you're legendary, man, how strong you're! I didn't know that you did these strange hocus pocus things like my sister! But you know I'm not very learned on these *oddities*, it's important for me to know that a boat 'floats' on water, this thing of microcosm and macrocosm are somewhat too complicated for my limited intelligence. Well, honestly, actually... I didn't understand much."

With his hands he gestured by drawing big circles in the air, trying to emphasize his assertions. But Marius didn't heed him.

"Kids, I think that little by little we'll come to discover something more about this trinket. But for now I suggest we continue on to Canobbio to do our shopping... Come on, Joshua, do not make that face. Listen, I can try to explain more simply what I was saying earlier. It is true that it concerned a kind of magic, but *we are magic*! Every living creature is the highest expression of *Magic*! The paradox is that we have forgotten in the passing of the centuries, while at the same time we lost, little by little, even the extrasensory faculties which we were equipped with. This is the real dilemma; hopelessly lost... only esoteric groups have continued to transmit the message, risking their lives! You know what happened during the Crusades, the Inquisition and then in 2022, following the change in the *Crystalline Grid*, where there were more contacts with other planetary civilizations. It was predictable: the governments have tried to cover up everything. Many artefacts have been destroyed, somewhat like the one you now hold in that bag, Chrisa. Everything was done in the hopes of not generating panic on the planet because if that had happened, the oligarchy would have had to capitulate. The few decided that people would never know the truth. But already during the twentieth century, the Elite of the Dominants who ruled on the planet Earth knew of the imminent risk which was being met. They didn't do anything to save the planet, but they arrogantly thought only of themselves and of those wealthy individuals whose financial support was important for the circle of 'the chosen'. They thought that digging deep bunkers and organizing a sort of post-disaster survival plan meant they could avoid the worst. But the catastrophe of the twenty-first century had long been predicted and was not with underground tunnels and anti-atomic shelters that people could survive. The first *Annwyn* had arrived on our planet at the end of the twentieth century; initially they were entities somewhat confused, certainly they didn't yet have the same skill as your sister Chrisa. But they had begun to bring changes in the collective knowledge: they founded the 'new age' and 'spiritual growth' groups and they tried using these to allow more and more people to increase their psychic vibrations. An interesting story, although initially it had been taken very lightly by the most famous philosophers and physicists. It wasn't until the beginning of the twenty-first century that there were more detailed studies on quantum physics that even the most sceptical opinion had begun to change. But by then it was already too late, damn too late!"

Marius is irritated; he looks interrogatively the young woman.

"Chrisa, do you feel something else that escapes me?"

The young woman became serious and thoughtful for a moment; her eyes were looking for something in the ether, and then she answers with a smile.

"No, Marius, the Energy doesn't tell me anything, unfortunately. I think you've discovered a couple of new 'puzzles' that, with patience, we'll try to assemble. I'll make some annotations in my *notebook* and then this evening, in front of a cup of good herbal tea, we'll try to catalogue everything we know. It's especially important to consider every little thing that will occur, even the most improbable. Staying connected with the Energy, the vibrations can scroll smoothly... even if everything happens on a subliminal level."

Walking towards the car, all three brood silently. Chrisa thought about the object that she held in her bag and its mysterious function; Joshua could already taste the homemade ice cream, prohibited like Fabrizio's honey cakes. The rest of the trip went quiet and they arrived in Cannobio, Marius's mood has been transformed back into the sympathetic and mocking old seadog.

Only Chrisa remains wary and suspicious, something is still bothering her, preventing her from smiling spontaneously.

"Come on, Joshua, leave me alone, would you?" Chrisa said, "I don't have time for the usual tantrums and if I'm in a bad mood it is because there are several things that I can't explain. I have a void here," she says, indicating her forehead, "something is going to happen, and certainly not because of tomorrow's race..."

Marius drives with extreme caution along the winding road, busy with countless tourists, especially Nordic visitors, who prefer the coast of Lake Verbano for their summer holidays. Enya's voice, as usual, filled the cabin with the sweet melodies of times gone by. It has been more than two centuries, but her songs are always pleasant and full of mystery. Marius' throaty voice sings one of his favourites:

"Dan y dwr, tawelwch sydd.
Dan y dwr, galwaf i.
Nid yw'r swn gyda fi.
Dan y dwr, tawelwch am byth.
Dan y dwr, galwaf i.

Nid yw'r swn ddim fwy gyda fi." ³

---

³ Beneath the waters, there is silence.
Beneath the waters, I call you.
There is no company with me.
Beneath the waters, silent forever.
Beneath the waters, I call you.
The sound is no longer with me.

Chapter 9

Vice

After having listened carefully to the lawyer's complaint, Dr. Sella let himself sink into a comfortable armchair. A thousand thoughts assailed his mind like a tsunami.

"I've got to find a way to talk to that girl. If she wants to or not..."

Evidently, there was nothing that could interest him less than what the lawyer proposed; he was very clear about the priorities. With a sneer, he looks at the transparency of Veronica's dress: she's in front of the window, observing the lakefront over the terraces. Then he let the butler pour him another glass of Hennessy Paradis. Meanwhile, he extracts his cigar case from his breast pocket and takes a *Lancero*, he passes it under the nose narrowing his eyes and then he turns to the woman.

"Honey, could you?"

With his upper lip curled into a grin, he makes a sign for her to approach. "Prepare it, the way you know…"

Veronika takes from her purse a small tube, very sharp on the tip and she pierces the head of the cigar, making a perfect hole.

"You're talented, you have experienced hands!"

Sella giggles while she passed her tongue around the other end of the cigar.

"Never make the hole too small... it might overheat and the smoke would have a strong and bitter taste... You are skilled in this and more, my dear Veronika."

From behind, the lawyer listens to the soliloquy of his 'client' while watching the woman reflected in the glass display-case in which are housed, equipped with a digital sign, rather unusual objects.

"Dr. Sella, I wouldn't want to appear rude, but your cigar smoke irreparably damages the scent of the flowers. Do you mind going out on the terrace? The temperature is still mild, and no indiscreet ear or eye will bother you."

The lawyer's voice is authoritative yet annoyed; something in the depths of Sella's soul advises him not to object and do what was asked. Sella winks at Veronika, who follows him like a dog. He stretches out his damp, big hand on the side of the woman and, with a vulgar gesture, he goes back down the buttock.

"Intrusive eyes? In my opinion, the least discreet of all are his own... isn't that right, my darling?"

But Veronika doesn't respond to the encouraging attitude of the man, she feels very confused and hardly able to conceal her agitation.

She sits under the large gazebo, which was adorned with many colourful veils that flutter in the slight breeze which comes up from the lake over the roofs of the town. Veronika put on the large black glasses hiding one third of the face, giving to her an air of anonymity. She sips the amber liquid from her glass. The cognac is ruined by too many ice cubes, but she doesn't care that much; behind the black lens she looks warily at Sella and, further, poorly concealed by the curtains covering the doors open onto the terrace, the motionless figure of the lawyer. She feels that

82

there is a stake of indisputable greatness in that game, but as with poker, there's one born cheater: and Sella is one of them.

The lawyer walks away, and passing by the two large paintings whispers to himself.

"That bastard, he thinks that the material world is the only escape for the satisfaction of the impulses!"

He goes down the stairs and quickly reaches another room that opens to the north on a courtyard containing a beautiful Zen garden. The place is accessible only by operating a liquid crystal device, the result of technological advancement of the twenty-third century. The surface of the wall, at first 'solid' was transformed by making visible the entrance, as if by magic.

The lawyer sits down and immediately presses with the index a button on the intercom to call Adam, his butler.

"In around ten minutes, please inform my guests that I had to leave on urgent business. Let them taste another glass of cognac and tell them to wait for me in the living room. I order you to insert the engineer video and sound-control. There're a couple of things that will be verified at a later time! Ahh, I highly recommend that you insist that they remain here. If Sella is in a hurry, surely he'll contact these people directly with the phone, and this is just what I want him to do. I will hold back in the *studio* on the ground floor, Adam. I have to finish a job that takes priority..."

Now his face lets bare his teeth in a strange smirk. If things go as he wishes, his client will be under his control. His gaze wanders for a moment to look out the window at the squiggles drawn in the sand, representing the element of water: it's a privilege to have a small Zen garden at home. The lawyer smiled disdainfully and ironically expresses his thoughts in a low voice, thus freeing his mind.

"This will be flavoured for good, it will be his undoing. Then, little by little, I'll try to dismantle the rest of his empire, and that of other Dominants! But revenge should be enjoyed lukewarm, never hot nor cold!"

Adam, with extreme discretion, immediately executes the orders of the lawyer. The old butler saw his master grow, in every sense of the word. He had long since become the only person the lawyer truly trusted. Something deep ties Adam to absolute loyalty to him: a kind of cruel and terrible blood pact, an alliance that has no anthropomorphic limits.

Before notifying the guests, Adam sets up the video system: in total a dozen tiny camouflaged cameras. They are positioned behind the great pictures of the room and into the sides of the beams which are embedded in the hollow of the old ceiling dating back to 1800. They are placed on the roof, under the pitched gutter, others under the gazebo, and between plants in the tanks. These mini cameras fixed at strategic points, allowing a 360° view.

*** Vitium Hominis ***

And after leaving the bewildered guests on the terrace, the butler returned inside the house with a face painted with a sort of wicked complicity.

"What kind of insolent!" Sella sneered, "And have you heard his old bastard bootlicker?"

Sella's voice is disdainful; his face became inflamed while measuring the length and breadth of the terrace floor, which were covered with mahogany slats. He kicks the large planter that contains many different species of cacti, obviously hurting his foot. Limping he reaches for the woman.

"Who does he think he is? 'Imperative urgency'... ahhh, give me a break. The bastard doesn't know who I am," he added in a choleric tone. "Nasty, insolent! He gets hundreds of thousands of Crowns from me at the end of every job!"

Veronika tries to calm him with her hoarse and sensual voice.

"But honey, you have to wait a bit, we can take some time for us..."

She approaches him, rubbing herself against his legs like a purring cat, and then she takes off her glasses and pulls him towards her. Sella, who already had a few too many cognacs, calms down a little, but stiffens. His eyes quickly go around the space about them:

"Veronika, honey... hmm, you always know how to confuse my mind."

Chapter 10

Ephemeral in the Flesh

Marius pondered while advancing with quick steps along the cobbled street, all curves that leads to the centre of the small town where his acquaintance's shop is. Only a couple of times, a little suspicious, he turns his head to look behind them. No one follows them, or at least not apparently.

"Chrysalis," he says, "satisfy my curiosity: do you really think that someone has deliberately left that object where you could find it? I wonder if this is the key to the mystery, and if this is so, I assume that the owner of the Matrix is not able to make it work, and he's sure that you know how to operate it. If indeed this is the secret, then we can imagine what the intended purpose of that person is: he's a scholar, or he's some other creature, certainly not of this planet."

Joshua looks startled at the old man while Chrisa shows a faint smile on her lips that doesn't make it to her eyes, still full of sadness.

"Marius, but if this individual is not an *Annwyn*, what does he want to do with the Matrix? Do you know what the function of this item was in the past? You said that your ancestors used it, but to do what?"

In her most intimate thoughts, the girl was asking herself if the Matrix could take her to the codes. In moments of anger she felt the desire to break the *Sacred Mirror*, but she was perfectly conscious that this would detached her from Joshua and from this apparent reality. No, she wasn't ready yet, she couldn't live without Joshua. She was convinced that one day, both could have chosen!

The air is stale, the walls of the old houses oozes in the damp afternoon and a dog is rummaging through garbage left to rot in a corner of the lane.

"How much rubbish, too much dirt everywhere, with the technological advances that we had achieved can't we overcome the garbage problems?" Chrisa thinks to herself while she tries in vain to pacify her pounding heart.

The wise words of a great prophet, Krishnamurti, come to her mind. A couple of centuries earlier, he had stated:

"There is a revolution we must do if we want to escape the anguish, conflict and frustration in which we are seized. But this revolution must begin not with the theories and ideologies, but with a radical transformation of our minds!"

Then slowly shaking her head, she turned to speaks to the two friends.

"I remember an anecdote that our mother had told us; she appreciated very much the thoughts of Krishnamurti. He said that once he was in his room, illuminated by the sun, surrounded by many freshly cut flowers. Accidentally, a butterfly entered into the room. The windows were closed and the butterfly could only see the blue sky beyond the glass, trying to escape to the open air and freedom, but always ended up against the glass. The insect had flown all around the glass to see if there was a higher way out, then tried at the bottom without finding an opening. Then

Krishnamurti opened the window and the butterfly flew away. I was always intrigued by the comparison that human beings are imprisoned in a crystal cage from which they try to escape. Yet, rather than an intense desire to go outdoors and look for the opening, the man wants to first know the type of glass with which the cage is built, he wants to discover the age of the crystal, the person who manufactured it and so on. Unlike the butterfly, men have no immediate desire for freedom and, with it, to achieve happiness! They are locked in the crystal cage and complain of the injustice and suffering in life. The men struggle and suffer just because they want to stay in this material cage."

*** In Carne Caducum ***

Joshua surrounds his sister's shoulders in a gesture of tenderness, while Marius whispers to her.

"Come on, my sweet friend. Don't worry and stop thinking about saving the world at once. Chrysalis, this is a utopia! There were several saints, prophets, sages, philosophers and fools... each had the hope that Man would repent and try to find answers to his questions through the mind. It's now centuries since we celebrated falsehood as a Missa Solemnis. There are elapsed ages of glory and light, others of darkness and misery, and right now we're in a medieval era without equal; although something has definitely improved thanks to the presence of the *Annwyn*. Forget about the role and reason of your presence on the planet, think that we love you, you are important to both of us... we don't want to lose you... for nothing in the world."

Joshua's face darkens and his voice chokes in his throat. He's aware that he shares something very deep with his sister. He is also aware that there was an ocean of differences that can't bring them together, besides their genetic heritage. He isn't an *Annwyn* and he experiences this fact almost as a sort of exclusion. He loved his sister immensely, he would sacrifice his life for her, but he doesn't want her to suffer because of her salvation's mission! And Chrisa knows, she always knew, that Joshua is the only person who can be trusted beyond death.

"Come on guys," Marius says, thinking to end the distress of his young friends, "here we are. Put away the sadness, and take a small taste of some special cheese?!"

He enters the shop; the owner is intent on rearranging tasty-looking fruit and vegetables in a large wicker basket.

"Hi, Giacomo! Is there something new in town? Come on, pull out a bottle and let us try out some of 'those exclusive' cheeses; tomorrow night my two young friends and I will be celebrating my victory, or theirs, at the race. Aeolus shall be on the side of the best!"

Giggling, Giacomo turns and embraces his friends, and then he takes a bottle of Tuscan red wine from behind the counter and lays it on the long, old wooden table laden with colourful first fruits.

"Hey, I recommend you to take a few pears, the pink and light green ones out there, while I look for the glasses. Nice that you came to visit me, today I was just bored to death."

Giacomo tells of his latest adventures with the Experimental Team; apparently, all the food that is placed on the market is controlled. Products not bearing the seal of the Unified Power are prohibited and those who sell unauthorized goods end up in huge trouble.

"But if you think about it? It is insanity, since all the crap with the seal of the UP comes from genetic manipulation! There is nothing, not even a grain of rice, that isn't from a mutation created in the laboratory. With this garbage, they're trying to change the structure of our DNA... you see? You don't need to be a learned man in the field to make one plus one... and once we are also 'faked' there the control's game is implemented! Puppets. That is what they want to make of the human race: puppets who sit quietly and helpless, not daring to oppose the system. Consider controlled procreation; okay, if this is to empower parents... but reproduction in a test tube has unfortunately taken the place of normal physiological reproduction... tell me, where's the spice of life?"

Giacomo looks around suspiciously; he takes a few steps toward the back room and pulls the separation's curtain. Then he goes to the entry door and also closes it, by lowering the strainer fitted with a garland of bells.

"I think they have at least three hundred years that kind of stuff, but if you just touch the door, their tinkling warns us that is someone out there. Ah ah ah, a touch of ancient technology in this kind of dilapidated shop. It's better to be cautious, even though Marco, down at the end of the square, checks the road during the day and informs his friends if he sees the Experimental Team."

The shopkeeper turns around and reaches below a shelf, where he detaches a hidden and presumably undeclared, and therefore banned, cell phone.

"But let's ignore these problems; by Giacomo, you enjoy the best! Here is delicious stuff, believe me... are you ready to make a mockery of the Experimental Team and damn your taste buds with something that could get me killed?"

In the merchant's company the three friends spend a couple of hours with no strange thoughts to darken their mood. Even Chrisa apparently manages to think about anything else, just every now and then her eyes are rummaging through the darkness toward the back room as if she feared that someone might suddenly emerge. Her shoulder bag contains an artefact to be preserved with care. Surely, with the help of Marius she'll be able to find out its purpose... since Chrisa is increasingly convinced: somebody must have deliberately left the *Vibratory Matrix* on the pavement so that she would find it.

Chapter 11

Moral Redemption

Chrisa and Joshua remember their parents with great affection! Every moment they spent with them was magical. Their childhood was a sort of exciting and fantastic adventure, where the support of their parents had always encouraged them towards very farsighted goals.

Mom and dad had realized that someone absolutely had to get out of the duality in order to understand the deeper meaning of his presence on the planet, and in doing so he was to reach higher levels of Light. Of course, Chrisa knew that, as an *Annwyn*, the reason for her presence on the Planet is just to support the spiritual evolution of humans, not influencing them directly. Unfortunately at the beginning of the third millennium and before the hecatomb, few were paying attention to the paranormal messages or the channelling from other dimensions.

The Higher Self in sentient beings had of curse grown in strength and great changes had begun, but many people remained anchored to the received education that was considered 'normal life', through the fault of the theological dogmas. They then disregarded these heavenly messages and didn't want to be guided towards the Higher Realms.

Only in those communities where there were many *Annwyn* had the evolution become perceptible and the vibration on Earth, increased at an ever faster pace, had enabled a small number of people to achieve a higher level of consciousness. But the catastrophe, however, had not been avoided... and this was a fact.

Now, especially when sadness and loneliness assail Chrisa and Joshua, both of them remember those very special moments shared with their parents. They had learned a great respect for nature and the animals, and through these teachings they had always managed to tackle even the most difficult situations when they were inadvertently spectators of vandalism or violence. Unfortunately this was the reality of that era: they had to rebuild what was destroyed in too many centuries of indifference and wastage.

Because of the greenhouse effect and after the terrible catastrophe of 2022, people got literally caught by panic. A sort of collective phobia had rekindled the hatred towards the whole social system in the minds of those who had lost everything, fomenting in them the desire to make barbaric acts with the maximum aggressiveness. This led to the rise of fierce extremist groups that rebelled against everything and everyone instead of working to restore proper institutions to face the future with positivity and intelligence. Only after the restoration of martial law and the creation of the Experimental Team were these groups persecuted and isolated, little by little.

With the passing of the first 40 years, around 2060, the situation derailed and humans had fallen into the abyss of ignorance, so the spiritual elevation was consequently blocked. Therefore, instead of raising their consciousness to another vibration state, the people no longer continued to try to break the chains of alienating forms of thoughts, but rather they further stimulated them. In some sense, this had occurred already several times on the planet when entire cultures had vanished into thin air.

*** Moralis Redemptio ***

Many had forgotten the challenge to become 'observers of themselves' to be able to dominate their thoughts and actions. Too few were able to review their old way of being and co-existing, by cutting the ties with some aspects of their annihilating perception that prevented them from rising to higher planes of consciousness.

All this was fossilized in a hopeless situation: aware of this, some members at the top of the great totalitarian nations, mostly theosophists, astrophysicists and philosophers, tried to repair the damage by providing the world's population a clear basis for free study and training in philosophical and scientific disciplines.

But they were, unfortunately, continuously opposed by the religious autocratic factions, who had taken on a sort of improbable role, comparable to the ancient medieval Crusades. They themselves joined the rampaging with the aim of encouraging religious hegemony to emerge against the newly created Unified Power.

There was a bitter and bloody conflict, where those opposed to the will of the Theological Sects were killed, exiled or imprisoned in a hospital designed to keep these people under maximum supervision and control. This increased the sense of general malaise in the populations, making them fall back again to the primitive levels of the early first millennium.

It was normal that in places most affected by geothermal influences reigned a kind of terror, and right there, in those weakened places where Nature couldn't help living beings, the various religious institutions had begun

94

more strongly to try to expand the totalitarian rule over the world. The same thing happened many centuries before, in many underdeveloped nations.

Unfortunately, the study of the past, from which we could learn from repeated past mistakes, had been almost banished from virtual libraries, with exception for some pirate sites that were regularly obscured within a few days. Few people had access to old volumes, which for more than a century, had been stowed in huge vaults to be preserved and protected from external chemical influences.

Then something began to radically change. In 2080, during a summit at the last Emergency Congress, it was decided to rebuild the headquarters of the Unified Power. One of the promoters suggested choosing Al-Hillah, *The Gate of God* of Babylon, as it was called by the ancient Sumerians.

The idea was that the biblical myth mentioned in the Apocalypse as a metaphor of evil would serve as a warning, to rebuild the Good! And right there, in the city of Ishtar, where Nebuchadnezzar had led his people to the conquest of Jerusalem and destroyed Solomon's Temple in the year 600 BC, it was decided to rebuild the headquarters of the new Power that would allow the unity of all races, of all nations.

Chrisa rearranges her thoughts after the introspection. Somewhat estranged, she looked around, realizing that she had just recalled a few centuries of history. She turned to Marius, and lowers her voice so Joshua would not hear her.

"Al-Hillah! *The Gate of God,* Marius... Your view of the Cross of the Scriptures is nothing but its key!"

Giacomo laid down another wooden plate filled with sausages and some triangles of black bread.

"That's organic, guaranteed! And as few you can still find in these times. My friend breeds his animals in the wild, even at the risk of having problems with the law. He doesn't care about the safety rules which would like these animals stuffed in aseptic environments. Although everyone knows that the meat that is sold is just an anomalous structure with a taste of flesh, in reality it is a molecular concoction that was never alive! My friend lives in an isolated valley about 3 hours from here, his pigs wallow in the mud and the chickens are chased by dogs. But shush... don't tell around that Giacomo sells prohibited goods. This stuff is worth its weight in gold, it's godsend for the body."

Chrisa smiles at the good man, then approaches and hugs him affectionately.

"Thanks Giacomo," she grins, "but my brother and I are vegetarians... However you could not make us a more welcome gift, you are an invaluable friend, not only for your generosity, but for the privilege of being in your presence. I know you don't understand, but you should know that this is very important for you and your 'evolution'. I'm sure that you will stay out of trouble, don't forget that the Experimental Team considers almost everyone to be infiltrates or subversives. Better not get into conflict with them, thus you avoid the Inquisition."

Then she became very tense and thoughtful. Marius chuckles.

"Chrisa be peaceful," he says reassuringly, "my friend is also smart and has extricated himself from trouble more than once. Apparently there is some 'good spirit' that protects him."

"Come on, with this hocus pocus," snorts Joshua, "I am starting to feel some discomfort. We shall be careful when we leave here; I wouldn't be bitten by some *jaglynx* that confused me with its prey!"

But if that should have been a joke, none of them smiled. They always blame the poor beasts, when someone ends up torn into pieces in dubious circumstances. But the suspicion of many is that behind the Unified Power there is much more concealed!

Chapter 12

The Primordial Beast

The lawyer is sitting in his Corbusier deckchair which, despite the lapse of centuries, had remained the same. He's watching the internal circuit with contempt, the monitor showed Sella and Veronika in the gazebo. He felt a strong disgust for the weakness of humans who are overwhelmed by the instincts of the ancient animal. When it came to the flesh, almost all behaved indecently and without thinking. The neural stimuli were only directed to mating, like animals in heat. Everything else was losing value and personal priorities and defences lowered below the desirable threshold, and then if you add a little alcohol, the cocktail became deadly, uncontrollable.

*** Prima Bestia ***

Is that possible, despite the presence of so many Beings of Light, that the social behaviour of humans had not changed? Although the *Annwyn* were able to influence the rising vibration of the planet, yet there were too many *lower creatures*... like Sella, specifically.

The lawyer receives a sort of snap behind the neck, a sure sign of detachment. The potential which binds him to the casing of his body can be driven at will through his Mind. He smirks, observing his body, which remains perfectly still and relaxed on the deck while the vibration of his astral body assumes a bright light and golden colour. That's a game. It's a sort of exercise that took him to a feeling of perfect pleasure, completely different from what is perceived by humans.

This was a singular faculty, the splitting: the detaching from the material casing which bound him to the Earth's gravity, the lawyer always felt a sense of divine omnipotence.

But there was no time to lose: the guests were having fun on the terrace, even if their game wouldn't last long... so ephemeral was the pinnacle of pleasure.

Alessandro is busy counting the tourists, mentally dividing men from women, children and elderly with white hair. Sometimes he's in trouble because, thanks to advances in medicine and the new discoveries made by science, it's now possible to extend the lifespan over a hundred years, maintaining an appearance considerably younger. Although the Unified Power had repeatedly tried to tamper the scientific progress, the eternal human desire for immortality always had the upper hand.

The young man didn't notice that something strange was happening beyond the boats' wharf. Tourists flocked in long lines outside the restaurants and bars, quietly waiting their turn to be admitted. A couple of kids with rollerblades were spinning around the deck of the young Alessandro, who eventually lost his temper.

"Hey! Damn you, can't you go somewhere else to play around? You'll end up into water, and I certainly will not come to fish you out, do you understand my language, irreverent miscreants?!"

Alessandro ends up losing patience and gets up suddenly. Only at that moment his gaze falls on the water's surface; near a mooring buoy, he notices something that floats. He forgets the two boys' rollerblading and takes off his dark sunglasses. A strange sensation takes the pit of his stomach.

"Damn..."

With a leap, he reaches the small boat which he usually use to bring the owners of the boats from the harbour to their boats. Suddenly even the two young people stop and follow the movements of the boy on the boat. Then one hears the screams and the panic ends in a general, real mess.

"What happened? Holy God, someone call the Experimental Team! Help the poor guy, alone he can't make it... Quickly!"

There is even more yelling until the arrival of a large feline with bestial roars drove away the curious, rushing at and bearing sharp teeth against those who tried to approach the harbour.

Slumped in the little boat, Alessandro, pale-faced, continues to vomit into the water, holding on to the edge of the boat with difficulty.

People hear some penetrating whistles while a dozen *jaglynx* arrived, accompanied by a large group of Experimental Team guards. The big cats seem crazy: in the general crush, tourists were leaning toward the outer side of the lake front. These are situations where it's surely wise to stay still and do exactly as instructed by the guards. No one dares to walk away, only the frightened children have taken refuge in the arms of their parents.

Alessandro is reached by a pair of guards with their silvery uniforms, which shines under the rays of the setting sun. They help him to bring the boat into the harbour while other guards were combing the area and dredge up what remained of the mutilated bodies of two people.

After a few minutes, a high barrier fence was raised around the port, so no prying eyes could violate the secrecy of what happened on the other side. Certainly no one would dare to even think about approaching, the *jaglynx* inspire fear just by looking at them.

"I have no idea of what happened," Alessandro continues to repeat, in a panic. "I stood there, counting the by-passers, I swear it! No one came over the protection barrier of the dock. Only a couple of young men on rollerblades were swirling around my deck at the time I saw that thing floating... oh my God."

With one hand on his mouth, the poor guy had begun to vomit on the floor, under the disgusted gaze of a guard who then passed him a paper towel.

"Okay, let him alone for now," said a nice-looking man dressed in a bottle green linen suit. He greeted Alessandro officially.

"I'm Commander Fenix. I formally ask you not to leave the town of Ascona until we get back in touch with you. Oh, one more thing, please. We know that the boat over there, the Avalon's Mist, is inhabited by two young siblings. Can you tell me where are they? We boarded, but the hatch is closed, apparently there is nobody on board. I also need the list of vessels that entered the port in the last 7 days. I must compare it with the government's one. That big boat, do you see that one on the right? On board we found charts of the area marked with the location of tomorrow's race, but there are no data to explain their presence. Inside it looks as if someone had dusted everything thoroughly, erasing all fingerprints, including these on the navigation maps. The owner is a certain Dr. Sella... can you tell me where he is right now?"

Alessandro, still bewildered by the events, continues to shake his head, unsteady on his legs, showing visible signs of illness.

"Don't you think you should see a doctor from the intensive care unit? A word of advice, he could give you a remedy. You're very proven... It's the first time that..."

The officer is interrupted by the young man.

"Holly God, Commander, please! I don't know where those two are; they left with their friend Marius, an Irishman who has always lived in Ascona. As for the boats, it's all shown in the list, you have access to the data on *Unynetweb*, as required by the Unified Power. I strictly follow the law with the utmost care, believe me, Commander."

At the idea of having to take a remedy from a doctor at the Intensive Care Unit, Alessandro immediately recovered. He knows what happened to people given those cures. For nothing on earth he would take that rubbish, he didn't want to see his brain affected. Rather, he preferred to be killed quickly and without any preambles.

The young man's face is sincere, the scrutinizing Officer's gaze doesn't notice any abnormal signs and, knowingly, he trusted him. Moreover, his *anthropomorphic badge* had already been checked and found to be free of criminal record, clean like a new-born one's from a perfect genetic selection. The Commander Fenix pulls from his pocket a metallic business card and extends it to Alessandro.

"This is my address, Al. Call me if you need my help or if you recover your memory."

Alessandro notes that Fenix has called him by his nickname and he asks himself the reason. Then the commander moves away, followed by the *jaglynx* which were waving their long and bushy tails, showing their teeth and making a path in the crowd.

Alessandro found himself alone on the pier. He takes his cotton sweater from the big box set on the electric scooter. The sun has already fallen over the horizon, leaving crimson brushstrokes in the dark blue sky to the west. To the east, above the peaks of the mountains that encircle the Lake Verbano, a few emaciated stars pierce the night's surface that within an hour would have stretched her shadow and her fears over the town. The young man is concerned about the Avalon's Mist. Where in the hell have his friends gone? In the penetrating gaze of Fenix had taken a strange twist when he had mentioned the two young people: apparently nothing escaped the Unified Power. Alessandro must try to contact Chrisa and Joshua to tell them what had happened. Perhaps it's an impulse, but Alessandro is convinced that it was not only the Experimental Team spying on the small harbour, and he's afraid that his friends could be in serious danger.

Chapter 13

The Soul of the World

Marius is absorbed in his thoughts: visions of Clonmacnoise returned to his memory. Childhood had not been kind to him, but had spurred him to grow up quickly and now, perhaps, a different fate awaited him. Of his land he especially remembered the green plains, the cliffs and rocks overlooking the sea. Those cliffs partly protected the island from the enormous flood of two centuries ago; but if in fact the island was partly spared by the great catastrophe, it was because of the presence of the ancient inhabitants of that place: the Celts.

Archaeological sites such as Clonmacnoise had the good fortune not to undergo major alterations; *something magical* had preserved it. Marius was convinced that in 2022 some areas of the planet Earth had been shielded and protected by extra-terrestrial entities, and not only by the legends on the ancient inhabitants. Who knows, maybe they were just the same *Annwyn* that, with different groups belonging to similar thought's sources, had laboured to save the planet.

Giacomo's voice has become an echo in the background; the old sea dog still thinks about Chrisa's phrase in reference to the possibility that everything was related to the *Cross of the Scriptures*. Subsequently there is no other choice; they must go as soon as possible to Clonmacnoise! Certainly, among the ruins of the Seven Churches they would find what they seek, and maybe the symbol related to *Vibratory Matrix* may reveal something that also explains the disappearance of his close friend, Steven. The image of his childhood friend returns to his mind like a knife that cuts a gash in the butter. Marius is vulnerable, this isn't good. He had dropped his self-defences and has the impression that day by day his *casing* is made more difficult to manage. He wonders if Chrisa perceives these changes; perhaps he should talk to her and expose all his doubts. Better yet, tell her everything, beginning with explaining the real reasons for which he himself had accepted the task of taking care of them after their parents died.

"Hey Marius, where're you with your head? Will you answer my question? Or do you also have extraordinary powers like the *Annwyn,* and left behind your physical body?" The amused voice of Giacomo awakens him suddenly, and then the gaze of the old sea dog crosses that of Chrisa, which became darker and more troubled.

"No, no," Marius grumbled, "I'm so sorry, I was distracted; I was thinking about a few things that I have not done yet. You know tomorrow's race has kept me quite busy lately."

He lied, shamelessly, and the girl knew it.

"Forgive my rudeness, Giacomo, I admit that today I'm not in the right mood to appreciate your hospitality!"

"Don't say that, old chap, it's because the years have begun to weigh on the back of both of us," the shopkeeper mocks him, winking at Joshua. "Don't soften too much, if you let go you end up like those who have being locked up in those nasty places. Those kinds of hospitals where you are parked before you get the last bite, when you're too old and your body would require a lot of expensive treatments. Brrr ... I don't want to think about that, rather I find another solution."

Giacomo looks sideways at the young siblings and avoids talking for a moment that seems to last for hours.

"Excuse me, but sometimes I can't escape from 'thinking'. At least a few centuries ago things were very different." Almost whispering, he adds: "the Unified Power doesn't just make things right, if you know what I mean."

The merchant looks at the digital wristwatch and makes a serious face.

"Wow, it's already six o'clock, I think it's better if I close the shop before someone come to snoop around here. It's usually check-time, where the Experimental Team bring their felines with the supersensitive sense of smell. Damn them! I have to hide this gift of God under the floorboards of the back room and then leave plastic boxes of those hideous dried fish from the government's cooperative that you aren't even sure that was once alive. But at least the smell is so strong that it hides the aroma of the cheese and of all the rest. Nowadays, everything is genetically manipulated, almost 80% of the food, now. Beautiful disaster, with the excuse that no one dies of starvation or thirst, the Unified Power has a monopoly on world food supplies. Come on, quick, quick! Dearest friends, came back soon to celebrate the winner of tomorrow's race. Too bad I can't come to Ascona, unfortunately I have promised my daughter to take care of my grandchild."

Marius embraces him with force; a tear runs along the edge of his eyelid.

"Cheer up. I'll call in a few days, on the other number, the illegal and unregistered one... and watch not to get caught, you must never, ever connect through *Unynetweb*.

If you get caught with an unregistered number, you will end up behind bars! Always use the code name, as we agreed."

Marius felt a new twinge in his stomach... maybe this could be the last time he holds his friend in his arms.

The young people turn to say goodbye to Giacomo, who holds out a few apples to them both.

"Here, just like those that your great-grandmother used to bite! They are juicy and full of vitamins." Then this time winking at Chrisa, he adds, "take care of him as well as he took care of you over the years. Marius has aged... Come, go, and hurry up!"

Along the small alley all three are silent, the air is fresh and the sun has already disappeared behind the mountains. The kids hid the apples in the capacious pockets of their jackets; they don't want to take the risk of getting caught with goods that doesn't bear the stamp of government control.

Fortunately there is no one on the path to the car, only the smell of food being prepared from a few building comes to their nostrils. As soon as they climbed into the electric car, Marius turns on the player with the recorded music he loves: Irish music. He raises the volume a little and looks warily out of the car, and then turns to look at Chrisa, who is sitting in the back with her legs curled up against her body.

"We have to go to Ireland, my friends... as soon as possible! I have a strange premonition that something is happening, and I think you are in danger. Everything is linked to the strange object that you found, Chrisa. There would be no time to return to Ascona..."

"Hey Marius, wait a minute..." Joshua interrupts, excitedly. "What about tomorrow's race? What's all this urgency? Are you starting again with the hocus pocus? I'm sick of these tricks. The both of you leave me alone!"

Very pissed off, the boy punches the dashboard, and then, having hurt himself, sullenly rubs his knuckles.

Chrisa remains silent, her face reflected no emotion. She looks at the apple that Giacomo gave her, and then bites into it with intense pleasure. Smiling, the young woman thinks back to some buffoon's old story, trying to explain why humans suffer and die, instead of living in Eden.

"Hmm, really juicy and delicious! That's right Marius, I perceive the same vibrations, but I don't think that we can travel around without the appropriate travel documents and permits; unless you are holding on to us some other surprises. Come on, spit out the bone!"

"This afternoon's vision was clear and I was validated by my instinct as the hours passed." Marius smiles, a little forcedly, and then adds in a strange tone, "we must go immediately to Ireland, but I think there is something more. I didn't want to tell you in order to avoid further anxiety. I received a strange message on my unregistered digital phone, from the Commissary, which will check tomorrow's race. I don't know why there is such an urgency to speak to me. He alluded to 'interferences'… he uses that phrase when the Experimental Team is involved."

After waiting several hours, the Experimental Team patrols return to the Central office. Fenix had left a magnetic note on the deck hatches of Avalon's Mist. It clearly stated that the occupants of the sailboat should appear as soon as possible at the Central office, bringing their identification documents.

Inside Fenix's office there is much excitement and the shouts of the guards are mixed with the groans of their cats, the hum of the *unycell*s vaguely resembles the sizzle of molecular food being cooked in basic solutions.

"Commander, you'll see that the boys will respect the order. Don't worry about them, or even for the old Irish man. We wait for the scientific team to do... hmmm... the autopsy of the remains of those two wretches. They were two criminals with several arrest warrants. However, I wonder how they could leave the hospital where they had been confined four months ago. We shall investigate as well over there: the two criminals should have been hibernated. The decision and the warrant were signed by the president of the Experimental Team, yet somehow they managed to get dismissed. The doubt arises that there are infiltrators or people who were paid to let them run away."

Fenix stares straight ahead, and then presses a button and waits for the dark liquid to come from the vending machine.

"It sucks! This sort of rinsing isn't coffee. Do me a favour, Sergio, go down to the restaurant on the corner and fill up the thermos. Damn, I think it will be a long night. No, I have no worries about the boys; the youngest is an *Annwyn* and knows her way around. It's the story about what happened to their parents that bothers me, a very bad story Sergio. Really bad!"

On the huge screen that serves as a dividing wall, the images found at the crime scene are visible. A computerized network of further documents, are arranged at the end of each streak of light, connected by additional segments. There are pictures of people, with data concerning their current coordinates, some specific details that included sexual orientation to shoe size and the brand of cigarettes they smoke, despite the worldwide smoking ban. To the Unified Power there aren't any secrets: once catalogued, a human being took the same value as a genetically codified animal at the beginning of the twentieth century. It all started with the creation of the company 'Igenea.net' through the Internet, a sort of rudimentary *Unynetweb* in use in the 21st century. Igenea had started an inventory of people, curious about their ancestry, through DNA testing and analysis. The game was done! Thanks to the ingenuity of more and more people, genetic cataloguing was started.

*** Anima Mundi ***

After the disaster of 2022, all survivors were required to register, and from that moment the control of their every move was necessary for the purposes of those who ran the hegemonic power.

"We should do nothing else but wait. It's necessary to immediately establish road block control, waterways control, and airspace control." Quickly moving the liquid crystal cursor, Fenix establishes contact with all suppliers of transport services, road checks, charging stations for electric cars and grocery stores. "If they try to leave our area of surveillance, they will be immediately intercepted. Their *unycell*s however, are not connected into the network, which means that they have switched them off, so we can't track them by satellite. We missed that too! They are clever, very clever... and the girl is an *Annwyn*, stick that well into your head!"

Chapter 14

The Magic of Music

Marius parked his car behind a thick bush in a secluded area, and now he must walk to the harbour, trying to avoid being seen. If they wanted to quickly leave Ascona, they must avoid being intercepted. The message on Marius's phone had definitely been a warning: the race's Commissioner is one of his dearest friends. They still don't know what happened during the afternoon, and they didn't imagine that the area was blocked by agents of the Experimental Team.

But Chrisa continued to sense those strange vibrations in the air.

"Marius. Better you don't go down to the harbour, there is something wrong... it is a feeling, but I sense there is danger... there is much fear and threat in the air!"

The old man stops, turns on his heels, and reached for the slightly trembling girl.

"Fear not, Chrysalis. I trust your intuition and you know it. What should we do?"

For a long moment also Joshua observes his sister with a serious and contracted face, and then intervenes.

"Listen, let us send a digital message to Alessandro. Both of us are in possession of an unregistered cell phone... I think it is too late to give a damn about the laws! I'll see if I can get some information on this story, the speedboat and the presumed spies, yes, and ask about any weirdness that happened this morning."

While Joshua is looking for his phone in his safari jacket, the thunderous roar of large helicopters flying over the town could be heard. Instinctively all three squatted down behind a bush, holding tight to each other. The large headlights were pointing in their direction, but after a few interminable seconds, the 'flying beasts' moved away, raising a mound of earth and dry leaves.

"And this confirms that Chrisa is right," Marius said. "It has been several months since we've seen the air patrols after dark. Come on, you try to send a message to the boy, let see what he says."

The air is mild and a sweet aroma of flowers that pleasantly tickles the senses hovers in it. Not far from there is a huge villa's botanical garden which borders the lake, the hedge of jasmine is several hundred feet long. The immense house belongs to a rich man, although it has been somewhat neglected for a decade, as if no one seemed to care. They were telling some strange stories about the former owners having the original nineteenth century structure restored in the year 2000. They had invested beyond belief, expanding the cellars flooded by groundwater and the rising lake. Outside it looked like a castle, with two large four floors towers, apparently accessible only from the outside through a door situated at 20 feet over the ground.

Chrisa and Joshua remembered having been there many times to play in that lush garden, when they were little. And they also went there other times with their parents, to attend to special parties. A couple of times a year, a group of gardeners came to cut right and left, making way through the branches. That certainly was a wonderful place to hide... if there had been a need.

"Who is the Experimental Team seeking? Here, I sent the message... see if Alessandro responds."

Long minutes elapsed, during which the two young siblings and Marius remain secure behind the hedge, then a flashing light and clinking of the cell phone suddenly takes up Joshua, who feels his heart pounding in his throat.

The boy quickly reads the words written by his friend in a low voice: *"Where are you? Holy Heaven... a real mess occurred here... body parts in the water... I felt sick... SS is looking for you... the port is controlled... I fear for you, don't come... Tomorrow, I'll get back to you. D."*

Marius shakes his head, running a hand behind his neck. He stands up slowly to stretch his legs, which had begun to ache.

"Damn. Now what? If we go down, we won't be able to unstick them from our butts, but if we don't return to the boat, it would arouse suspicions... and I don't like the Experimental Team nosing around on my catamaran or on your sailing boat. Although something tells me they already did it. We must decide what to do, and fast! Listen, it can be very risky, but one way or another I have to get something from my apartment. Perhaps the only thing they know is that you came away with me and that maybe we stay away for a few days... hell, if we weren't registered in tomorrow's race…"

The old man takes some steps back and forward, then suddenly stops

"Listen, I will walk down to my flat, take the papers and a couple of other things that could be useful. Then I'll send a message to the race Commissioner on *Unynetweb*... I will use the registered mobile phone and then detach the connection to prevent them from tracing of the sender. They must have put it all under control. I will invent a credible story to fool any researcher. If it's as I think, the Commander Fenix will be informed immediately. If I have problems, I will send you a digital message on the other, unregistered cell phone, okay with you two? You'll be fine, don't worry. Stay here, but don't return to the car. We'll go together when I get back, and then we leave immediately. Afterwards... well, I would have another trusted friend that can possibly help us to leave the country very quickly. Ah ah ah ah... I'm a good poker player, guys. Oh yes, the old Marius is quite smart!"

Joshua strikes his usual pat on the old man's shoulder.

"Try to hurry. The hocus pocus awaits us!"

Chrisa grimaces at her brother, not believing that was the right moment for sarcasm, while understanding that the situation has become exasperating.

"Joshua! Please try to avoid wasting your breath. It's not a game. It seems to me that you don't want to realize it. I guess I know to who the corpses they dredged from the lake were: I told you somebody was watching us from the luxury speedboat. I'm convinced that those are the people killed, but I don't think they fell into the water only to be prey of some voracious pike. The whole story is certainly to be linked to this object!"

Chrisa taps the shoulder strap hidden under the linen jacket. After a brief pause, she adds, "I wonder if we can get to Clonmacnoise. I have my doubts, even though I trust in that fox Marius and in his strange circle of friends! Hopefully he won't encounter any *jaglynx* on the way home, they are cute animals when they are alone, but if there are cops in the way, they become bad, as this is what is expected from them. Once I *mentally* talked with one of them. It was a big male that hadn't castrated yet, waiting for the guard to whom it had been assigned. It evidently didn't hold much esteem for the man. But did you know that they are castrated to prevent them from establishing a sense of the pack? They are all born in the laboratory after a unique cloning, in the presence of the guard to which they will be bonded. I promised myself that one day this will change. The day in which the *Annwyn* will have reached a sufficiently high number, and consequently also the vibration of the planet will be further modified."

Joshua looks at his sister with a bewildered look, but he doesn't say a word. He prefers to play around with his cell phone on which he uploaded good, relaxing music, a couple of very old Chopin's piano concertos: *Les Nocturnes.*

*** Musicae Ars Magica ***

Chrysalis smiles at her brother and then with one hand she strokes his head.

"Hey, what if one of these nights I take you with me? Do you think you can try to maintain your composure and show courage to follow me into a dream? You asked me long ago, Joshua, now I think the time has come. If in Ireland we have to look for something that is not otherwise accessible to sunlight... then we can use the moonlight. Like some stories of vampires and creatures of darkness, ah ah ah. You know those stories still fascinate gangs of youths who don't stop to think that immortality is the panacea for all ills!"

Suddenly the phone is blinking, an incoming message.

"It's Marius... he's inside his apartment. There were no problems of any kind; there are only a bunch of agents at each corner. They've left a magnetic message on his door and urged him to appear at the Police station. He says he'll send a message to the race commissioner and then come back to us, he'll be here in a maximum of twenty minutes."

Chapter 15

The Concealed Power

The butler coughed several times to attract the attention of Dr. Sella and his escort. Tired of waiting, he forcefully slams the balcony's doors; the noise is such that the two indecent guests quickly recomposed themselves. Certainly it's a very embarrassing situation, and this leaks from the butler's glance full of irony mixed with disgust.

"My master asks you to join him in his office, he apologises for the absence."

The old butler turns on his heel and walks away quickly, muttering under his breath, "worse than animals. I agree with the judgement of my master. These two should be hibernated or be submitted to the correct therapy!"

The lawyer entered the studio with a briefcase and a large brown envelope held closed by a burgundy ribbon with a black wax seal. His gaze is impassive and betrays no emotion. Slightly raising the jacket on the back, he sits on the chair. He puts his briefcase on the floor and places the large envelope in the centre of the immense walnut desk, covered with a layer of briarwood and floral designs in ebony and mother of pearl. He doesn't say a single word, his silence becomes oppressive. Dr. Sella, pissed at being kept waiting and then being disturbed during his perversions, is red in the face. Veronika, with damaged makeup, doesn't know how to compose herself. She's also dizzy because she had been guzzling cognac.

"Madam, I beg you, you may use the bathroom. My butler will accompany you; I think you need to regain your composure... if so it can be defined. You can't walk out of my house in that condition!"

Only then did the lawyer flaunt a wry yet scornful smile. Sella doesn't even breathe a word; he tries to stay calm and convinced that soon he could return the snub with the interest at the man whom he began to loathe from the bottom of his heart.

As soon as the woman moved away, following Adam like a puppy, the lawyer turns and glares terribly at Dr. Sella.

"Who do you think you are? I remind you that among us there were very clear agreements. You were paying for legal advice, which I provided to you and your many companies. Everything is accurately reported, I like to be precise, and you know perfectly well that this is my value. The various *favours* that I have asked of you over the years have always been rewarded with lots of money. And this was also recorded with sagacity. But now things have changed, Dr. Sella. I no longer need your presence. It has become cumbersome. However, I can't stand the idea that something terrible could happen to you, and maybe the Experimental Team could lay the blame on me. Now I have to give commands, and you, you little bastard, should only carry out my orders."

With an upset face, in the throes of an uncontrollable rage, Sella suddenly rises, reaching the lawyer's desk in two steps.

"You! How dare you? With what imprudence can you make these observations? Son of a bitch, to whom... but watch yourself, and do me a favour. I just need to make a phone call and you will regret having been born... You fucking bastard... you may stick your fucking threats where I say!"

*** Occulta Potestas ***

Dr. Sella goes to leave, but in spite of himself he cannot move his legs. With a piercing pain in the head, he realizes that he is paralyzed. A myriad of thoughts are whizzing in his mind while he gradually realizes that the nature of the lawyer is far from that of an ordinary mortal. He senses a funny feeling, fear seizes his stomach. He experiences a strong need to vomit, but holds himself.

"Well, I warned you Sella," growled the lawyer. "Now listen carefully. It's not a joke in bad taste. There are several things that, even with your influence and money, you couldn't discover. But even if you had discovered them, I'm sure that you couldn't have understood. You're too much bound to greed and your material body... But never mind. However, you aren't sufficiently endowed to understand, your mind is not 'ready'. I have you in my hands, Sella, and I can destroy you. But I'll not annihilate you because something tells me that you also have registers with my name marked on them. You see, in some way I'm attached to this town, these places, and I'd like to remain here for some time more. Now relax, draw a deep breath and put aside your pride. People like you don't deserve to live, yet people like you give a bad example to the inhabitants of the planet, so that they decide to change their vision. It sounds simple, right? Yet the world of the 21st century was full of scoundrels as you, and you saw what happened, but then people have changed their vision. A small step towards the Goal, isn't it? Sella, now I consider you just a *tool*, a trivial checker that I can move across my board at my leisure... and your strumpet... who will return in a few minutes, unaware of everything. So, do you want to 'cooperate', or would you prefer me to use more persuasive methods? You can't even imagine what my real power is, Sella. You can choose, but I suggest you choose faster."

Dr. Sella can't move, the lawyer's eyes keep him paralyzed, and the only thing he can do is try to rearrange his thoughts. Mentally, the idea of having fallen into the trap forces him to see no other alternative but to yield to the threats of the lawyer. By doing this, as if his opponent had the power to read minds, his body melts and he's able to regain the armchair.

About thirty seconds elapsed, during which Dr. Sella looks in to his jacket pocket, searching for a handkerchief to wipe the beads of sweat running down his face and neck.

The lawyer looks at him with grim eyes, his face with ethereal features shows no emotion. Suddenly the place appears to Sella a sort of limbo, he feels a lot of pressure inside his chest, as if his heart was about to implode at any moment.

"Okay, okay, stop it and leave me alone," cries Sella, in the throes of a sort of panic. "You're a monster, you aren't human!"

In pronouncing the sentence, the pressure in his chest loosens and he can again breathe without effort.

"What do you want me to do?"

The man's gaze rests on the glass cabinet behind the lawyer, a strange object appears brighter than the others, but without any light source from entering the board. What the hell is happening? Sella feels again a strange sensation in his head while turning again his gaze toward the lawyer.

"Forget about that, Sella, learn not to ask too many questions. I have already said that you can't understand. You're solely driven by impulses of the flesh and your mind is darkened by hatred and greed. All that I ask is that you leave that girl alone! It's not through the power of an *Annwyn* that you'll be able to increase your power. Try to remember, store it well in your depraved brain. I swear that if you even try to interact with Chrysalis, you'll regret being born. The girl and her brother are under my protection, am I clear enough? And now, I highly recommend that you pay a visit to Commander Fenix. There is a risk that if you don't, your anthropomorphic ID will receive data that could adequately prepare your admission to one of the beautiful structures of the Unified Power. You know what happens in these hospitals, don't you?"

The lawyer leans comfortably against the backrest of the armchair, swinging lightly back and forth. His face is decorated with a grim smile that reveals white teeth, then with a gesture full of grace and elegance, he gets up to welcome Veronika as she enters the study.

"Ah, my dear, perfect. Yes, how beautiful you look! When you leave my house, they can't think that I have abused your grace!"

The man gives a significant look to Dr. Sella, who preferred to look down and remain silent.

"Can I let Adam bring you a cup of green tea? Although tea time has already passed, I suggest you avoid alcohol for a while. Dr. Sella has just said that he should pay a visit of pleasure to the Head office of the Experimental Team. I informed him that Commander Fenix had tried, with some urgency, to get in touch with him."

Chapter 16

Between Heaven and Earth

Almost running, Marius returns to the two young friends with a big handbag, a shoulder strap and a large plastic bag with water bottles.

"Never go on a journey without taking along water and some small supplies," he smiled at Chrisa, "in the car we have vegetables, fruits and cheeses bought from Giacomo. I'm not a fan of raw fennel, but I think this time I'll make an exception!"

Marius throws the handbag at Joshua, adding, "I did some deviation between the lanes, then passed under a porch, and jumped the fence. Since the entrance of the building was watched, I thought I would use the 'service entrance'. It isn't easy to descend from the gutters and cross the tightrope to the balcony barriers, considering my age, but I avoided the patrols. Actually they have already entered my apartment, but they left everything in order. I have some documents and I got some crowns set aside for emergencies. We can't use our *unycell* or even the credit cards; otherwise we'll be tracked with extreme rapidity."

Chrisa looks at her brother hesitatingly; she grabs the bag and puts it on her shoulder, then turns to Marius.

"Did you send the message to the race Commissary? May I know what nonsense did you tell him? I fear that the Experimental Team won't buy it."

The old man smiled slyly. "I told him that we have visited some friends in the mountains and that Joshua was sick during the trip due to congestion after eating a dozen chocolate croissants!"

Chrisa blurts out a laughing. "Ahhh, I am certain *that* they will believe it. I remember the last time he gorged himself on sweets; Commander Fenix brought him back to the boat. I think you couldn't choose a more truthful pretext for our excuse; however, it seems very unlikely that you two will not participate in tomorrow's race. Hopefully he'll not even consider this, and not decide to look for us in every village above 2.600 feet of altitude."

"I would say that the friendship that keeps me from the race Commissary is very strong," Marius grins again, "most likely tomorrow the Marenca wind will rise, the weather forecasts have been formalized and they will be forced to cancel the race! So there will be no suspicion, considering that he will contact me by leaving a message on my *unycell*... which I left under the pillow on my bed!"

Whistling happily, the old sea dog goes to the electric car, opened the trunk and puts in the bags and shoulder bag.

"Well, at least some of the problems are apparently solved, but tell us, how do we get up to Ireland? They haven't yet designed teleportation, even though we're in the twenty-third-century," Chrisa frowns. For her it wouldn't be a problem getting around during the REM phase through dimensional space, but she had some doubts that she can take both fellow adventurers with her.

"Be quiet my girl, one thing at a time! Now let's get to the other side, near the riverbed where the old ruins of a dilapidated farm are situated. Remember Martino? Yeah, that little squinty guy that always goes around with a white silk scarf saying that he's the New Red Baron? His airplane is ready for departure, silent as the night breeze... and tonight the moon is covered by dense, ugly clouds. We must move. He has assured me that he would fill up the tanks to the brim, so we have a sufficient flight range to arrive in Dublin! Forward: Ireland awaits us!"

Martino walks back and forth along the perimeter of the gate that isolates the stretch of the grassy runway, which is mainly used by fanatic and nostalgic aviators whom occasionally visited the area of Lake Maggiore. When he saw the car headlights, he began to wave excitedly.

*** Inter Mundia Coeli et Terrarum ***

"Hi, you old wretch, what have you done this time? I hope you don't stick me into a mess, I care for my integrity. Hello as well to you two. Hey, but you're Joshua, that moonstruck who juggles very well on the water, appears worthy of Marius. And you, who're you?"

Chrisa stiffens, but tries to be polite and answers with a hint of a smile. She hates this kind of character; they wet themselves if the Experimental Team is around, but then they gloat over the first opportunity to go against the tide and break the law.

"I'm the sister of the unfortunate fresh water sailor! My name is Chrisa, my pleasure."

Martino squeezes her hand firmly, and then he stares at her from top to the bottom before moving away without a word. Loaded like a mule, Joshua drags his feet along the path covered with wood chips which leads to the hangar. Chrisa observes every shadow with extreme caution and casts furtive glances over the perimeter enclosing the grass runway. But her instinct didn't reveal negative presences and she gradually relaxes. Marius hid the car in a sort of sunken underground structure and then covers it with a camouflage tarp and lastly he lays bundles of dry branches and a pile of other debris over it. He smiles, thinking that's the best hiding place, proof from curious eyes, which he already used a couple of times in the past. With a bunch of small branches, he cares to erase the prints left by the car tires in the last section. Everything else has been intentionally covered with wood chips and bark of trees that camouflage every track perfectly.

Arriving in the big shed, the most absolute darkness envelops them. A few feet away, Marius coughs slightly, as if there was some dust particles that irritate his throat.

"Well, we arrived! Joshua put down the bag, Chrisa remain on this side, now this madcap Martino will make us a little light, so at least we see where we lay our feet."

The pilot takes from the back pocket of his trousers a dynamo of small size but with a beam of striking light.

"Well, my airship will take us to the destination without problems. It dates back to late 2150, a little old to be always on duty, but fully functional for a fan. It's from the aeronautical engineering Airbus in Toulouse, to be exact... a prototype that was too expensive for the purpose intended by the designers. Well, American competitors didn't boom, not even sixty years ago, my boys! Airbus has the best designs, but unfortunately only ten 'Dragon's Fire' were built. For this reason, they abandoned the idea to build it in a series. Ta-da... here she is, in all her dazzling beauty!"

Chrisa is quiet, a strange feeling has taken possession of her and she would have gladly turned on her heels. Joshua drops the bag on the floor with a thud and a cry begins to leave his lips, but Marius cuts him off.

"Well, I guarantee she can bring us up to Ireland, or further afield. I have already boarded her several times... it works like a dream, try it!"

Joshua takes a turn around the aircraft, before crying out through clenched teeth.

"Are you really sure that it was only constructed back in 2150? I think this thing must have been built the last millennium, an 'abortion' in the mind of some mad aeronautical engineer."

Martino receives the observations without a murmur, and then angrily retorts: "well, if you don't like it, you can go back to where you came from. Or take a nice walk on foot, but Ireland is far away! It seems to me that there are several *jaglynx* and some henchman of the Experimental Team hunting you. See you then, the decision is yours!"

The airman unwinds the scarf from his neck with a bored gesture and then sits on a chair covered with dust, and his face betrays no emotion of any kind. Chrisa watches the scene trying to go beyond what she can tell by her perceptions; there are several questions which arise in her mind. One thing is certain, however, Martino is an honest person and is offering them an opportunity to escape; doing this, the man also puts his own life at risk.

Chrisa throws a furtive glance to Marius, who answers back with a nod of the head.

"Sorry Martino, you're obviously the expert and many times in life you only get involved with what your eyes perceive. If you say that you can bring us to Dublin in a short time, I'm convinced that your 'Dragon's Fire' conceals some mysterious tricks that aren't visible to the eye. Like I said an hour ago, even if we momentarily have a kind of alibi, I'm convinced that Commander Fenix will search for us far and wide. Explain to the kids how you overcome the problem of radar and move interceptors!"

Martino hoists himself on to his long legs, that make him look like a spider ready to wrap his prey in silk thread, and takes a sharp breath. With both hands he smooths his hair on the head, which is long, down to his shoulder, slightly wavy and a dark blond with some coppery reflections. With a sly, elfin smile, he puts a finger over his lips and whispers: "ahhh, my friends, but this is just beautiful! My 'Dragon's Fire' is actually *invisible*!"

Chapter 17

Role playing Game

A strange light filters from behind the thick centennial curtains, laden with dust and faded from the intense rays of the sun.

Fortunately, in that hour of night, there are no prying eyes to see the curious people who rummage through bushes bristling with thorns and tall trees that have invaded everything around the large residence. Ivy creepers, with large red and yellow leaves, had covered the exterior walls, making the austere house almost perfectly camouflaged. It appears partly hidden by a forest of rhododendrons and azaleas that have grown beyond measure since they had not been pruned properly for years.

In truth, it was mainly tourists that were interested in the fate of Villa Var Darquen de Aguillar. The inhabitants of Ascona were no longer interested in it. For many years the inhabitants were also accustomed to the strange stories and legends that were told about who knows what bloody events and paranormal happenings.

Years ago, Chrisa and Joshua had taken a liking to exacerbating the rumours, telling some particular fantasy made more plausible by the facts that promptly recur when an *Annwyn* found herself involved in some strange story.

There had been several children playing in these huge gardens which bordered the lake. They spent whole afternoons playing the 'End of the World', a kind of excluding game that emulated the events of 2022.

Joshua and Chrisa's parents didn't approve of this type of fun; they had said that it could not be as simplistic as even the fate had affected this happening. But many things, as always, had been carefully concealed and then, over the centuries, people had stopped questioning the real reasons for the death of 2/3 of the world's population.

The musty smell fills the room as soon as the hatch is removed, and two excited people mumble while a third one carries a bulky, iridescent container.

"Do you think anyone has noticed your arrival?"

The individual, who opened the door in the floor, hangs out with his hands in the air. The voice is shrill and resembles a *Unynetweb* mechanism just turned on and in the process of spatial tuning.

"His Excellency doubts about my abilities?"

"Ah, but obviously you are infallible creatures!" The third person snaps, even more angrily. "With all the men of the Experimental Team that were unleashed with their cats, your putrid smell hasn't been ignored."

For a moment, the individual with the package assumes a glassy appearance, the same colour of the container that gradually disappears through the hole in the floor. Then, resuming composure, he speaks with an authoritative and touchy tone.

"His Excellency, I execute specific orders and I can assure you that it's impossible that someone has seen or perceived my presence. Now, if you will allow me, I want to finish the task that was assigned to me."

Saying this, he falls with a flick through the trap door then closes it with a faint pop. The other two people, while one is shaking his head in obvious discomfort, retrace their steps and leave the room. Down the long staircase that ends 50 feet below in a luxurious hall paved with slabs of black and white marble. A very intricate design representing a labyrinth, as was fashionable in the late thirteenth century, emerges in its irrepressible beauty and magic. Then they enter another spacious room in which stands a monumental fireplace, sitting opposite one another in order to continue a chess game began a few hours before.

"If this continues, with all these errors of judgment, you end up losing your queen."

"No, Lord Warden," the man with greying hair, dressed with an expensive *fresco Lana* in pearl colour, responds with an amused smile.

"I don't think so... it's not a simple game of chess. Basically, we just have to give them a little more time. I'm sure that your sharpness will allow you to achieve the purpose of her presence much more quickly than expected. She is a *real* Queen, a white *Annwyn*."

*** Ludus Partium ***

Lord Warden gets up from his chair and strode to reach the library, which covers the entire wall on the side of the huge fireplace.

"Then we should rewrite the history! I think that what happened was unmistakable and inevitable, we certainly can't be proud of our past, my friend. The human race had unfortunately derailed, like a train into a frantic race that ends up butting against a mountain in which it was supposed to enter a tunnel... some kind of escape. What is certain is that during the eighties of the twentieth century, at the arrival of the first creatures of Light, they had tried to convey the message. But Men are stupid, arrogant, selfish and cowardly! That was the proper punishment, but too much, really too many, they are still saved. There wasn't a selection on the merits…"

In the fireplace the fire crackles, throwing around frightful shadows. The two figures appear to come out of a nineteenth century painting. It seems that the past four centuries have remained frozen in time; even their features are of extraordinary class, an aristocracy that knows no limits, carried by the Unified Power or the martial law that had marked the planet.

"Lord Warden, whereas here we go in lazy contemplation for who knows how long, don't you prefer to leave aside the chess and devote our time to some less amusing practice? There are several volumes, see, just the ones, leaning against the mirror with the plaster frame covered with gold foil. They are very old, just brought from our 'friend' who has managed to smuggle them from the underground storage of Ishtar. Don't ask me how he did it, no doubt some of *them* have managed to find a way to avoid the checks. Or they are able to cross *The Mirror*! There are several treaties that had contemplated this possibility, more recently, dating back to the twenty-first century. I keep all this 'compromising' documentation on the lower floor, in the laboratory. I was working for months. When that despised being Sella began to interfere, I had to set priorities. You see, Lord Warden, I am now convinced that something has diverted his intent, and when he becomes aware of what happened at the harbour, I think he'll leave Ascona. One thing intrigues me: for whom is Sella working? Who is behind him?"

The interlocutor watches him weirdly, then with a snap of his fingers, calls a presence not well defined, which remained crouched in the darkness. The creature approaches, sniffing the air cautiously, then nestles at the Lord's foot.

"Ah, yes, my dear Hathor, I think that through our influence the Unified Power will not disappoint our expectations. Sometimes you only have to be patient, very patient. The teachings of the ancients estimate this merit very considerably. The exercise of patience is in fact a kind of gateway to beauty, albeit ephemeral, which allows an anthropomorphic being to be seen with other eyes and then considered differently. Ah ah ah ah... to digress a bit on the subject, let's take a presence like that of our friend above: did you think he might in some way enjoy the beauty of his ephemeral material existence? No doubt his presence can only be revolting and horrific, segregated into darkness. Yet these devilish creatures have potential far more vital to those of humans: they are invulnerable, or so they believe... they can procreate, even if in their own way, a possibility that is denied to the *Annwyn*. Don't you think this is a real shame? So much perfection wasted by supernatural laws that relate in this case as way to control. What I'm trying to understand is: what are the unwritten laws? Unfortunately, all the books talk about these things in such a hermetic and occult way! Do you have an idea? If you allow me this arrogance, how would you find a way to permit an *Annwyn* woman to procreate? Clearly, by the union of beings of the same kind…"

The man looks at Lord Warden with a sinister gleam in his eyes, the animal groans and hisses at his feet, turning on itself as if it were to be interrogated. A strange flash of light is reflected from the eyes of the beast, which begins to speak.

"Probably, Hathor doesn't agree with you. An *Annwyn* cannot procreate with *"any other Annwyn"* since there is only *"one matching soul"*. Not genetically speaking, of course... There are several concepts that have not been considered yet with sufficient determination."

Lord Warden blurts out a loud laugh, and then reaches for the animal, that begins to change its physical structure.

"Well, well, I see that you finally learned something! Now show us what you can reproduce, Vamaran. I wouldn't have wasted my potential!"

Chapter 18

Beginning and Ending

Chrisa went away with the excuse of having to use the bathroom, but instead of following the corridor to the end of the hangar where the services were located, she turns immediately to the right through a dark tunnel that the young woman knows leads outside. She needs air, fresh air, as happens every now and then when the situation began to be alarming.

The young woman is convinced that she can trust Martino: all Marius's friends are of the same mould, eccentric people, but reliable. Obviously, many of them don't fit neatly into the pattern designed by the top tiers of the Unified Power.

A gust of wind ruffles the long, amber hair of the young woman, the breeze brings scents of the same flowers they could smell while waiting for the return of Marius. But partly hidden by the jasmine's aroma, Chrisa noticed a different smell, very distinct and strong, an unmistakable *predator's* smell!

Immediately her senses are awakened, heightening her hearing to perceive any sound cleanly and incontestable.

The chirping of crickets becomes exasperating, then all of a sudden, the silence. Some low cloud full of rain slips in front of the moon, obscuring part of it. The smells of the wild becomes more pronounced. The wind comes from south-west. Chrisa believes that the animal lies beyond the grassy track, where the beaten earth was dotted with fir bark, where it runs along the perimeter of the small tourist's airport. The girl tries to get in telepathic contact with the presence, initially believing it was a *jaglynx* who had decided to take a stroll without its human companion.

Suddenly a wave of adverse energy inflicts excruciating pain in her head. It wasn't an animal from the Experimental Team. Holy God, it is something quite different, a kind of creature that Chrisa had already met on several occasions during her dream travelling. She panicked and quickly ran back to the burrow and secured the iron door of the entrance.

Trying not to hit anything in the run and making use of her highly developed tactile senses, almost with closed eyes, the young woman arrives out of breath in front of the little group in the hangar.

"Quickly! We have no time to lose! Martino please put the plane in motion and get out of here as soon as possible. We aren't alone and there is now something which is stalking us, and it isn't the Experimental Team."

Martino looks Chrisa right in the eye, where he reads fear without needing Chrisa to explain. Without saying a word, he grabs a couple of packs containing the various plans and maps, and ran to the ladder, followed by the others. Fifteen seconds later, a slight hiss fills the space in the hangar while the roof opens in two halves, releasing a square hole of about thirty feet. At the same time, the 'Dragon's Fire' is already five or six feet of vertical height. A dark spot of undefined outline comes running in to the hangar. Martino shudders, but doesn't waste time trying to figure out *what* it was. Sitting next to him, Marius blurts out an expletive in Gaelic while trying to adjust the seat belt.

Behind them, the two young people are still settling the bags under their seats and luckily haven't watched the gruesome scene. But Chrisa senses something, and with tears in her eyes she whispers into the Joshua's ear.

"Just in time: luck is on our side, or that thing wasn't planning to harm us. I have the impression that it's not a fortuitous presence... but still I cannot be certain."

Martino gives the signal to close the hangar's roof, then, at a depth of few feet above the foliage, pulls slightly the stick and turns a few degrees to the north. The aircraft emits a faint hiss that could be confused with a gust of wind and passed between the trees. Indeed, at that height they would not be intercepted by radar and since it is night, the special paint which covers the aircraft, reflects what is around it like a mirror.

"It's a perfect camouflage, my boys; such a material makes this plane invisible," Martino gloats, although beads of sweat adorn his brow. Evidently he doesn't want to talk about the apparition, and his fellow adventurers are grateful for this.

Chrisa broods on what she can remember. Unfortunately, the totality of all her memories is only disclosed to her when she's in the REM phase. She smiles, thinking that there hasn't yet past twenty-four hours since her last journey on which she, certainly not by chance, has found the *Vibratory Matrix*.

In the dim violet light of the front-board instruments panel, Marius turns to contemplate the faces of the young people.

"All okay, guys? We are already in the vicinity of the Alps mountain chain, Martino must go up in altitude and it's possible there will be even stronger turbulence. I've done this trip several times when... Well, maybe isn't the time to talk about it. It's a long and convoluted story. I think it's wiser if you relax. How about trying to sleep? Chrisa... however I don't think it would be wise to use your powers, not now, much less inside an airplane."

"Be calm," Chrisa smiles to Marius, "this type of exercise I keep it for later. Something tells me that when we're in Ireland we'll need it!"

The old sea dog turns around and begins to chat with Martino. The journey will last a little more than two hours, if the weather remains favourable and if there will be no interferences.

*** Alpha et Omega ***

The young woman pulled the black moleskin diary from her bag and starts to scribble notes. Joshua realises that his sister is also sketching, with the pencil moving crazily around the page. However, he is wise enough to avoid peeking, and prefers to take a nap. He was really in a great need of sleep, damned! That was a day full of events, and he was sure that the following day will also be one of surprises.

Joshua stretches, then he pulls out one of Marius's old sweatshirts, very worn on the wrists and elbows, from one of the bags under the seats. Glad to have gained a little more heat, the young man takes a big swig of water from the bottle before he curls up in his seat. After about ten minutes, he falls asleep, lulled by the slight gusts of wind that dominate the alpine zone.

Tired of taking notes, after a while Chrisa follows her brother's example and falls asleep with her head in her arms, resting on the folding-table.

Further north, after the Saint-Gotthard massif, large red stains on the radar allow Martino to predict the turbulence.

Unfortunately, the rest of the trip was less quiet, but even these weather conditions would have a positive impact, in some way. Who would venture out to face an imminent storm coming from North which was going to collide against the Alps? Only fools, of course... As soon as Marius realizes the gravity of the signals sent by the board's instruments, he gives a frightened look to his friend the pilot.

"And now? Do you have any solution for this unexpected situation, my friend?"

Chapter 19

The Lie Rules the Weak

Fenix dreadfully punches the top of his desk; the cooled coffee in his cup gave a concentric ripple as when a drop of rain reaches the water's surface.

Red in the face, the man is breathing heavily, with a sudden gesture loosens the tie around his neck. To hell with appearances: now isn't the time to remain dressed up in the presence of bastards.

"Look Sella, I appreciate that you came here of your own accord, believe me. This, however, doesn't change the situation, although it is certainly a smart move that spares you an unpleasant arrest warrant. I sincerely hope that you're aware of *my power*. If I wanted, I could shut you up in one of our hospitals! I hope not to be forced to do so, but I will obtain your cooperation. Your girlfriend is unaware of everything, obviously. The woman, Veronika, she's apparently only a small pet which lets herself be carried around right and left solely to please you. Females such as Veronika are not very well perceived by the top of the Unified Power. Indeed, let us say that the Unified Power seeks to *remove* this infected society appendix, if you can understand my meaning. I believe that the lady has two options: she changes her habits, or our doctors will make her change it... you know, don't you, how persuasive and effective the specialists in psychologies and mental illnesses can be?"

Dr. Sella angrily swallows, his saliva becoming uncontrollable. He was well aware that with difficulty he'll be able to hold off the rush that is gripping his guts. Even if what Commander Fenix is telling him is the absolute truth, he can't bear that his woman is merely regarded as a whore. Had it been another place, in other circumstances, he would have spit at the face of his interlocutor... he would use the knife of his *Lancero* to slash Fenix's face, or castrate him, although Sella hated to deprive another human being of carnal pleasures. Yet, Sella tries to contain himself, tries to banish his anger by focusing on the certainty that the blame didn't lie with the poor stooges of the Experimental Team, but rather with that bastard, his former friend, the lawyer.

"Commander Fenix, I repeat that I do not know those two... well, dead bodies... in other words... those human remains that you have fished from the lake."

But the eye of the commander is turbid; evidently he doesn't believe a single word professed by Dr. Sella.

"Listen carefully to me. Thanks to DNA control we have gone back to trace the anthropomorphic card of the two corpses. They are registered as escaped convicts from a high-security hospital."

Then, turning to two of his staff, Fenix gives orders. "Sergio, display the data of the two guys who were *fished* out yesterday afternoon. You, Sella, look there. That's Augusto Danoni," Sergio enters the data with great speed, and on the display appears the images of the two wanted criminals. "The other one is Paolo Ceretti, both escaped from the hospital in Vienna. I think you may perhaps explain the reason for their presence, a couple of days ago, on your yacht?"

Sella is visibly upset; a twitch of the jaw betrays his apprehension while his gaze moves from one picture to the other, both visible on the display that takes up an entire wall. The redness of his face becomes more marked while with his hands pulls at a lock of hair from over his eyes in an angry gesture.

"What is this? I will speak only in the presence of my lawyer... I want to call a lawyer!"

"No," the peremptory voice of the Commander Fenix makes him wince.

"You won't just call any lawyer; this 'variant' has been granted me by the highest authority of the Unified Power. You're aware, Sella, how my work is commended for keeping the scum away from this country. If you respond in an appropriate manner, I will give you a concession and will not shut you away. At least, for now... As for your friend, I'm sorry to inform you that she will take part in a basic reprogramming. I think in three or four months she will be reborn, evidently not quite the kind of person you're used to having as escort."

*** Mendacium Infirmos reget ***

In declaring this decision, Fenix smiles challengingly. Dr. Sella pales, all of a sudden he realises that something has gone wrong, very wrong. He feels the earth under his feet fall away, and had it not been for the promptness of Sergio, he would have fell to the ground unconscious.

The cop helps him to sit in a chair. Sella is visibly frail and with all the strength that he had left, he was trying to maintain a respectable demeanour. Commander Fenix isn't impressed at all. In fact, he enjoyed catching a big fish that had been too long out of his net! Now he takes his revenge, he doesn't care much if these two thugs were killed in that

140

horrible way. Indeed, in his opinion, all criminals deserved to meet the same fate!

From an adjacent room, Sella is startled to hear a familiar voice. For a moment the impulse to jump up and reach the separating door becomes unmanageable, and then he slowly regains self-control and remains sat on the uncomfortable chair.

Fenix observes every muscle of the man. In a second phase he would look to the movie too, which, unbeknownst to Sella, they're still running. This type of verification during an interrogation allows the experts to evaluate the physiological reflections of the interrogated, by means of the vibrational display obtained with special filters. But the commander realises that this is the man they are looking for. He's almost convinced that even the disappearance of Chrysalis and Joshua and the old sailor are linked to him. The race's official had heard that they are stuck somewhere in the mountains, apparently it snowed at a low level and they didn't go down to the valley because the boy has *gorged* himself, causing indigestion. He smiles, thinking about the time he had to bring the young man to the sailing boat because he had been sick for the same reason. He'll deal with the disappearance as soon as the bastard who stands in front of his nose finally decides to spit it out. The prostitute had already been unwillingly sedated and loaded on to a car that will take her to a specific institution in the region of Turin.

"Look Sella, I will give you an hour, sixty minutes, do you understand? Examine yourself and put everything down on that sheet. Sergio, please give him the whole notepad. I really think he'll have a lot of things to confess!"

From the other room Sella hears a laugh that he recognises. The man feels betrayed, while a sort of chaos is opened in front of his perception. The terror began to creep into his brain and gradually he reconsiders the events that occurred in the last 24 hours. He's aware of being hunted and realises how important Veronika is to him, even if in a remote corner of his brain, he fears that she will somehow betray and harm him.

Chapter 20

Breach in the Past

Crossing the rising storm, the 'Dragon's Fire' continues for nearly an hour, flying to the north at an altitude of about 2.800 feet. Martino had shrewdly avoided any radio contact, and fortunately no control tower had intercepted the presence of the plane. Everything went smoothly, but they did not rejoice before they reached the goal!

Over the English Channel, Chrisa feels a slight vibration coming from her shoulder bag while a faint light is filtering through the fabric. Initially, a strong sense of discomfort captures her, but she tries to calm down while she looks in her brother's direction. He was sleeping blissfully, indifferent to what happens inside and outside of the aircraft, and Martino is too busy entering the latest data in the electronic board's computer. Fortunately, no one has seen the glow. The young woman doesn't want to unnecessarily alarm her travelling companions. She'll discuss it with them as soon as they arrive at Clonemacnoise.

About ten minutes later, Martino lowers the aircraft further, now the ruins of the place of worship are visible in front of them as the first glimmers of dawn began to dye the eastern horizon peach and purple. The stones, whitish opalescence, get almost eerie. Maybe they really were meant to intimidate those who arrive in these places at the rising or setting sun.

"There she is," says the pilot, "not that much is left standing, unfortunately. The passing of centuries has destroyed much of the archaeological record everywhere. But it feels good, anyhow! I never had been here at dawn, not just Stonehenge, kids, *that's really* an impressive place. Too bad the Unified Power has locked it in a glass and steel structure to protect it from climatic degradation."

Martino is excited as an elementary school kid; as a good pilot, he manages to land with extreme precision his 'Dragon's Fire' in a space about ten yards from the River Shannon, that, in the last two centuries had shrunk to the size of a stream.

"Well guys, we arrived safely. Now I wonder... well, without wanting to disprove what Marius has been reported, obviously... But I really didn't buy the *trip for pleasure story*. What the hell are you doing here? I can't simply let you up here with your bags; this isn't the kind of service I reserve for good friends."

*** Transitus Memoriae Via ***

Martino takes a brief pause. He clears his throat and tries to take an attitude that will ensure the highest of professionalism. Marius shakes his head, and then finally decides to speak.

"Look, my friend. You have already done too much for us. We can't take advantage of your kindness, it's too risky. We need to verify a few things, but it'll soon be daylight. I would impulsively put myself to work immediately, but the brain tells me to wait, that there will be more tourists to mingle with. Then, if we need to, we could always pay a visit here at sunset. What do you guys think? The time now is 7:00 AM; we can leave our bags in that grove, among ferns and scrub, and then take a walk here around without exposing ourselves too much. Maybe we move into the undergrowth to the north, descend to the ruins at around 10:00 AM."

Martino remains silent while reassessing everything, from one side he's aware that he can't remain there with his aircraft; he would attract the curiosity of passers-by. Then he bursts out laughing.

"Gosh, I'm a fool! I should have thought of that before... look, I propose a more intelligent solution. Leave your things inside the 'Dragon's Fire', I have several trustworthy friends among those crazy Irish. Marius, do you remember Steven's grumpy fellows? And then there's your cousin Sibéal, I could take your things down to her. She lives a few miles further south, in Shannonbridge... I can *park* the 'Dragon's Fire' in the barn, no one will notice its presence. When it's not activated, unfortunately I can't run the *mirror device*. I wouldn't like that, for some nosy walker in the countryside, deciding to look at it too closely. Although the Irish have a reputation for minding their own business, I wouldn't be the one to break this good habit!"

Marius looks at him weirdly: he has known Martino for decades, as he knows well enough those dissolute friends of Steven. His cousin could certainly be trusted, he wanted to visit her later. The idea of Martino's is perfect. Then Marius thinks of his friend who disappeared years ago, and a cloud of sadness covers his face.

"Steven! Who knows what happened... and yet... something tells me that he isn't dead. Martino, I think you're right: maybe it's wiser if you stay here with us. Go down to Shannonbridge. I know all too well this citadel. Bring our stuff to my cousin Sibéal, while we walk around the woods, and afterwards we take a look around this place." With his head he indicates the archaeological area.

145

"There, somewhere must be some *symbols* that will help us shed light on several things."

Marius throws a furtive glance at Chrisa which lowers her eyes.

"And this good girl will show us how to use the *Occult Arts* of my ancestors!"

It promises to be a beautiful day; there are no clouds in the sky thanks to the slight breeze which just bends the blades of grass and makes the leaves dance on the branches. That's the Irish dream, a Treasure Chest in which had been kept the spell of a ruling era filled with magic for thousands of years!

With all the worries that beset his mind, Marius feels responsible for the youths, but perhaps being in Ireland allowed the old sea dog to look at the new day with confidence. He always has been of the opinion that there are no problems and that we have only to look for solutions that may allow us to deal with our earthly journey with a good dose of optimism and genuine gratitude. Of course, disasters, diseases and bad things happen, yet this wonderful gift that is Life deserves to be taken with positivity. Only in this way, and over time it was tested by scientists, the positive projection may serve as a magnet: that is the 'Law of Attraction'!

Chrisa's hair is ruffled around her face. Tired of moving it with her hands, the girl takes a big clip and ties it back. Joshua looks at her with cunning eyes.

"Hey, but look at her, if she had a long dress and a veil wrapped around her body, you could confused her with a Druid priestess!"

"And who says that maybe I'm not exactly something like that?" Chrisa retorts, sticking out her tongue, "do you know that here the Druids were worshiped a lot? There are several legends that Marius told us... discussing the antique myths of *islands shrouded in mist* and therefore invisible to

146

the uninitiated. Why do you think mom named our sailboat Avalon's Mist?"

The smile suddenly vanishes from the girl's face; a gust of wind comes harder as if to emphasise what she had just reported. Joshua shudders and looks around with a serious face.

"But, but... brrrr, sister please, let us put down these things for now. Everything seems to be connected: Nature, the elements!"

Marius wraps himself in a sweatshirt worn by time, and then he throws around a furtive glance. Now the whole country, watered by the first sunshine's rays, is turning into a huge emerald.

"Yes, everything is connected and especially here... in these places. Come on, now we let Martino go, he'll try to land without being noticed. Say hello to the gang, I'm convinced that when we get down to the Old Druid Inn, the whole bunch of you will already be there, filling your belly with malt beer or cider. If we run into any problems we can't deal with immediately, we'll contact you on your private number. Ah ah ah ah, if only the Experimental Team knew how many of their bans we flout!"

Marius approached his friend and hugs him strongly, then hit Joshua with the usual pat on the shoulder and, followed by Chrisa, ventures into the thick grove which in the distance becomes an eerie brownish stain.

Martino is still waiting for several minutes until his three friends have gone through the shrubbery, and then in a run he reaches his 'Dragon's Fire' which sets into motion, emitting a faint hiss. You only can see the grass a little bent by the disturbed air, but there is no trace of the plane. Martino had immediately switched the device that makes the airplane invisible by reflecting what is around.

"Hey Marius, what's that about the name of our sailing boat?" Joshua asks, a little sullenly, "is it some fantastic

147

story again or some of my sister's 'out of this world fairy tale'?"

Marius continued to walk briskly, pretending to have not heard anything. Then the young man runs after him and pulls his sweatshirt to make him stop. The elder man hangs on before he answers; looking up to where the trees begin to be sprayed by the rays of the sun.

"Shush... the creatures of the woods have witnessed many historical facts, Joshua. Don't mention the *Legends* in a so inconsiderate way! The ancients had immense respect for them, my boy. Yes, I'll speak of Avalon... and the Promised Land... although I think your sister knows much more about what has been hidden by the Unified Power in the basement of Ishtar. They had not reckoned with the mnemonic power of the mind of an arcane *Annwyn*."

Despite having heard Marius's comment, Chrisa keeps walking, also pretending to have heard nothing. Her strap bag vibrates subtly, but concealed by her jacket, the faint glow became more intense as the hours passed.

Chapter 21

Dark Powers

The fire continues to crackle in the fireplace, while the old pendulum wall clock strikes half past three. Its sound is creepy and so icy that Hathor for a split second has the vision of a huge expanse of ice. Lord Warden looks approvingly at the dancing flames as the creature called Vamaran transmuted into an anthropomorphic form of rare beauty. A male of approximately thirty years of age, 190 cm tall, with a slender figure, big eyes, very dark hair to his shoulders and a sensual, full-lipped mouth.

The presence is covered by a dark velvet suit that puts even more emphasis on the pallor of his complexion. A large ring with a black stone decorates his slender and well cared for right hand.

"I'm speechless, Lord Warden!" Hathor places the large book, bound in black leather on which is etched, in gold, a title written in something similar to Nordic runes. The lawyer warily approached Vamaran and reaches out to touch him.

"If I was you, my dear Hathor, I wouldn't try to touch it... don't forget that you are an *Annwyn*! A 'dreamer', therefore, the mutant before you is the only person to have recognised the *codes*. To my knowledge, he's the only creature that came out of the projection breaking of the *Sacred Mirror*. Vamaran *was an Annwyn!*"

Hathor retract his hand quickly and sticks it in his pockets, laughing.

"The Devil take you!" Hathor said, turning to Lord Warden. "Now I understand why you kept all your alleged studies secret! In fact I don't think you ever honoured me with your trust. Many of us are desperately trying to get out of the projection, the purpose of escaping the cycle of death and rebirth... and you? You have found what for centuries we have been looking for... or maybe it's just something abominable, reprehensible and certainly not completely in accord with the *Annwyn* morals? No, Lord Warden, don't reveal to me anything. I prefer not be acquainted with the artefacts you have used. But I'm perfectly aware that if Waterhouse Pandora's painting, which I keep in my studio in the old centre of Ascona, was unable to unlock the *codes*, they are obviously hidden somewhere else."

Behind him, the soft and melodic voice of Vamaran fills him with a certain primitive discomfort:

"Hathor, I think this is the error. You didn't seek in the appropriate way. Actually, I can confirm that the *codes are hidden in the painting of the beautiful Pandora*, but the type of examination that you did wasn't the right one. If you observe the image of the portrait by applying the 'hermetic vision', you'll understand what I mean."

Vamaran smiles in a kindly manner. His behaviour is graceful and sweet, with a touch of femininity. His presence intrigues the lawyer, who perceives in his mind the words of the great Plato when, through Pausania's words, had spoken of the beauty of Eros and the vision of the androgyny.

Centuries have passed, and yet Lord Warden had certainly made use of the teachings of the great philosophers, and even of Hermes's *Emerald Table* in which he had left traces so that *the selected* could rise to the True Essence! But what Hathor can't understand is the analogy of the components: had he then collected useless objects for hundreds of years? Had he stolen from the vaults of the Unified Power objects that don't really serve any purpose?

*** Tenebrae Vires ***

Lord Warden observes Hathor, without seeking a verbal confrontation with him. With shrewdness, the old Lord knows it isn't yet time; everything would be cleared as soon as the pieces were arranged on the board as set out by the precepts.

After 200 years, after waiting for this moment, Lord Warden is confident that the young Chrysalis would allow the *Queen* to make the last move: the definitive one. And this had been clearly expressed to Hathor. The Unified Power has so far served his purpose, but its presence has now become outdated and cumbersome. It's time for posting: Gaia must go back to being The Heaven after passing St. John's Apocalypse. Those who are ready will definitely get out of the projection. This is basically the twisted vision of the elderly Lord: he's only craving a sort of New Kingdom, perhaps vaguely comparable to the ancient Kingdom of Heaven.

Hathor Var Darquen de Aguillar manages to steal scraps of the old Lord's thoughts; Chrysalis's image was more than once outlined in his mind, and now he knows with certainty that the girl is in serious danger. The lawyer takes the big bound book that has just leaning on the chair.

Meanwhile, he caresses the cover with the tip of his fingers and observed Vamaran with a peculiar smile.

For a moment he creates an eerie tension in the air, as if the unpronounced challenge between the three men became explicit. Vamaran runs his slender, white fingers through the black silk of his hair, a gesture that even Hathor notes as extremely sensual. He's struck again by a strange thrill as the vision of Chrysalis causes of his martyrdom, is torturing his mind.

"I understand that everything changes, Lord Warden." The *Annwyn* turns to face the old man, passing his eyes across the mysterious presence of the mutant. "And what guarantee do you have that I will not oppose you? You know the value of that young woman to me... for my future... as long as I'm confined to this dimension."

Lord Warden observes both contenders without betraying his thoughts; he remains in absolute silence, allowing the clock to beat the certainty of time that inexorably elapses.

Even the smell of burning wood becomes more pronounced; something is moving, and something subtle and terrible hovers in the air. Another doubt assails Hathor: why has the other creature not yet returned from the basement? What else keeps him there? He only had to carry his heavy burden far from the light of day... His musings are, however, diverted by Vamaran suddenly speaking up.

"Why do you care so much about this *Annwyn*, Hathor? I suppose she is, hmm, very pleasant and attractive; maybe with a few touches she could really become irresistible to any living creature. On this I agree…"

"Vamaran, I don't allow you to bring over your arrogance!" Hathor shouts angrily, while his presence seems to fill the room; the fire becomes restless, darting between the marble slabs of the immense fireplace. High, crackling flames flare up, making the faces of those present almost ghostly.

"Chrysalis is under my protection, and I absolutely have no intention of letting... to allow your abominable appearance to... I'm certainly not allowing you to touch her!"

"Well, gentlemen, now you're both exaggerating. It seems to me I'm attending a duel between *troubadours* extolling their seductive arts, or maybe you want to try your skill in the use of swords?" The Lord Warden laughs throatily.

"We don't need this kind of contention, gentlemen, not between *Annwyn*!"

If Hathor had lost his composure, he would have certainly hit the Lord strongly, causing him irreversible damage; he was still coming to terms with his creation and Hathor didn't know his exact strength.

A whirlwind of thoughts overwhelmed his mind. Vamaran was an *Annwyn*, but who knows what magic or extraordinary confluence of artefacts he possessed, since he had passed through the *Projection*. It's obvious that Lord Warden had kept many details about his alchemical studies hidden from him.

"Again, you're wringing your brain unnecessarily. Hathor, Holy Heaven, but you're really convinced of being Almighty! Certainly not because an *Annwyn* can live almost twice as long as a normal human, you must think that this would enable you to acquire reckless forces. We were saying just before the coming of Vamaran: move the pieces on the chessboard! Too much depends on the young woman now, this matter has become quite tricky and I don't think it's appropriate to let time go uselessly. I realise that the Unified Power has other objectives and is against us. I get to move several pieces, Hathor, but you must keep your oath. I'm not pleased to have to remind you of that.

The Pact of Alliance can't be acquitted just because you're in love with that mischievous and impertinent girl. For the last time, I guarantee that we won't harm her! The young woman just has to turn on the *Vibratory Matrix*, as agreed... and when passes the *Projection*... Vamaran will take care of Chrysalis. The accident that happened to her genetic creators was certainly not caused by me... I repeat for the umpteenth time! It was a careless mistake, a mistake that has caused us considerable delays. Now the young *Annwyn* is at least 23 years old, it will be difficult to tame and shape her how it should have been done years ago. Hathor, I understand that you have met her several times in her dream travels, but you never managed to approach her because the young girl is terrified by you! But look at you: I agree you are of refined appearance, but when you enter the REM phase, well, you saw what you are capable of. Ahhh, those two poor, depraved souls ended up feeding fish! That's what Chrysalis perceives, your bloody, innate violence."

Hathor breathes heavily; perhaps for the first time in his life he had in front of him an antagonist that would not easily be circumvented by word or deed.

"I admit that I'm not always of light touch, Lord Warden. But we had already clarified the issue about the girl some time ago. I want her more than anything else in the world, and I'm ready to go through the hell to try to get her love me back. I have been waiting for this for ages. There have already been several reincarnations since then... Chrysalis was my beloved ten centuries ago, but I keep the promise to eternally love her!"

Visibly moved, Hathor let himself fall miserably in his chair, his hands still holding the large volume tightly. Then, with a wave of sweet tenderness, he caresses the back cover.

"If I'm deprived of Chrysalis, for me it will be like crossing the *Sacred Mirror*! I don't want to close the circle of life and death; I don't want to think of life without the presence of the woman I love."

Vamaran throws a strange look to Lord Warden, who remained seated in motionless composure.

"You should opt for a choice, Hathor. I never appreciated melodramatic scenes and this, believe me, is pathetic. Vamaran was forged to help me reach the ultimate goal, and your presence, Hathor, is now irrelevant!"

Chapter 22

Ancient

At 9:30 AM, not far from the entrance to the ruins of Clonemacnoise, the three adventurers sat waiting, hidden by the undergrowth's foliage. Marius is a little relaxed, even if a certain fear pervades his mind. He tries to drive back the anxiety he feels at the idea of 'profaning' those holy places, but recognizing that 'nothing is left to chance', evidently he's there in that place because in the Microcosm he's an integral part of the game.

With the arrival of the first tourists, Marius begins to show signs of restlessness as he walks among the ferns, while twigs of wood scattered on the forest floor crack and break under his weight.

"Well, kids, it's time! Listen, we're approaching the entrance, down about 650 feet south-west. I'm going to buy tickets and then we'll meet where the stones are placed under the protective waxed sheet. I counted 25 people who entered, of which only four were kids... children usually are the most curious and tend to stick their noses where they shouldn't. The Cross that we are seeking is housed in the Museum's Visitor Centre, outside should be a reproduction, an exact copy. First it's necessary to analyse the copy, then we evaluate when to get a closer look at the original for more details. The Cross of the Scriptures is about 13 feet high and is divided into two panels, with scenes taken from the Christian Bible. There is a depiction of the Crucifixion, the Last Judgment and Christ in the sepulchre. Jointly at the entrance tickets, they give us a sort of explanatory brochure. But the story of Clonemacnoise runs in my blood... I have been bound to it since my childhood." Marius starts with a firm step: "come on, hurry, we haven't time to lose!"

Chrisa and Joshua lengthen their strides, trying to keep pace with that of the old friend. As they approach the entrance, Marius beckons to the young ones to stop and wait. He enters the Visitor Centre and then leave a few minutes later with flyers and entrance tickets.

"Well, not that these written things will help us that much. You'll be guided by intuition, Chrisa, these explanations can't serve you, but these are shown to satisfy the usual curiosity of tourists who gather here to seek some kind of mystical past. They didn't understand anything! Since too many archaeological findings were destroyed, the multitude of fools who remained alive had only turned the cards on the table and, thanks to the manipulations of the Unified Power, has brought immeasurable damages. But read about it here... *Mysticism... oppressed civilization... divination and witchcraft*. Whoever wrote this nonsense? They have all drunk their brain, of course."

Marius starts warming up in his soul and Chrisa gives him a meaningful look.

"Come on... don't try to give a reason for everything, Marius. If you fish back in the past, there was almost always someone who has tampered with the information. This is inherent in the DNA of humans... a kind of depravity that cannot be eradicated easily. Come, let us go, we shall really trust to my intuition to guide us."

The young woman goes forward, sure-footed, wandering among the heaps of stones, many of which are arranged in perfect order. Above the place hovers an eerie sense of magic harmony.

Suddenly, the watchful eye of Marius sees, behind a wall in partial ruin, a strange figure clad in a slate grey tunic. Strange signs are painted or embroidered on the front, above the heart. The old man shivers, noticing a bizarre feeling of helplessness to take possession of his perceptions. In a blink of an eye, the apparition vanished. In Marius's soul lurks something strange, maybe it's only a feeling, but he, in those mystical places full of his past, knows he can't leave everything to fate.

The old sea dog gets very circumspect; while Chrisa approaches the copy of the Cross of the Scriptures respectfully, he makes a tour around the nearby ruins. Joshua realizes that something has changed in the attitude of his friend.

"Hey, what's wrong, Marius? It seems like you have seen a ghost! Come on... take it easy, everything is under control. It's sunny; there is nobody from the Experimental Team around... just a mound of stones piled up a bit here and there. Hey, are you listening to me?"

Marius turns, reaching the young man in four long strides. Bringing his finger to his lips he whispered, "damn you, kind of a cocky kid. You don't know how to keep your tongue! Joshua this isn't a race with 'flat wind', lest you can remain quiet, you can go back in the grove where we came from."

Suddenly the old friend becomes very serious; Joshua notices a strange fire he never seen before in the eyes of his protector. That frightens him and immediately he takes a good attitude, trying to curb his tongue.

The old sailor smiled, and then with an affectionate gesture, he ruffles his hair.

"My child, you don't know what moves in the Unknown Worlds. The *Holy Doors* may be many, to enter them requires courage and preparation... you and your sister are, in spite of yourselves, tied in a double knot with..."

Marius became suddenly silent, seeing Chrisa pass her hands over the surface of the big Cross. Followed by Joshua, he approaches the girl, always throwing around suspicious glances.

*** Vetera ***

"Is this a faithful reproduction of the original?" Chrisa asks, smiling.

"I think so, Chrisa," the old man replied after a few seconds thought. "It should be... but as I've said before, the original is housed in the Museum's Visitor Centre. Come, we'll go in to take a look at it."

The girl turns around with a strange smile.

"It's not all, Marius. Something important has been concealed. I perceive it... it's as if each presence tries to send me an encrypted message, only understandable to an *Annwyn*. I'm the only one here. Evidently the *voices* wish to communicate with us..."

In silence, all three enter the small museum where the most sensitive archaeological findings are stored, where they were protected from the weather. In the middle of the room, from four feet high, towers the marvellous Cross of the Scriptures. As Marius suspected, a rope acts as a circumference to prevent people from touching it. The lighting from the ceiling is muffled; sensors all around would have prevented the approach of even a fly.

Marius again felt that weird feeling of helplessness, in noticing an abnormal shadow in a corner. Trying not to give it too much attention, the old sailor approaches the two young.

"Hush, do not turn around," he whispers. "Just continue to observe the cross. I noticed something again that worried me already when we were outside, now I will try to find out what or who it is. For no reason should you turn around!"

Following the orders of their friend, though with visible fear, the young people continue to stare straight before them. A few seconds later, Joshua, almost in a panic, turns to his sister.

"What devilry is this? Sis, I'm beginning to get really scared. Can you tell me what's happening?"

Urged by her brother, the young *Annwyn* narrows her eyes and lets herself be taken, for a few seconds, by *'the dream'*. Always remaining still, fixated on the Cross of the Scriptures, the young woman uses her powers to see what's happening behind them. She recognizes the shape in the dark, now bright in her vision. She sees Marius, who walks backwards step by step, pretending to take better look at the cross, when in reality he was getting closer to the presence hidden in the shadows. Suddenly Chrisa sees three sharp runes embroidered in red on the presence's breast.

OTHALAN - ISA - LAGUZ

Everything seems to happen in slow motion. Marius whirls around, managing to prevent the escape of the now discovered man. First, the stranger tries in vain to cover up his head with the hood, then with a burst of anger he remains motionless in the shadows.

Chrisa and Joshua are, however, at their place, the girl holds her brother's arm.

"Quiet, everything is okay. He's a druid Brother. We will remain here until Marius allows us to reach them. Leave them alone, I think they have a lot to clarify…"

Chapter 23

The Ireland of the Libertines

Martino reached the Inn, which had remained almost the same as the last time he had visited it, perhaps a decade before; the usual buzz of excited voices, some laughter, and then the melody of Gaelic songs recalling the exploits of brave heroes of the past. The man takes off his jacket, throwing it over his left shoulder. Sawdust was thrown on the floor to dry the water brought in by visitors. Ah, what a beauty for the spirit; everything seemed to have remained the same, although the years had gone by.

A powerful voice startled him.

"Hey, good old Máirtín, for all the dragons of Hades... what the hell are you doing here in Shannonbridge?"

The pilot turns around, a bit fearful, searching through the dark faces of those present for the voice that had startled him. A big, fat man with red hair and beard nears. Two eyes behind thick lenses are watching him with curiosity; the big man took both his hands on his hips and, in that posture, looks him down from above.

"Riordan? It's that you... you old slacker rascal!"

The two men remained for a few seconds to look at each other prior to embracing with enthusiasm.

"May the devil take you! You're just a huge beast, I see that you are still the same; you smell of beer and Irish whiskey... and most of all, you have two bottle bottoms for glasses! The clock is ticking for you as well? What news do you tell me?"

Riordan looks at his old friend, wondering how many years had elapsed since the last time they met.

"Well, don't act like a vainglorious braggart. You spend your time dreaming in the clouds! It will be at least ten years since I saw you here. With the troubles caused by the Unified Power, obviously it is not too surprising that someone disappears from the face of the earth without a trace. Here, you see, things have remained almost identical. We kill time, try not to mix into too much trouble and stay away from the Experimental Team. But you, rather, don't tell me you're here for a pleasure trip... I won't believe you!"

Martino was initially a bit taken aback by the enthusiasm and almost told Riordan the true reason for his presence. Caught by a flash of common sense, he bridles his tongue and tells the first lie that comes to mind.

"Some acquaintances have asked me to bring a chest of single malt whiskey aged in oak barrels left to swim in the sea... you know, that one with the smoked flavour so unique it sticks to the roof of the mouth. They pay well. In short, smuggled stuff, that certainly isn't in the food list that passes 'the convent'. Ahhh, well, the Unified Power is trying to avoid consumption of alcoholic beverages. Too much brain damage, they say. Mental and physical addiction, that leads to the continuing deterioration of the human race."

Then Martino blurts out a loud laugh.

"They can hang me up by the skin of my buttocks, but those cowards who only drink lemonade can go straight to hell."

Obviously, the clear, despicable and disparaging remarks of the pilot had eased Riordan's tension and curiosity. He embraced him with ardour and takes Martino in the middle of the pub.

"Hey, friends, I present you with Máirtín. A Red Baron of our troubled century, he came from the continent, where the Unified Power has taken deep roots. I offer a toast to this brave man who flew over the Channel to come to get few boxes of our liquid gold!"

Martino's presence has attracted the curiosity of a man leaning lazily over the counter. The middle-aged man fiddles with a Crown coin by turning it skilfully over the knuckles of his right hand. His hair is straw coloured and his face is very thin, with a poorly treated beard that inflicts a sinister aspect to his face. The coat he wears is worn below the elbows and conspicuous dark spots pollute the area around the slit pockets. The boots of brown leather wrap around the legs just above the knees, a sheath of the same colour is attached to a loop that runs around the left thigh. The watchful eye of the pilot notices the man immediately because he doesn't fall into the picturesque atmosphere of the inn.

*** Hibernia Luxuriosae Multitudinous ***

Trying to appear polite, Martino answers the innkeeper's inquisitorial questions. The innkeeper appears genuinely amused to host an Irish whiskey smuggler in his own tavern.

"The Devil may take me by the feet! But come on, come on, it's my treat! You'll try the best malt whiskey on the island... of all the islands, even those hidden in the mists... if you know what I mean."

The big man winks at Martino, who, a little embarrassed, responds with a smile. The urge to laugh is gone to hell; since he noticed the guy with blondish hair, his mood has darkened. He thinks about his friends' mission and the danger they will face if, arriving unexpectedly at the inn, they come across the shady type... and if he's a spy of the Experimental Team?

Martino sits at the counter and drinks in one gulp the amber manna that the owner pours into his glass. The pilot is a tough one, accustomed to swallowing concoctions of dubious origin, since the Unified Power has a watchful eye over all the substances considered 'abusive', including alcohol. Then immediately in his mind looms a diabolical plan: it's clear that he must try to find out who that dirty guy with a dangerous look was.

After the second glass, hungrily gobbled, Martino pretends to become more talkative and began to stage his possible intoxication.

"Hey, be generous, look at that man over there... yeeessss that one with the hair colour of the summer's sun, offer him a glass on my part. He seems to need it!"

The landlord immediately provides, and at once the individual turns toward Martino to thank him with an unconvincing grimace.

In fact, after drinking the contents, the man gets up and leaves the tavern, rubbing the floor with his feet and raising a cloud of sawdust. The air that enters through the open door raises even more sawdust and also brings in a lot of dry leaves. Martino immediately drops the pretence and resumes his usual attitude, except shutting himself in a conspicuous silence. Fortunately, no one pays attention; they all are too absorbed by their own affairs and blather about how time was going to bring rain from the ocean.

The pilot doesn't like this eventuality too much: rain from the West meant trouble. He prefers the Atlantic flat as oil, and Martino had already encountered too many hallucinatory experiences. He meditates on what to do, there isn't time to waste, now more than ever, and for two very clear reasons he must find his three friends. First: he didn't like that shady guy and he rarely makes mistakes in judgments of people's character; second: if the weather changes, it's wise to put their asses on the aircraft and quickly return on the continent as soon as possible!

Although the innkeeper had initially protested, Martino reassured him by saying he'll return in the evening for another round of whiskey and, of course, will consider purchasing his illegal goods.

Outside the inn, gusts of wind are brought on the land by the silver-coloured clouds, but enough sunlight illuminates the trees and radiates pleasant warmth to the skin. The pilot quickly thinks about what to do; he certainly can't go back on foot all the way up to Clonemacnoise. He decides to call Marius and explain succinctly the situation and then go directly to Sibéal's cottage. It's almost 11:00 AM and ahead lies a day that will be difficult to forget... Martino feels this on a subliminal level.

Chapter 24

Beyond the Shroud

Certainly, the druid hadn't planned being taken red-handed by the people whom he had been spying. He had carefully observed them since their arrival at dawn and their attempt to hide in the undergrowth next to the ruins. But these forests, once worshiped by the ancient inhabitants of those places, have a power in itself. The plants are *alive* and have their protectors, people who, like Ualtar, ensure that the ancients may rest in peace and no mortal has the opportunity to pass, without permission, the *Holy Doors*.

Othalan, the first rune on his embroidered tunic, means 'the Last Guardian of the Threshold'... that one whom guards the entrance into the kingdom of the Gods. The second rune, **Isa**, is the manifestation of the moonlight, the divine feminine matrix venerated by the ancients, while the last rune, **Laguz**, is the Water seen as magical initiation, the rune attributed to mediums and witches.

"My name is Ualtar, I'm the Keeper of *The Sacred Door*!" Joshua and Marius look at Ualtar in astonishment, and he adds, "for some reason I imagined you guys a little different... like saying, well, I thought you would be more austere. Instead I find myself with two young people and an old man."

The old sailor smiled a bit forcedly. He notes that Ualtar looks at Chrisa, then the druid smiles before continuing.

"Well, she's the one I was waiting for, a young *Annwyn*. It's quite a long time since I felt something in the Air, in the Water, in the Fire... and the Earth also reminded me of the *Legend*. I know why you're here... but where is the man that must accompany her beyond the Threshold? He should be one of her kin, a male! A couple of months ago, a very distinguished and educated man had sought the brother's right here at Clonemacnoise and Shannonbridge. He knew that to cross the Sacred Threshold he had to be accompanied by his 'other half', as required in the *sacred rite*. I was only told that he must speak with the woman. He had promised not to be late, where is *He*?"

Ualtar looks with amazement at Marius and Joshua, then approaching the young woman the man's gaze rests again upon her.

"They aren't *Annwyn*, you can only make use of the aid of an *Annwyn* man to cross the projection, my girl."

*** Super Lodicem ***

Chrisa is left speechless. She's just been trying to understand what use the mysterious object has. She seems very confused and maybe even a little bit scared. Certainly, it's true that she wants to find the codes, but she didn't expect all these mysteries!

"But... but I, perhaps there is a misunderstanding. I only followed my intuition, which proved through meditation. Marius, the old man who is with us, isn't an *Annwyn* is true, but..."

Meanwhile Chrisa speaks, Marius get closer to the girl and then surrounds her shoulders with his arms.

"Ualtar, I belong to the congregation that binds us to Othalan... my lineage is of these sources, while the time spent at Avalon has changed the course of the *Legend*. I can't pass the Projection, but I can keep open the '*Door*' through which you exit the projection. My time spent in this dimension is finished, Ualtar. I remained here only because I had promised their parents," he nods toward the two youngsters, "a promise that is now over because they have attained the age of majority."

Suddenly Chrisa understands the words of the ancient mariner, and tears flow from her eyes, and she doesn't even try to hold them. With a boost, and perhaps even a bit of anger, she takes refuge in Marius' arms.

"Why have you always concealed your true nature? I felt that there was more about you, Marius, my friend, but I only thought it was Wynne and other Celtic legends. Then the other day on the Monte Verità, I saw the colour which your aura took... I understood that you are something other than human, even if you are not an *Annwyn*. It is true that this isn't your real world!"

Marius smiles, caressing Chrisa's hair with his trembling hand.

"Ah, little Chrysalis! How could I leave knowing that you and Joshua were left alone in the world? You know, we often joked about these things with your parents. Nagged by saying that, I had no one in the world, and therefore you were my family. This is why I stayed so long. Otherwise, I

169

think I would have followed the fate of Steven already, ten years ago."

Ualtar looks around warily, a slight agitation took his gestures.

"We shall try not to attract too much attention. Chrysalis, I feel that you have with you the *Vibratory Matrix*... You must be very careful because for anything in the world, this object must not get into the hands of the Unified Power. We can't proceed now, there are too many people and the activation of the Cross of the Scriptures requires a specific rite. We must return here with two brothers... this night. However, the rite requires the presence of a male *Annwyn*. Only a couple can go through the projection and pass through the *Sacred Mirror*, to finally move away from the cycle of reincarnation. But is that exactly what you want, my child? Do you know what this means?"

Ualtar looks at Joshua and Marius sternly, "once the *Vibratory Matrix* is activated, it will be my job to watch over the *Sacred Door*; this is the task of Othalan, the last Guardian!"

From Joshua's face, it is clear that he absolutely doesn't like it. The young man bites his lip hard, pale-faced, he even doesn't want to reiterate Ualtar's words and then, with lowered head, he follows the group outside. His feelings bubble, the young man is a coward and has an aversion to anything that he doesn't understand. The mystical arts fall into this category.

Ualtar converses softly in Gaelic with Marius. A cool breeze has risen and several clouds have obscured the sun. Chrisa looks at the pale star and below, to the west, the tops of the trees begin to fidget with extreme force, taken in the grip of the current.

"Everything is connected here," muses the girl, "or here more than in other places... I feel a sort of apprehension,

Joshua. But don't worry, I'm with you, I'm here to protect you."

"Oh what a great protection," the brother replied quietly. "You heard what the Druid said? Once out of the *Sacred Door,* you won't be able to go in and out like you want... This isn't one of your astral travels, sister. I am so scared that we might be separated... forever!"

Chrisa takes her brother's hand in hers and kisses him gently on the forehead.

"No Joshua, don't worry, nobody will separate us. There isn't any male *Annwyn* that can force me to cross that threshold... But I think it's right that if there are on planet Earth any *Annwyn* who wish to return to the land of our fathers, and never have to reincarnate again... well, I think this is good and just. I would like to talk again about that with Marius; our old protector apparently didn't tell us everything about himself! I'm also gradually beginning to understand other fragments of this strange puzzle. Years ago, in Ishtar, I heard strange *prophecies* and then I read stories in some very old, dusty books. But what I don't understand is the reason why the Unified Power keeps all these things hidden. There is the wisdom of centuries underground in those libraries, to which only very few *Annwyn* have access. Joshua, I fear that the death of our mother and father is connected to the *Vibratory Matrix…*"

The girl's words meet the puzzled and bruised face of the young fresh-water sailor. But her brother has finished the sarcasm. Joshua, perhaps for the first time in his life, realised that there are too many things he doesn't understand and in which, in spite of himself, he's embroiled. He thinks of the man Ualtar spoke of, who was he? He couldn't be Steven because he has been missing for several years now, and then Steven was just a crazy Irishman, while Ualtar had reported a male *Annwyn* and a man looking very handsome and elegant! Chrisa reads her brother's thoughts.

"Yes, I was thinking about that detail, Joshua. But I haven't the slightest idea who this man can be! And I don't like that... Ualtar said that he had to be accompanied by his *other half*, as required by the sacred rite. The idea of being the half of someone who I don't know just makes me sick. Joshua, this night, before we decide what to do and maybe come back here with Ualtar, I must enter the *Dream*, but I will not go alone. Brother, you're coming with me!"

Chapter 25

Betrayers

Hathor takes leave of Lord Warden, who, followed by Vamaran, exits the big front door. For a while the lawyer remains in the doorway, watching them walk towards their car. Only when the car runs along the avenue lined with unkempt large Japanese azalea bushes, does he turns back to the villa.

The man is visibly shaken; the idea of having a competitor, for the most with a fascinating aspect and a quite chatty speech, annoys him terribly.

"What's happening? I was convinced I had supremacy over them, too... but I realise I have been hoodwinked by Lord Warden. And what if Dr. Sella is involved in this story? Mhhhmm... Actually, now that I think, what could he want from the young *Annwyn*? I don't think he was trying to get only a diversion, he knows a lot of women like Veronika. Why bother with a prey that is unapproachable? I thought he aspired to get some extra-sensory powers... I should have submitted him to a tightened interrogation using my powers, and not only because he was threatening Chrisa. I was dumb!"

Hathor went back to the library where he had just discovered the true identity of Vamaran; he retrieves the black leather book from the large low, table. He furiously slams the double doors that isolate the library from the music room. In the latter, the man lets himself fall heavily into the Scottish tweed blue and green armchair. An old Grotrian-Steinweg piano dominates near the window with the heraldic family emblems in Murano glass and tin. Large floral arrangements with his favourite lilies are well arranged on the sides of the piano, the perfume is intense and pleasant, but goes completely unnoticed by the angry man.

It looks like an animal chased by hunters made invisible by the dense foliage of the forest. Images of the early twentieth-century return sharp to his ancestral memory: he remembers a bloody tiger hunt with elephants in northern India. But this time, Hathor is not on the elephant, but rather feels that he's like the tiger, frightened by the echo of the last words uttered by the old lord.

"Ahh, is my presence so irrelevant? That old, cocky bastard! Even Lord Warden must have some weakness... Let us go to see if my *friend* has done with arranging things in the basement. It's been some time, he should be back upstairs, I have yet to give him the final instructions and give him his reward".

*** Proditores ***

Hathor reaches the basement through a passage whose entrance is concealed behind a door of carved wood between two eighteenth century paintings, whose huge, golden frames appear as gothic trappings. He slips through the panel and finds himself in a room of about six feet square, he raised the trap door hidden in the narrow oak floorboards and then he goes down a steep staircase that seems to sink into the abyss below. He immediately notices the stench in the air.

"Holy smokes, I shall have it cleaned up down here, there will probably be a few rotten rats".

However, the spectacle which presents itself to his eyes when he reaches the basement with an octagonal vaulted ceiling is horrifying. Hathor brings a hand to his mouth to hold back a retch.

The ground was littered with shards of broken glass jars and the remains of the biological experiments he had been working on, lying witness to savage abuse. A slimy, foul-smelling substance dirties here and there, even sprayed over old manuscripts dating from the thirteenth century. Anger begins to creep into the mind of Hathor. With trembling hands the *Annwyn* picks up the remains of creatures which had been stripped of life, *his creatures*! Living forms collected during his travels through the astral and other dimensions for which he was trying to find a place on the planet Earth. These creatures could make a contribution to the myriad of problems that afflict the human race. Hathor believed to be close to the solution.

"Why harm these innocuous creatures?"

While Hathor contemplates the result of this act of vandalism, behind a shelf of oak that reaches the high arched ceiling, the man notices a pair of black shoes followed by the legs of its owner.

The *Annwyn* recognizes the livery pants of his trusted butler, Adam. In his anguish, doubt assails him, confirmed a few seconds later when he sees the large puddle of blood where the man lies.

Someone had wanted to harm him and profaning his existence, first taking away his love of Chrysalis's dream and now the love that bound him to his creatures and to Adam, and had thus achieved his goal.

Not far from the villa Var Darquen de Aguillar, Lord Warden and Vamaran converse.

"Vamaran, do you think that Hathor will try to oppose us? I'm convinced that I had found his weakness! It's obviously the deep love that binds him to the young woman, but I didn't know, however, of his union with her, a dozen centuries ago. This small detail, seemingly insignificant, could hamper our purposes. If Chrysalis learns the truth about her past with Hathor, this might change our plans!"

"Ah, but she still doesn't know the immeasurable power of my charm, Lord Warden," Vamaran smiles, rubbing his hand with sensual pleasure in his hair.

The two accomplices reached the hotel by the lake, where Lord Warden had the most beautiful suite on the top floor. Taking the elevator to the suite, the two men went out on the terrace, paved with precious blue Mesopotamian marble and sit comfortably in chairs covered with soft silk cushions. Vamaran head indicates the glimmer in the east.

"You see, the sun will rise in just over an hour. The four adventurers should have already landed in Ireland, Chrysalis and her human brother, their protector, the old sailor, and his pilot friend. When I went in person to verify this at the hangar, before they took off, I managed to crawl into the mind of the pilot. I discovered where they were going, and I felt that Chrysalis has with her the *Vibratory Matrix*, Lord Warden. However, I don't think she'll manage to activate the Cross of the Scriptures because for that ritual you need two *Annwyn*: a woman and a man!"

A rough sketch of a smile models the shape of the face of the old lord, evidently much pleased.

"Ah well, this is a good news. I'm unnerved by having to adopt outrageous attitudes... you do understand me, don't you? I hate violence, but even more I hate those who force

176

me to use it to protect my intent. Only when I have uprooted the evil from this physical dimension, will I dedicate myself to something more enjoyable... hence, Vamaran, shall we play a game of chess, so we can consider our next move?"

Chapter 26

Immortal Soul

Joshua's bewildered look is more than eloquent. Chrisa scrutinizes him with infinite tenderness, then strokes his cheek, whispering in his ear.

"Don't be afraid. I'm sure that it will work; I have met other *Annwyn* who were accompanied on their dream-trips by people they love... if it is love that enables this, it shouldn't be difficult for us."

The girl smiles and again caresses his brother gently pushing back his curly and rebellious hair.

"But sister, you don't understand, I doubt my abilities! I'm terribly afraid of doing this kind of 'thing'. You know what I think of magic in general and of all those events that have no rational explanation... It's always been like that, I don't think I can change now."

Both look at each other intently, then moving to some antiquities displayed in a shroud, they remain for a moment, silently contemplating the Celtic's artefacts.

Ualtar follows the wall for a while and disappeared to the north, behind a heap of piled stones. Marius, smiling, reaches the two friends.

"Well, I got some more information from the *Guardian of the Sacred Door.* He described the features of the man who he had met here in Clonemacnoise months ago. Unfortunately it was not very helpful; I don't know anyone who resembled the description of a man between 30-40 years old with dark hair, slightly greying at the temples. There are many such men, even among the *Annwyn.* The only detail that intrigued Ualtar is the noble and refined appearance of this individual. It could be an aristocrat, and then the circle shrinks a lot. Few *Annwyn* belong to this social class, since most of them preferred to choose to reincarnate in bodies that were not constrained by specific codes related to membership of noble blood. Have you any idea, Chrisa? I know you don't have much contact with your fellow *Annwyn,* your mom had already explained the reasons to me. But maybe you remember having met someone who belonged to a noble family, perhaps those times when you were summoned to Ishtar by the Unified Power?"

*** Sempiternus Animus ***

Chrisa shakes her head, she doesn't recall anyone... but it's certain that the following night Joshua and she would discover something more.

"No, Marius. I don't remember anyone in particular..."

The old friend shrugs and nods with his head to the young woman's bag, well hidden under her jacket.

"Ualtar also recommended keeping it well hidden. Its value is immeasurable, and is the only one left that can be used to activate the Cross of the Scriptures. All the others are lost or seized by the Unified Power for mysterious reasons. There are *Annwyn* who possess some, but in very poor condition, most are only fragments. Ualtar and his *brothers* have viewed a total of a dozen in the last 120 years, but only one was whole... and it belonged to the man Ualtar has just reported!"

A curtain of darkness settles on the heart of the young woman, while her mind seeks into the hidden depths of her ancestral memory for a possible answer. She doesn't want to confess to her old friend her idea of taking Joshua on a dream-journey, she fears that Marius wouldn't approve. Yet that's the only way to recover the truth. Of course the mysterious man was in possession of the *Vibratory Matrix*, the same one which she now holds. For what obscure reason? And why did *she* found it?

Ualtar has already disappeared from the horizon, when the three adventurers reach the exit of the archaeological zone. Several electric taxis were waiting, parked under a huge oak tree. Speaking to a driver in Gaelic, Marius fixed the price to carry them up to Shannonbridge. After about thirty minutes, they arrived near the cottages inhabited by relatives of the old mariner. The man is visibly moved, he pays the fixed price to the driver and then all three went out and headed up the driveway.

Many fruit trees, carefully numbered and marked with a Unified Power's approval label, are perfectly aligned and are lost in the distance, down where the River Shannon is following his now miserable and peaceful course.

A lean and tall woman, wearing a long greenish cloak fixed at the waist with an original belt, walks to meet them. Her hair is white as snow, but although she's certainly more than seventy years, her face looks timeless. She immediately recognizes Marius and addresses him in Gaelic, and then she tightens her arms around him with great enthusiasm.

"Meet Sibéal, one of my many cousins. Her name in Italian would be Isabella, but don't you find the Gaelic much sweeter and more melodic?"

For a moment, all worries vanish from their minds; Sibéal prepares a good cup of tea that is served with slightly salty scones with a taste of cinnamon. Joshua, as expected, fills his belly and after he asks the old lady's permission to take a couple 'for later, in case he is still hungry'. The woman laughed.

"But I would like to invite you for dinner; they gave me fresh sheep's cheese this morning, to be served with black walnut bread, and then I would prepare some pastry with hot stew of crab, salmon and various fish in sour wine and dill sauce."

"Hmm, I'm not so fond about sour sauces," Joshua pouted. "What's for dessert?"

Chrisa glares at him angrily and that immediately shuts up the boldness of her brother. Marius chuckles and speaks to his cousin in Gaelic.

"Más fiú é a dhéanamh, is fiú é a dhéanamh i gceart!"

Irritated the young man snorts, convinced that Marius is taunting him. Realising the misunderstanding, the old sailor explains to the boy.

"No, translated what I said means 'the simplest things are the most extraordinary, and only a sage can see them'. Joshua, I'm referring to the Irish food, certainly very different from the Mediterranean to which the three of us are used to... but to let you in on the surprise, Sibéal cooks divinely!"

In the meantime Marius and the two young people help Sibéal in the kitchen; Marius gets a call from Martino. From the beginning, Chrisa perceives that something has gone wrong; the old sailor's face usually tanned and shiny becomes dull and pale.

"Guys, Martino will arrive in half an hour. We were right to come here rather than moving directly to the Pub... Martino has just reported that he found a strange guy who gave him a bad vibe. He'll turn around a while in the old neighbourhood, to see if anyone follows him, then if everything is okay, he'll join us here at the cottage."

Chapter 27

The Truth about Bartók

The Commander Fenix throws inside the paper shredder a couple of messy sheets. On his face are evident signs of a sleepless night spent analysing records after records, projected on a digital screen that covers the entire wall.

Pissed off for not having got a toad from Dr. Sella, he gets angry with those around him. Evidently his colleagues know him well and they try not to contradict him.

"Do you have any news about the two young siblings and the old sailor? I am really starting to worry about their lives. I'm sure they aren't directly involved with the killing, but something makes me believe that one of the three, if not all three, is the real target. Is someone ready to intercept if there are any communications through *Unynetweb*? The race-commissioner reported that they went to the mountains... Damn it, there are mountains all around, there is no sure destination. They can be gone to Gstadt or St. Moritz. Then the boy was sick, gorging himself with who knows what, and they haven't returned yet. And now that the race was cancelled due to bad weather which will arrive in the afternoon, they certainly will not come back to Ascona."

On the screen appears the image of Chrysalis when she was a little girl, with her brother and their dead parents. Fenix gives a depressed look to the old image:

"Damn it, was a nice family. Why did someone kill the parents? What was the real reason?" He raises his voice excessively, to be heard by all, and begins to give orders: "I want to know where they stored the information on the *Annwyn* girl's family. Is there anyone among you who remembers something special about the investigation? If I remember correctly, the victim, their father, was a prominent genetics researcher. Bartók or Bar-something... I think the name was Jeremiah or Isaac or something like that, with a bloody religious connotation. Damn it, how can you have a name like that and procreate one of those *things*... an *Annwyn*. The case was filed, unsolved, but maybe the Unified Power didn't want too much to be revealed."

*** De Bartók Veritas ***

Fenix turns around and he realises that his soliloquy had caused confusion and a few smiles among his employees. The commander let himself fall back in the swivel chair, with the head in his hands waiting for a young recruit to type in the different connections, then with a remote control device he begins to fathom the graphical representation containing ten gigabytes of information and photographs.

The officer Sergio, a thermos in the hands, approached with some caution as he enters the office and closed the door behind him.

"Commander, I brought you fresh coffee. I hope you like it... and these, if I may, are the anthropomorphic cards of the family. There are also references and links on the *Unynetweb*, the different departments and areas of interaction. In No. 4 are highlighted Dr. Bartók's scientific research and his governmental responsibilities. His wife isn't stored in any specified area; exemplary mother, a little bit original in her ideas, but apparently being called '*diviner*' was normal for her, and she had contact with other *Annwyn*. Excuse me, Commander, I'm not very competent in this matter... there is Xernon, an official of the ministry in Turicum who carried out extensive studies in Ishtar, about the presence of the *Annwyn* on the planet. Do you want to contact him for a video-call?"

Fenix chews his left thumbnail, and then throws a sinister look to Sergio.

"Someday you shall remember that it is usually me who get the solutions, it's also always me who makes decisions on how to proceed. No. I won't hear this Xernon. We do not need to involve people from the North side of the Alps in our research! I already had to ask for surveillance of over half square acre. Turicum is full of boastful wiseacres, better to have them away from our bottom. Believe me, Sergio. I speak from experience!"

The commander takes the thermos of coffee from the hands of his subordinate then heads to the door.

"Thank you for the coffee. Now I want to go over a couple of things on my own, though if any of those out there think of something, even the smallest nonsense, then send the information directly to my screen."

Sergio goes without saying anything, he snorts passing the desks of two colleagues who are making digital scans of paper documents and cataloguing them in the relative anthropomorphic cards.

"Fenix is tired and is being particularly unpleasant, try to avoid going into his office," he whispers without stopping. When he arrived before the check-point, he turns to the secretary.

"I will take a tour in the area, with Selene and Solaris. I'll leave the coordinates when the two *jaglynx* are ready to go out."

The woman passes him an *earth-frame* monitor with connection to the *Unynetweb* and his identification plate.

"Damn, I would rather go home but my shift ends at 12:00."

The fingers of Commander Fenix are nervously drumming on the top of his desk which, to the sight of an observer, looks like a forest floor invaded by autumn leaves, as if a gust of wind had passed through the open window behind him.

The man perceives that there is something escaping him, everything is there for his eyes and he just had to try to steal that very nasty detail that's apparently occluded to him. Fenix reinserted the Bartók family photo, increasing the size. Now the background is clearer, with the cursor he moves to the beautiful late nineteenth century building... then enlarges even more on a side of the English park with dense and luxuriant vegetation of rhododendrons and azaleas.

"It must have been the end of spring, to judge from Mrs. Bartók's dress," the commander whispers to himself. "Um, a beautiful woman, the young Chrysalis actually looks a lot like her mother!"

Again he reviews the little details and copies them on a digital card.

"Ahh, behold, there is also the shadow of the person who took the photo, someone who wore pants, probably a male. Okay, here we are. Depending on the time of capture, we can calculate the exact size of the photographer and his weight on the basis of other data extracted from the shaded area. I will run a macro enlargement of the pupils of the people portrayed here. Maybe their eyes have caught the reflection of the photographer! Hmm, well well, look here in the corner... no wait, it's slightly curved because of the wide angle lens they used; behind the driveway, it seems to be a vehicle."

Taken from his meditations in a low voice, Commander Fenix had not even noticed that one of the secretaries was peering from behind the glass, motioning with her hand. A little irritated, he presses the speakerphone button and asks her to enter. The woman blushes slightly, evidently a newcomer in the centre, moved from some other area.

"Excuse me, sir. Your men have finished with the witness Sella. They ask if they can let him go since there is no evidence to enable us to retain him for a longer time."

The commander looks up at the ceiling. From his lips escape out a curse. "Call back Sergio... he's the person to whom I had entrusted this matter!"

His voice is altered, shrill; the woman stammers with visible embarrassment.

"But he's already out... Shall I immediately contact him on his *unycell*?"

Fenix pretends not to hear; he removes from the mess on his desk a bundle of magnetic cards and places them in a metal box with digital locking. Then, leaning forward, trying to keep the authoritative demeanour, hisses: "no, forget it. Sella can wait a bit. Tell him we're waiting for authentication... in short those upstairs may invent something plausible. Until 12:00 o'clock, we can hold him here at the Central, and then I will decide what to do with that scoundrel. But don't let him contact anyone, not even a lawyer!"

Nodding, the woman turns on her heel and strode away, as if she had the devil at her tail.

Fenix looks again at the image projected on the screen. With a nervous movement of his body, he leans forward again, noticing something that had escaped him before, a detail that now seems obvious: the tower of the villa! It is not any tower... he had already seen that one. You bet he already had seen it! He passed in front of it every evening when he took Elvira, his wife's dog, for a walk! It was on the property of Var Darquen de Aguillar, right down at the bottom of Ascona's lakeside promenade.

"Holy cow! I'm an idiot, foolish to the cubic root... why haven't I noticed it before? Here my stubbornness pays off..."

Chapter 28

The Beauty of Nature

Chrisa is secluded on the porch behind the kitchen; she wants to remain alone a moment in the hope of being able to rearrange her thoughts. The glass roof of the *Jardin d'hiver* is slightly milky to occlude the strong rays of the sun and prevent them from damaging the many plants housed there.

Once she had entered the strange and slightly damp environment, Chrisa clearly perceives the energy emanating from the beautiful plants that cover the entire wall to the house and most of the ceiling. Everything vibrates a specific frequency that humans have begun to understand and study further. Nature was cultivated with great care and love; humans had been discovered to be inextricably linked to Gaia, the Great Mother, but it had taken centuries before they understood the importance of ecology! Large, brightly coloured bougainvilleas were perched along special brackets which allow the extremely long branches to grow freely. Different citrus plants are grown in huge clay pots. Chrisa recognizes different kinds of kumquats, tangerines, oranges, lemons and limes of brilliant colours in shades of green and yellow. A couple of bergamot trees are laden with small, round fruits with an unmistakable smell when rubbed.

The aroma is intense and Chrisa, after closing her eyes, let herself be carried away by her memory. She sees herself back in Tuscany, many years before, in the company of her mother and father. She now remembers with clarity that her parents loved those places that, thanks to the efforts of the farmers, had been able to flourish again as they did at the beginning of the twenty-first century. Only here and there were traces of the catastrophe of 2022 still visible: deep scars that have disfigured the earth's soil.

*** Locorum Amoenitas ***

Chrisa sits in a corner inside an old woven willow armchair, lined with a soft pillow printed with lilies and iris. For a moment she remains still, as though imprisoned in her memories, then she takes from her bag the inseparable moleskin diary and pen.

With rapid and minute lines, she carefully notes few more details from the day before. Everything happened so suddenly; only thirty hours had elapsed. She rereads the notes of her astral travel, details regarding the discovery of the object that turned out to be a very ancient and non-human artefact.

Suddenly, she sees in her mind Hathor's face, that being that she despises with all her strength. The gaze of that individual now looks different, but perhaps this is only her impression. Chrisa feels the heart pounding in her chest. Everything was fast and on the journey from Ascona to Clonemacnoise, on board Martino's aircraft, she was able to doze just a little. Now she feels very tired, sick of pretending to herself that everything is under control, unnerved to try to keep everything at bay.

The arrival of Sibéal startles her.

"Hush, it's me, baby! I feel your deep concern... I have the power to read minds... including the minds of the *Annwyn*, Chrysalis. Perhaps the good old Marius has not told you everything, apart from a lot of fuss about my culinary skills and my healing powers."

For a moment the two women look at each other with great intensity. Chrisa clearly perceives the thoughts of the woman, without her expressing them in words. The young allows Sibéal to view her memories and thus to experience the same strong emotions tied to the death of her mother and father. Then, very gently but with determination, she closes her mind to the woman.

"I learned the hard way not to trust anyone, Sibéal. Many times I have gotten into big trouble because of my naivety. I don't want this to happen again. Not ever..."

"No, Chrysalis," she smiles kindly, shaking her head slightly. "By doing so, you don't avoid the problems! I'm sure your parents have told you that several times. I met them both, though it was a long time ago; you and your brother hadn't been born yet. Will you now listen to what I want to tell you, or would you like to stay a little bit longer alone? The time is ripe, my little one. You have to make very serious and important choices... and the strength of Marius is low, like mine, for that matter. There is no time to lose."

The woman turns very slowly, the long, silver dress caressing the polished stone that covers the floor of the spacious veranda. After a few seconds, only the echo of her last words remained... *there is no time to lose*.

The girl closes her diary with an elastic band, and then puts it inside her bag. The light of the *Vibratory Matrix* looks fade, but the flickering is always noticeable. She looks toward the west corner of the veranda, where the late afternoon sun breaks through the kaleidoscope of windows to spray a large dragon tree with pink and purple leaves.

Suddenly, in the reflection of the sun, appears clearly a large flower which reminds Chrisa of the Japanese giant peonies, extinct for almost a century and no longer produced in the laboratories.

The flower takes on an iridescent outline and seems to swell as Chrisa watched. She stiffens, then, more and more intrigued, she approaches the dragon tree unsteadily. Now the scent is noticeable and mixed with the smell of the citrus plants; the fluorescence appears alive and gradually each petal is separated from the stamen to flourish in its perfect beauty.

When the girl notices that she was being completely spellbound, the flower has reached its full flowering and disturbing beauty. Suddenly it begins to wilt, petal after petal: the pale pink turns first translucent and then take beige and earthly shades. As it had appeared, it disintegrates in the air, leaving only a faint dust, barely noticeable.

Shocked, Chrisa turns on her heels and goes back to Sibéal's large kitchen. In one corner, leaning against the north wall, the great clock reminds her that only thirty minutes had elapsed since she had entered her host's greenhouse.

In the adjacent room, sitting comfortably in armchairs, her brother, Marius and Martino are talking and laughing happily.

"Have you somehow made sense of your ideas, Chrisa?" Marius asks her with a smile.

"Sibéal told me that you preferred to be alone, and because of that we didn't come looking for you. Martino told me some details on the guy he met at the pub, you know, that man dressed in a strange way. From the description, he might belong to some distinct *group*; by now Ireland has for centuries been a free land and here burrow all those who escape the Unified Power."

Chrysalis looks at him, thinking about Sibéal's phrase *'the strength of Marius is low'* wondering what she was referring to. Taking courage in both hands, the young woman turns to his old friend.

"Yes, I have clarified my ideas and I think the time has come for you to reveal to us a couple of important little facts, don't you think Marius? I would also request the presence of Sibéal; if it's important that we activate the *Vibratory Matrix*, then I want to know the whole story... from the beginning to the end!"

"Hmm hmm," Martino coughs slightly, "I think this is none of my business, if I can put it that way. I prefer to mind my own affairs... so, if you'll excuse me..."

"Oh no, my dear," Marius replied firmly to his friend, "you're in this up to your neck, I think it's only right you know the whole truth. Or rather, at least that part of the story to which we can give a meaning. Unfortunately there are a lot of things that escape me. Today in Clonemacnoise I met a member of the Brotherhood of Othalan, his name is Ualtar and he's the *Guardian of the Sacred Gate*."

Martino's face becomes dark, and deep lines are drawn around his eyes and forehead.

"But then there is some truth in *Othalan's prophecy*... and you three, what do you have to do with it? I was convinced it was only one of these ridiculous Irish legends, washed and coloured by too many glasses of whiskey. Sometimes, years ago, Steven had also mentioned that *Holy Door*. It was said to be on Avalon, beyond *The Mists*. The same old stories become legends and then myths... isn't it? These are just fairy tales to quiet the kids at night when they don't want to sleep, Marius... or is there more?"

The aviator is visibly restless; he regains his place in the chair. Pours into the glass another shot of whiskey from his small flask, hidden under his jacket.

"Just a little more, I think. It will help me to digest something that will probably be difficult to assimilate."

Joshua throws a pleading glance around, and then his eyes met those of his sister.

"Here we go again, sister. Is it possible that you aren't able to take life with a certain philosophy? I had a good meal of biscuits, and since I slept badly last night on the plane, I want to get relaxed and get some rest. As far as I understand it, it seems that at the rising of the moon we must take a ride up to the ruins of Clonemacnoise... then I rather be well rested!"

"I agree, Joshua," Marius sighs. "But first I must tell you a couple of important things; Chrisa is right. I can't remain silent anymore!"

Marius sits on the other chair and calls out for his cousin.

Chapter 29

Over Control

Hathor feels such a rage that he barely manages to control his heart rhythm and the vital functions. He can't make sense of it, he doesn't understand the reason of the event and, even worse, he doesn't know who could have done it! His first suspicion is the creature called Vamaran, and if Lord Warden is his creator, of course, the instigator could only be him... but why? Just because he had put up resistance at the idea that this new contender could take Chrysalis away from him? Yet he had accompanied them to the door and watched them leave.

"But why was it necessary to kill Adam and destroy my laboratory and the decades of researches? What were they looking for?"

With his head between his hands, the lawyer is humiliated and cracked in the soul; he went upstairs and through the secret passage and finds himself in the music room. Then he attempts to make up his mind, trying to remember every single second of those hours spent in the presence of the Lord and his strange companion.

Hathor then returns to the big room where the fire is almost out, the iron fire pans contain the now charred pieces of a large spruce log which had burned throughout the night.

The sun has risen a couple of hours ago; the man sits in his favourite leather chair, trying to keep his composure. Deep wrinkles on his face make him look old and weak. Hathor looks for the book with the golden runes inscription; he found it under the cashmere plaid where he had left it. He takes it in his hands and presses it hard against his chest.

"Chrysalis, I'll find you... your life is in serious danger! I underestimated the true meaning of freeing the *Vibratory Matrix*. Evidently its power is much greater than even your father had dared to imagine. Poor Professor Bartók!"

*** Super Hominum Dominium ***

His voice, deep and emotional, is a slight whisper. He reaches the kitchen where two servants are busy cleaning and tidying up. Clearing his throat, he turns to the oldest.

"Madame Rosengarden, please prepare the usual suitcase. I go away for a few days, but first I'll pass by my office and inform... Adam."

In pronouncing the statement, Hathor thinks with pain of the lifeless body of his faithful servant.

The woman nodded, without asking anything else; she had worked for the lawyer for forty years and she has learned that her job is very well paid, as are her confidentiality and respect for silence.

Hathor, before rising from the secret underground room, proceeded to hide the dead body of Adam and the other creatures in the hypothermic cell in which he kept, in a state of hibernation, other scientific research subjects. He then cleaned away the shards of the glass jars and with the

196

pressure water pump carefully has washed the floor, walls and ceiling. In vain, he tried to make telepathic contact with the creature he hired for the recovery of prohibited artefacts. He had made detailed rearrangements of all the volumes and cards into different vaults. This fact, that had initially made the lawyer suspicious, led him to believe that the murderer was not that creepy being. Why would he bother to put everything in perfect order when he was going to destroy and kill?

Always with the book in his hands, Hathor returns to the studio where he draws from the desk a couple of leather cases worn by time. He thinks of the many different possibilities, but without being able to work out which was fact. Another thing is clear: how could Lord Warden or Vamaran be with him upstairs and at the same time carry out the butchery in the villa's dungeons? Something else made him suspicious; why was Adam under there instead of being in his office in the centre of Ascona, as Hathor had requested?

In his opinion, Vamaran was just trying to scare him and persuade him to give up Chrysalis... while the old Lord was just too full of himself to waste time with Hathor's genetic experiments. And above all, Lord Warden hated violence! No, of course... the two couldn't be the suspects: both aimed merely to use the *Vibratory Matrix* for hegemonic and selective purposes. But why had the Unified Power not sought to intervene in some way, considering that finding indiscretions were their strength?

"All right," Hathor sighed, more and more confused, "I'll order my ideas later; now I'm announcing my official departure... then possibly I'll modify my destination for *technical* reasons."

The lawyer typed the phone number of his secretary and asked her to organise his flight to Paris, as well as take care of the visa application process required when you go out of the country and share the required information to the Unified Power.

"Blessed technology, everything is so fast thanks to the *Unynetweb*, although at the expense of privacy!"

A twisted and painful grimace crosses his face, while sighing to himself.

"Ahh, Paris! How I wanted to bring Chrysalis back there with me... we had a wonderful love story in France, a few centuries ago."

He closes his eyes for a moment; leaning back against the chair losing himself briefly in the ancestral memory.

"Everything is possible; I just have to be able to show her the Book..."

Mrs. Rosengarden enters the room with the handle of the suitcase clutched in her right hand and the coat placed on her left forearm.

"Sir... the car is waiting in the driveway. The driver has already taken the documents from your office; the flight will depart from Lugano in two hours... if you allow me..."

The maid retreats a few steps and waits for Hathor to join her.

"I wish you a good trip, sir. Don't worry, everything is under control."

Hathor would want to hug her, he's so happy to be able to rely on the expertise of his housekeeper. He takes the suitcase and then squeezes her hand.

"Thank you. Your reliability is well known to me, dear Madam Rosengarden. I'm very grateful; I'll inform you as soon as I arrive in Paris. The usual hotel and the usual customer commitments..."

She sketches a slight smile and shakes her head slightly.

"Can I do anything else for you, during your absence?"

Hathor, walking toward the big door, turns around and tells her with great kindness.

"No, Madame Rosengarden. I don't need anything else. I'll be away only for a couple of days, there isn't any urgent business pending and everything can wait for my return to Ascona. Do me a more welcome gift: let me find the usual beautiful flower arrangement on my return."

The old housekeeper nods, then she watches the lawyer walk down the stairway leading up to the vehicle, her eyes veiled by a strange fear.

On board the business jet Hathor tries to relax, but the presence of a couple of members of the Congress, distinguished by their uniform, bothers him.

Although he enjoys the highest esteem within the ranks of the Unified Power, it's not reciprocal. The lawyer, over the years, had successfully found a number of highly confidential documents that could create major problems to the Unified Power if they were ever made public.

Being an *Annwyn*, he enjoys the accursed gift of longevity, which sometimes can't be appreciated because the shell, though much more slowly, deteriorates over time. In this existence, Hathor absolutely must be able to complete his mission. All in spite of the Unified Power, in spite of Lord Warden and his rival, Vamaran.

Thinking about this creature, that was once his kin, Hathor feels a deep sense of frustration. He had spent years studying Waterhouse's paintings, which he had obtained by means that were not complicit with the law. Recalling the *Pandora* painting, he is forced to think of Dr. Sella and his face darkens again.

The initial certainty of finding the key to the symbols on the painting turns into frustration. Not to mention that for at least 60 years, Hathor had been collecting countless pieces of antiquity that he jealously guarded in his study and, for those with greater value, in the crypts secluded inside the Villa de Aguillar.

One thing is certain: Hathor Var Darquen de Aguilar has immeasurable power in his hands, and this is well known even to the top of the Unified Power.

The landing in Paris is a bit turbulent, a strong wind got up from the Atlantic, bringing one of the usual early summer storms.

On reaching the old city, Hathor breathes greedily that air charged with pleasant memories mixed with pain. He takes a taxi and let's himself be led to the Île de la Cité. At the end of rue Lagrange, the lawyer asked the taxi to stop. After he directs the taxi driver to the correct hotel to deposit his suitcase and personal belongings, he leaves a large tip and departs. His hands tighten around the case in which he had placed the leather book with carved the golden runes. He makes sure that he is not being followed and then goes straight to the cathedral of Notre Dame, crossing the Pont au Double.

The old Gothic building, built in the twelfth century on the foundations of a Gallo-Roman temple dedicated to Jupiter, still stands in its majestic beauty. Hathor feels a pang while, almost running, he enters the Gate of Judgment. He walks the two hundred feet along the central aisle and stops for a moment to catch his breath. After passing the lateral wall, he heads right up to the fourth aisle, in front of the entrance to the sacristy.

The place is fortunately deserted; a deep silence is sometimes disturbed by the flapping wings of a bird that had nested inside. Faith and religion had lost all their appeal and meaning after 2022, and in the majestic temple only the animals protected themselves, and is now a place only visited by the romantic or the mad.

Smiling at his fate, the man rests his left hand on the marble door frame, polished from wear, about five feet from the ground. His ring embeds itself perfectly into the low relief that, with a slight pressure, triggers an opening mechanism.

Hidden at several key points, usually in places defined as sacred, *Gates to the other Dimensions* allowed the reaching from the physical plane to anywhere in the universe. Since ancient times, great minds had discovered secrets of unimaginable magnitude through alchemical studies and investigating symbols and codes handed down over the centuries. But because all these secrets were passed down orally by the members belonging to occult and powerful congregations, very few were aware of them. Much, much more powerful than the Unified Power!

Hathor moves a few inches, looking with the upturned eyes, towards the perfect framing just above his head. From the darkness there was a bright circumference and, in a fraction of a second, there was no trace of his physical form: Hathor had dissolved. A couple of pigeons, startled by the luminescence, flap and rattle their wings furiously. A few minutes later, they land safely back to earth, looking earnestly in the dust, for crumbs to eat.

Chapter 30

In the Human Soul, the Truth

Chrisa and Joshua listened to Marius and Sibéal's explanation with particular curiosity and attention; Martino, exhausted by the night spent flying, falls asleep almost immediately. Both young siblings are shocked by the revelations of their old friend. They never thought that many of the legends that they listened to when they were small, were in truth a precise and chronological succession of events that had involved the planet Earth.

Chrisa has stopped the narrative a couple of times to ask for clarification, then, in her head, she began to understand many things that had for a long time seemed absurd and impenetrable.

"Marius, how can I reach Avalon?"

The question comes as a flash of lightning in a clear sky, the old sailor looks with severity at Sibéal before responding to his protégée.

"You can't reach Avalon... not in this material body... Beyond *The Mists*, there is a future reserved for few: human, *Annwyn* and creatures belonging to other spheres. This place, over the millennia, has been named in hundreds of different ways, my children. And maybe, once you open the *Holy Door* and broken the projection, the mists will thin out and Avalon will be accessible to our immortal minds."

Sibéal approaches Marius and surrounds his shoulder in a tender embrace.

"One thing is for sure: each of us is the maker of his own destiny, and therefore may act only on the basis of his own karma. But sometimes events happen that may completely change our Path, thus determining in an indirect way the trip towards the Last Destination. Unfortunately, humans are always too busy brooding on the past and grieving over mistakes. They are also obsessed by the future, which is ephemeral and uncertain... forgetting that what really matters is the present in which every action and thought can change their Path."

Joshua begins to be more and more confused, he has great respect for his host, and for this reason he avoids asking embarrassing questions. He looks at his sister with apprehension, sure that later she'll be able to clarify a couple of little things that didn't fit into his simplistic worldview.

"This evening," Marius added in an authoritative tone, "with the help of the *Guardian of the Sacred Gate of Othalan* and another druid brother, we'll activate the *Vibratory Matrix* through the Cross of the Scriptures. Ualtar told me something about the runes that should be read counter clockwise... I wish to check a few things. Chrisa, could you please give us the item you keep inside your bag so that Sibéal and I can 'prepare' it? Now I think it is wise if you two go to rest."

Marius looks at Martino and smiles. "Well, he has been asleep for a while. I believe our stories have reconciled his sleep!"

The Irish woman led the young people into a private room down the long corridor. The large room is decorated with floral wallpapers representing lilies and has two beds against the northern wall. A large window opens upon the vision of emerald green fields and to the west, you can see the large barn where Martino's 'Dragon's Fire' was hidden.

*** In Anima Veritas ***

The scent of vanilla in the air reminds Chrisa of her mother's favourite fragrance; the young woman half-closes her eyes for a moment, smiling in her heart at the thought of her mother.

"Thanks, Sibéal. We're very grateful for your hospitality and the love you brought to our parents... and now for the tenderness that you show us. Here, under your protection, we'll certainly sleep in peace."

Joshua snatches, in the words of his sister, a bit of caution; he felt that Chrisa is trying in every way to conceal her thoughts from Sibéal so that she doesn't find out the truth. How would the old woman react if she knew that Chrisa wanted to make a 'dreamlike journey'... and wanted to take him, too? Sibéal exited the room, and with a big sigh, Chrisa sits on the bed.

"Well, then? Do you trust your sister enough to get involved... to follow her in to the *dream*?"

The young man turned pale, and drops of cold sweat decorate his forehead, and then slide down his cheeks like pearls.

"I'm afraid. I'm bloody scared, and that certainly doesn't make things easier!"

Chrisa gives his brother a big hug and kisses him on the forehead.

"You'll see," she says, softly, "it can also be fun! When I was a little girl, I imagined fairy tale worlds... there were gnomes and elves the next *I entered* the dream! It's a lot of fun, believe me. It's just important to maintain contact with this dimension and come back, afterwards. All this can happen in the REM phase, but surely there are other mysteries connected to the power and presence of the *Annwyn*, obscure notions that we still don't know. The *Annwyn dreamer* can do things that may appear conceptually impossible. But this is also, at the same time, an apparent reality; they had discovered it just over 200 years ago in the quantum physics. But it was already too late, what obviously had to happen to the planet Earth had occurred without being able to avoid the cataclysm. Ohh Joshua is better to forget it. If I try to explain concepts that aren't even clear to me... you would end up with increasing fear, which I already can see on your face! Now lie down, find a comfortable position and let sleep envelop you. The love that binds us, this feeling so wonderful that it can really do wonders, will allow me to take you with me. Initially, you'll experience a strange feeling and you'll feel light, then you will become conscious of what is around you and you'll, with a little patience, be able to interact with me. Okay? We take these as well," she placed a candle and a box of matches in her bag.

"Now let me lock the bedroom door, there is nothing more annoying than having to return forcefully to your material body when someone, thinking you're asleep, tries to wake you up."

Chrisa laughs making a couple of dimples on the sides of the mouth appear.

"You can't imagine the times that you've forced me to return from a *dream trip* just because you have appeared on the sailboat making a lot of noise! I beg you only to remain close to me, better if you hold me by the hand, thus avoiding losing yourself somewhere. Now lie down and go to sleep. I love you so much, brother."

Chapter 31

Healers of the Earth

In the large kitchen Sibéal looks out of the window. The sun has already disappeared behind the trees at the edge of the fields and the sky turns pink to the horizon.

"Cousin, you feel very tense, now that you have the chance to enter *The Mists*... you appear to me frightened."

Marius approaches her, contemplating the landscape outside; the wind has risen, but Martino's earlier idea to leave has been shelved. They can't wait any longer, the time was ripe and they must act without delay. In a few hours it will be late night and they can't just turn around and go back to the mainland at the first doubt; Ualtar was clear. The *Keeper of the Sacred Door* of Othalan's Order had been waiting for this moment for more than a century and now, thanks to the *Vibratory Matrix*, all of them can help the planet to make the vibration change.

Marius turns his gaze to the middle of the kitchen. The object is placed on the big walnut table, wrapped in a moss-green cloth decorated with golden embroidery representing Nordic runes. The presence of the object makes them both restless, but its abnormal although faint light, is concealed under the fabric.

"Marius, now that all this is possible, I feel that there are dark forces out there... These are very dangerous entities, certainly worse than the Unified Power. I was called to Ishtar too, almost eighty years ago; have you forgotten where you came from? I saw their astral bodies, I know their power! They aren't *dreamers* like the *Annwyn*, but have gained further potential over time. These creatures have advanced genetically, generating strange life forms; they were very smart and certainly didn't put themselves on a pedestal! They can bend the elements to their will, even if the Great Mother is opposed. Since we apply the Othalan Order's law, we felt the mutations in the air and in the water... we saw the fire change and reveal to us those visions of Hell. Marius, do you really think we can get them all back in their dimension? Do you think the Cross of the Scriptures together with the *Vibratory Matrix* has enough strength?"

"I don't know," Marius' face darkens; he runs his right hand over his wrinkled and tanned face.

"I don't know, Sibéal, I really don't know what to think! There is another question which forges suspicions in my mind... Dr. Bartók... the father of the two kids, he had reached a remarkable achievement with his research. All had been delivered, fortunately, to his friend and partner, Var Darquen de Aguilar. But neither Bartók nor his wife were able to refer all the details to me... they were victims of that weird incident. I informed you, as I was hoping you could help me with the children, which at that time were still very young. Maybe I dreamed that time would heal the wounds, that somehow we could erase everything and forget. Maybe I should have brought them here and kept them away from the mainland. At the bottom of my heart I just wanted both kids to have a 'normal' life like everyone else, but also wanted to keep the promise I made to their parents, that if anything happened I would take care of their children. Then the idea of the sailboat had calmed me down, I could be close to them without having too much of an effect on their lives. But in my mind arises a terrible doubt; something tells me that Dr. Bartók imagined that someone was trying to interfere with his studies! On a couple of occasions, he told me that he wanted to be able to trust Chrysalis by telling her, as he was sure that she would have some sort *of insight about what to do*. Chrisa at this time was already been summoned to Ishtar, it was his opinion that her mind was ready. Unfortunately, things went differently and that damn accident suppressed Dr. Bartók's plans. But it was not a misfortune, Sibéal. Chrysalis and Joshua... if I, at the last moment, had not insisted on taking them to the mountains for a ride, they would have been in the car, too!"

*** De Morbis Terrarum Liberatores ***

The woman gives to her cousin a heartening smile, then approaches a plant in the corner, and turned her palms, one facing towards the sky and the other the earth; a strange amber light glowed between her hands, enveloping the plant. The plant assumes a particular brilliance, as if the rays of the sun had focused upon it, and, little by little, very large flowers begin to bloom.

"Our *gift* is wonderful, Marius. See what is our power? I believe that every creature has its place in this universe. The problem occurs when someone seeks hegemony and control over all forms of life. Perhaps it is as you say, for reasons unknown to us, someone wanted to erase the presence of that family. I'm convinced that Bartók and his wife have deliberately allowed the entity we call Chrysalis to come in to this dimension... maybe just to activate the *Vibratory Matrix*. Evidently Dr. Bartók had acquired knowledge, a power too great for a human, and someone had arranged his death. But obviously things didn't go as their killers planned, thanks to your intervention. The two kids were saved. What most intrigues me is the reason that someone ensured that Chrisa came into possession of this item. And why did he or she wait so long? I fear there are other things related to the potential of the artefact, I'm afraid we haven't deciphered all the runes engraved on it correctly. These writings date back to more than 4000 years ago, so it is not the catalogued, common Celtic runes."

Marius approached Sibéal and takes her both hands, forming a circle around the plant, and the light grew more intense.

"Cousin, maybe there is nothing to decode, it isn't our job. Dr. Bartók had contact with someone who is part of the Order of Othalan. He talked to me in secret at his return from a study trip, more or less ten months before his death. I haven't yet had the opportunity to discuss it with Ualtar, obviously it would be important to investigate even this eventuality. It's quite possible that the scientist had been aware of the possibility of raising the vibration of the entire planet by means of a specific item! Come now, Sibéal, let us prepare the *Vibratory Matrix* for tonight's ritual!"

As soon as Joshua fell asleep, Chrisa watches him carefully. She hopes in the depths of her heart that she succeeds to take him along her dreamlike journey. The girl relaxes, and focusing on the flow of life energy within her body, slowly slips into the REM phase.

The air around her field begins to alter, taking a very intense golden colour. Gradually, the energy of the astral field is separated from the material one, as had happened two nights before. Once she had complete control of her movements, Chrisa approaches her sleeping brother and sits next to him on the bed. Following a ritual never used until that day, the young woman manages to capture the astral field of her brother and draw it to her vibration's level.

Gradually, Joshua's boundary is detached from his body, which remains inert on the bed. Initially, the boy looks around, as if trying to figure out where he is and what is happening, then he notice the presence of his sister and takes her hand.

"Perfect. Welcome to my world," Chrisa smiles, "a sort of parallel reality, little brother! Let's not waste too much time, outside the night is slowly coming and I wouldn't stay too long in this 'half dimension'... because this is the first time for you! Is everything okay? Can you see me and do you hear my voice? You can move at your leisure, also fly... but hold on to my hand, so we can be a little more secure that there won't be any interference."

"Yes, it seems to me," Joshua stammered, although he seemed a little dismayed. Then he pulled a smirk and after a deep breath he adds, "I feel very strange, as if I had taken a strong blow to the head. Even my voice echoes in my head in a strange way... But I'm ready."

Chrisa gently caresses him on the head.

"Let's make a quick move," she whispers. "Almost as if we were running, up to Clonemacnoise. The gates will be closed, but leave it to me, we can easily pass."

When Chrisa finished speaking, everything seemed to happen as fast as when lightning darts across the sky, releasing pure energy into the ether. Within seconds, at the speed of light, both siblings are thrown into *space-time* and arrive at what remains of the Monastery of the Seven Churches. Passing over the fence of the ruins, the two youngsters are inside the place they visited with Marius during the morning. The lack of light doesn't facilitate their task, and it takes a while for Chrisa to find the door to the museum where the Cross of the Scriptures lay. Once inside, the young woman looks in her bag, searching for the candle and box of matches.

"Unfortunately I cannot radiate enough light," she says, smiling, "but we need some human artefact and candles fit like a glove!"

The dim candlelight allows the two siblings to find the location of the Cross. In a split second they are in front of it.

"Let's get some light down here as well. Now you can see the inscriptions even better... you see, on this bottom section? The Celtic runes are in bas-relief, it's strange that Marius wasn't able to decipher them, even more anomalous that not even Ualtar knows what they mean!"

The cross appears to be out of a medieval vision, and in the flickering light, the bas-reliefs appear animated. Joshua squeezes his sister's hand and with his right he takes the candle before kneeling to better watch at the bottom.

Both young people can't imagine, however, that at the same time, over the English Channel in Paris, inside the cathedral of the Notre-Dame, a person had used one of the portals to penetrate into the parallel dimension. This man is Hathor Var Darquen de Aguilar, and he's desperately looking for Chrysalis.

Chapter 32

Illusions

Sergio, accompanied by Solaris and Selene, walks along the lake shore in direction of the port of Ascona. Every now and then, his *earth-frame* is connected to the *Unynetweb*, sending details about his position. Suddenly, the sound of an incoming call disturbs him and, a little unwillingly, the man responds, gasping and cursing.

"3482 listening." His tone changes immediately when he hears the voice of Commander Fenix on the line.

"Sergio, they have told me that you went down to the lake with two *jaglynx*. Can I ask you to go to house number 117 and take a few pictures? Enter them directly into the *earth-frame*; I proceeded to put the path and mark the positions from which you'll have to take the shots. This is urgent..."

Looking skyward, evidently more than just a little irritated, Sergio responds in monosyllables.

"Yea, okay, I got it. No, no problem, I'll insert the digital detection directly where you ask. I'll let you know if there is anything abnormal. Okay, bye."

Talking with the two felines, the policeman of the Experimental Team expresses his nervousness.

"Gee, after a night of interrogating a depraved mind which, if it were up to me, should be immediately locked up in a hospital, instead of finishing my shift with a quiet walk, I find myself with other irritating troubles. Everyone knows that the decaying property at number 117 has long been neglected! Damn, there are bushes everywhere and the plants have not seen the shears of a gardener for decades! That obnoxious lawyer lives over there, though fortunately he minds his own business, surrounded by his servants. What does the Commander think we may discover in the villa Var Darquen de Aguilar... maybe some mouldy corpse or some monster, popping out of a bad nightmare?"

As if responding to their master, the two *jaglynx* start growling ferociously.

"Hush... behave, be quiet. I'm just kidding, if there will be some big steak wandering around the park, you will be the first to be served!"

A nervous laugh escapes from him, which contributes nothing except to make it even more unpleasant to his already bad mood. Solaris starts to tug on the leash, causing Sergio to lose his balance, barely holding on to the lead.

"Damn me, when will I learn to keep my mouth shut? Be quiet, come on, stay calm... they won't give us a prize if we get to the villa in less than 10 minutes."

Sergio enters the data in his *earth-frame,* enabling his identification plate.

Commander Fenix, after giving the new directives, careless of his officer's reaction, returns to observe the Bartók's Family photo carefully.

"Good! If this is the villa de Aguilar, certainly they weren't there by accident..."

With a leap, he gets up and runs to the door; he throws it open with such impetus that it startles his employees in the other room.

"Bring me the digital systems analyst immediately!"

The inspectors who are still on duty watch each other warily. The secretary presses the pager and after about a minute, that seems to last an hour, turns back to the Commander.

"Valery is coming, Commander Fenix. She will be here…" She looks the displacement of the micro-chip codex on earth-frame, "in about 12 minutes, if she doesn't find any hitches."

Then she tries to smile, which turns out to be very difficult for her, and when she realised she was being observed by the others, she blushes dramatically.

"Thank you," the Commander blurts out in a shrill voice. Then he turns and regains his composure and returns to his office.

Sergio tries to calm Solaris, who is particularly agitated.

"Courage old boy, don't do that… show a little good manners and set a fine example for Selene. Look, if you get too edgy, you can cause big problems. Hush… be reassured!"

The officer passed his hand gently on the head of the large *jaglynx,* which almost reaches to his waist. The strength of those animals, genetically crossed to create a new species that could be trained to maintain public order, is impressive.

An adult can, with a bite, remove the head of a man. Even the dogs bred to be over 100 pounds and trained to kill aren't able to win against a *jaglynx*. Tame by nature, sometimes even managing to become attached to their curators, establishing some sort of relationship with them like what happens with the smaller feline, the domestic cat.

For five years, Selene and Solaris had been entrusted to the loving care of Sergio; they have learned to blindly trust their guardian and to obey him. On the other hand, the officer relies on the instinct of the two *jaglynx*. This sort of symbiosis was generated by the imprinting that occurred through his presence during the birth of the two felines. By genetic manipulation, the scientists were able to select and alter the DNA, producing specific, suitable characteristics. The *jaglynx* lacked the faculty of speech, although it is well known that the *Annwyn* can communicate with them. Sergio was more than once tickled by the idea of seeking the help of an *Annwyn* to help him communicate with his two entrusted, but this practice is strictly forbidden by the Unified Power. The penalty for transgressors is life in isolation... or even worse.

Reaching the end of the road, Sergio enters a narrow path lined with tall beeches. Approximately 500 feet further on, the Villa de Aguilar is protected by a high wall covered with evergreen shrubs. This isn't the first time that he has inspected these places: in fact, this spot has become such a tangle of vegetation that smugglers often take refuge among the plants in the hope of escaping from the law enforcement agency. They ended up abandoning the goods, mostly alcohol or tobacco, afterward to find themselves being hunted down like rabbits by *jaglynx,* who followed them up to force them to surrender.

"Well, my faithful companions, now let's take some pictures as requested by Fenix. Okay..."

Sergio makes a brief stop and fiddles with his *earth-frame* to locate the exact points of which his chief wanted the photos.

"Okay, another ten feet to the east and we have the first reference point, then along the wall down there behind that

215

thick pink and white bush, there should be a large entrance gate to the property."

Solaris split from his sister and protector, approaching the perimeter wall with his head up, sniffing the air. The big tail shakes with irregular jerks, and Sergio realizes that the animal has smelled something.

"Good boy, Solaris, well done!" He stimulates him with a sweet voice, "now quiet, don't you get away from us, let me take the pictures, and then you can show me what you've found."

*** Errores ***

The big cat growls softly, then he retraced his steps and walks over to Sergio. He squats next to Sergio's legs, then rub his head vigorously on his thigh.

"Good job, well done Solaris. You're the best: you and your sister are infallible. Now, however, stay still, otherwise I can't do those blasted pictures..."

He reaches out to stroke the *jaglynx's* head, "you know that Fenix can be a real pain in the ass when you don't immediately follow his orders. We still have several reference points to locate on the *earth-frame*... bless these tools, they are certainly a big help. Can you imagine if we had to use a topographic map, maybe with the help of a compass? This technology of the twenty-third century is a true prodigy."

Sergio blurts out a loud laugh, thinking of the great advances made by technology during the last two hundred years.

Selene and Solaris are glued to his legs, one on the right and the other on his left. They walk to the beat of their curator, stopping when Sergio stops to take pictures or to control his instrument. Suddenly, a beep announces a call from the police headquarters.

"Yeah, what is it now?" Sergio asks in a voice marked by boredom. "We're near the Villa, as requested, but I haven't finished taking pictures. We're almost up to the gate. Shall we need to disturb the owner and ask for a cup of coffee with cookies?"

The sarcastic tone of Sergio suddenly changes again when on the other end of the call isn't the operator, but rather Commander Fenix.

"I see that you have regained your usual mocking tone, Sergio. There will be no coffee with the lawyer Var Darquen de Aguilar, I was told he left for Paris about an hour ago. We checked the flight records on the *Unynetweb* and all the rest. Regarding your attitude, we'll speak about it when you return to the headquarters... or are there more qualms to add? Your working shift ends in less than one hour, but before returning to your home, I ask you to come back here. Valery, the analyst of digital systems, has arrived... there are a few things to adjust. Regarding Var Darquen de Aguilar, he should be committed on business for a couple of days; on his return we will take the time to disturb him and make a couple of visits inside the villa. How many shots do you have left? There are five photos marked on the *earth-frames*, those of the west side. Beyond the gate, following the wall, you will get the location of the tower. Try with the infrared images, insert a shot automatically every 5 seconds... no wait, Valery specifies that you must try to capture even the ground below, too..."

Then the silence... Fenix's restless voice continues with a more peremptory tone.

"There is something 'down-under'... at the bottom of the tower, Valery is sure. She examined the digital photo's data, and she's of the opinion that you must return to us a record of that specific point. We will send you the exact location of the perimeter on your *earth-frame*, Sergio, it's important that you fix the target and let it open automatically. Valery here in the headquarters will do the rest. Is that clear?"

Sergio swallows, feels a strong note of acidity in the mouth.

'Here's how to get a stomach ulcer,' Sergio thinks to himself, 'the coffee rolls over in my guts.'

Thinking of his stomach, he responds to his chief trying to keep his voice under control.

"Commander, all clear, limpid and cloudless." It was evidently difficult for Sergio to leave aside the irony, particularly when anxiety dominates all his sense of deliberateness.

"I also wanted to tell you that Solaris is behaving in a strange way... you'll have noticed it on the display by means of the microchip. He smelled something in the air, but here everything is quiet and there aren't people around. Maybe it's a wild animal... but now he's at my side, waiting for a command to inspect the area 'his way'. I'll keep Selene with me, so that the two won't scare some bird or rodent. From the mess that reigns in the garden, I could swear that millions of rats and small animals have taken refuge there. A gardener hasn't set foot here for years!"

Fenix was watching the projected image on the LCD display on the wall in front of him. The beautiful Villa De Aguilar appears in its most majestic beauty: the manicured English garden with brightly coloured rose bushes, flower beds and the lawn looks like a carpet of emerald green.

"What happened?" Fenix asked himself in a low voice. "Why has the lawyer left the villa and garden to decay? It is definitely not money that he lacks, without considering that in recent years he spends his time holed up in the villa or in his studio in the centre of Ascona. Never has a woman, only a few visits from his wealthy clients..."

Then he broods, still looking at the first data recorded by Sergio that appear at the bottom of the display.

"I think Valery has discovered something interesting. I hope that the hot-headed Sergio can carry out the orders. Lately I've noticed that he reacts more and more angrily. I'll talk with him about it in private. Well, maybe it's the stress; basically I understand it, and these things annoy me too. It was a night full of nasty surprises... all because of a couple dead bodies dug up from the lake."

"Mhhhm, excuse me, Commander," Valery's gentle and sensual voice brings him back immediately to the chaotic reality of his office.

"Sergio has arrived at the pinnacle's location. He's sending the data as requested. Look; I'll make a projection directly in the frame on the right. That's it. The image is clear, now transformed into three-dimensions... everything is recorded so that we can directly analyse the scene with the computer."

Discouraged, Fenix watches the images, on one hand the succession of the pictures and on the other the details of the frame into three-dimensional development. Had it not been for the presence of the attractive Valery, the commander would soon have fallen asleep. He isn't cut out for technology; honestly he preferred to delegate these tasks to those who have the brain prepared to understand the functioning of instrumental innovations. He uses his brain to think and find solutions!

Suddenly, he thinks about his wife, who had certainly been waiting for him at home for at least a couple of hours.

"Damn misery!" Fenix cursed suddenly, "I forgot to inform her that I would be late... she'll be annoyed by having to take out Elvira... she doesn't like to pick up the dog poop along the way!"

Chapter 33

Arcane Soul

Lord Warden finds himself with Vamaran in the hotel lobby.

"I reserved a table in the garden under the palm trees."

The old Lord winks, showing a strange smile that inflicts him with a Mephistophelean appearance.

"My friend, we shall share our last dinner..." his companion replies with a seductive and knowing look, "then next time, you will be my guest at the *Tylwyth Teg*, the y People!"

"Of course," hisses the Lord, "as in the ancient Welsh legend, Gwynn ap Nudd, *'the White Son of the Night'*, but with a dark and very sensual look, I would say, my dear Vamaran. Very dark and terribly luxurious!"

The two men start along the wide and sumptuous hall of the hotel, they went out on the porch and immediately a waiter dressed in livery accompanies them to their table.

The waiter leaves the menu on the damask tablecloth and then backs off a few steps. With an extremely obsequious voice, he turns to the eldest.

"Lord Warden, what would you like to drink? Can I get you a cocktail?"

The afternoon sun gives the plants a shiny and lush appearance; the eyes of the Lord are lost over the inflorescences of a large bush of Madagascar Jasmine, whose scent was inebriating. Vamaran is watching him in a curious yet dark way, then, as if awakened from a dream, Lord Warden replied in a faint voice.

"Bring me some green tea. Some *Mattcha*, the Maître knows my taste."

Vamaran relaxes. For a moment, he feared that his friend could become rude, knowing the peculiarities of the Lord and his sometimes violent reactions. The waiter departed, Lord Warden sighed through his teeth.

"They should know that I don't drink alcohol, that I refrain from eating meat and that I lead a life devoted to chastity." He smiles at Vamaran, asking cryptically, "do I maybe miss something?"

The *Annwyn* doesn't respond to the provocation; he takes in his hands a piece of origami paper that he had found in the attic where they were staying. Gently, he begins to fold the silk paper several times, with extreme precision and care. Lord Warden stares at him with a sly smile.

"The skill of your art is awe-inspiring, my friend. It never ceases to amaze me! There are countless peculiarities hidden under your sensual presence."

Vamaran returns the smile, and with a flick he folds a couple of corners of the Origami. A beautiful orchid flower appears in his pale fingers, as fragile and seductive as a real one, while his large ring shows a dark reflection.

"Chrysalis!"

He sighs while the features of his face appear dim, as if his was only a vision's image.

"She's in Clonemacnoise at this very moment. I have to wait for the night, Fintan *the druid* was clear... Ualtar will be surprised to see me. The Keeper of *The Sacred Door* of Othalan will be disconcerted to be in front of the man who dared to cross the threshold of Al-Hillah, *The Gate of God*."

Vamaran's milky hand tightens around the flower with a faint crackling, a few seconds later a silver flame emanates from the man's fingers, slowly consuming the bullet of shapeless silk paper.

*** Arcana Anima ***

The breeze rises from the lake, the edges of the damask tablecloth sway while a gust of air, laden with fragrance of jasmine, wrapped around the two men. It may seem superfluous to put into words Vamaran's thought: his eyes are languid and his full lips softly drawn.

"I'll burn for her; I'll leave the flesh in this tormented and distorted dimension. It has been so long, I have a strong doubt. That *Annwyn*, Hathor, I perceive that he'll try to hinder me. Lord Warden, you didn't tell me how he was tied to the young girl. Why? I sense that you have always known it; you didn't appear surprised when the lawyer warned us to leave Chrysalis alone."

"And what if I had told you?" The old Lord grins. "What would change, except to increase your desire for supremacy? I don't want to be involved in a duel between mythological giants. What is at stake isn't irrelevant, isn't the *woman*, but *the Door* that may be opened with her presence. Don't forget this, Vamaran! Make sure that your manner is as wise as wise could be; have the harsh discipline through which you had to pass: The *Tylwyth Teg*, the Fairy People await your return, Gwynn ap Nudd... don't deny the Legend."

The White Son of the Night sketches a slight smile; two small dimples on the sides of his mouth change its appearance. With a wave of his hand towards the lake, the breeze turns.

"They say that the *Marenca* blows with particular strength around here... They had to abandon the race, apparently."

The young waiter returns to their table with a tray of solid silver on which are two Chinese porcelain bowls, a cast-iron teapot and a blue pot with boiling water. A floral arrangement of Oriental lilies completes the presentation. The boy laid the flowers at the centre of the table, and then he pre-heated the lightweight transparent china cups and serves the *Mattcha* specifying: "first flush of April from Shizuoka, as you wished."

The Lord dismisses the waiter with a smile and a wave. Lord Warden takes his cup to his lips then savours the intense aroma before tasting it.

"Perfect! It's simply divine... This is the elixir of life, as simple as the plant Camellia sinensis that provides the raw material."

"What will you do?"

"The lawyer Var Darquen de Aguilar actually didn't seem very inclined to let the young *Annwyn* go," Lord Warden said, laying his cup on the table. "I first knew Hathor sixty years ago during a conference in Ishtar; I've never seen him as upset as he was last night. I think that he has concealed several things from us, starting with the volume adorned with the strange runes which he continually held tight in his hands. There is something I'm missing, Vamaran. I wouldn't have the lawyer play us some bad joke. I repeat: you know how much I hate brutality... When do you plan to reach Chrysalis in Ireland? And can you guarantee that the girl will trust you? Don't you forget that she is with her brother and that old sailor, their protector! And almost certainly there will also be the pilot; you saw them in the hangar just before they escaped. Although the intercepted information says they are somewhere in the mountains, evidently they wanted to hide their tracks. It was chance that you had the sense to see for yourself. Ahhh, blessed is the power of ubiquity, so easy to evoke in the most varied forms."

Their conversation is interrupted by the arrival of the Maître d'hôtel, who bows respectfully in front of the old man.

"Lord Warden, is the choice of tea to your liking? What would you like to be served for lunch?"

Lord Warden wipes his mouth with the linen napkin before answering.

"François, everything is perfect. I couldn't fault it… for lunch? Yes, indeed it's already noon... Time flies! Let us be prepared a mixture of vegetables, ah, I would also like a soup with smoked tofu! I have been coveting it for some time now..."

Then the Lord glances at Vamaran, as if to study the reaction of his guest, but he remains in perfect silence, his face impassive. His long fingers caress the white petals of the Oriental lilies with their inebriating and overwhelming fragrance.

"Undoubtedly, my guest will also like to share the same specialty... neither would he consume dead tissue. That would damage the physical and cerebral activities, which I already explained, if you do remember."

The Maître nods and bows again.

"As His Eminence desires, Lord Warden. Our Chef will be pleased to fulfil your every wish, as always."

The man in white livery and gloves goes away and quickly disappears behind a large earthen pot containing a huge orange plant full of juicy fruits and aromatic white flowers.

"I like this place very much: it's quiet, very few can afford this luxury, and here everyone treats me with the due respect. Have you noticed? The tables around ours have remained free, but all this respect has its price, in the end. The lease of the large attic cost me a small fortune. The only problem is that, for obvious reasons, I can't stay too long in one place, my longevity gives me problems, if you understand what I mean."

Vamaran nods before finishing the contents of his cup.

"Of course, it's not always an advantage, but not for long, very little... now I'm convinced that with the *Vibratory Matrix* will change this, too."

The *Annwyn* thinks about the druid, Fintan's words before adding, "I hope that the Celtic legend handed down the centuries doesn't reserve us some unpleasant surprises."

Chapter 34

Over the Sight

The trembling hands of the young *Annwyn* caress the bas-reliefs found on the Cross of the Scriptures. Her astral body gives off a pulsing, slightly amber light; not far, Joshua looks enchanted.

"Tell me that this is not just a dream! Sorry if I keep being sarcastic. By golly, I do feel so weird, little sister. It's always like that for you? I mean, when you walk in the dream you always manage to do all these things: fly, move at the speed of light and all these other tricks? Gosh, I have so many questions for you, these things are starting to intrigue me a lot!"

But the young woman apparently didn't listen; she's too absorbed by the idea of being a few inches from the Truth. Unfortunately she isn't familiar with the runes and she couldn't even imagine how to go about interpreting the obscure and perhaps distressing message. Chrisa runs the palm of her hands along every inch of the bottom of the ancient sculpture, dating back to 900 AD. Although it's past 1322 years, the time has not irretrievably erased the traces of an important message for the future civilization. Fortunately, some wise man had protected the Cross from the weather and neglect during the past two centuries, when ignorance and fear had driven civilization backward.

The twenty-third century has been compared to the middle Ages, and for a good reason. The Unified Power for years was buying up all the artefacts that could incite the inhabitants of planet Earth to seek for their true origins. Even if they don't burn people for witchcraft or blasphemy anymore, the Experimental Team does much worse in the hospitals, using persuasive and not strictly orthodox methods.

All these thoughts whirl in Chrisa's mind, carrying on her great uneasiness.

"Joshua, I didn't find anything relevant. My mind is closed and doesn't feel anything at all on the vibration's level... as if this 'pillar' is deliberately trying to protect its true identity. If I weren't sure that is carved into the sandstone, I may think it's a living entity..."

The young woman shifts a little away from the cross and puts back the cordon set on pedestals, and then approaches her brother.

"Come, we better go down to Shannonbridge before they're aware of our disappearance. We'll rest a bit before returning here with Marius and the two druids... maybe they will be able to figure it out. Or maybe we should have taken with us the *Vibratory Matrix*! Perhaps that object will trigger some hidden mechanism. Most likely!"

*** Super Aspectum ***

As soon as she finished the sentence, something unusual happens, and suddenly in a corner of the museum, an amber light of high intensity materializes. Chrisa is overtaken by fear and for a moment she's paralyzed. She clings to her brother and whispers: "there is someone...

227

someone like me, who knows how to use astral travel. Whatever happens, keep close to me and don't let go of my hand for any reason."

A soft voice from the darkness tries to reassure the two young people; the vision looks like a *Kirlian* photographic image, the distribution of charges on the surface, it reflects the internal movements of electricity and bio-photons of the body.

"You must not be afraid, Chrysalis. Don't escape from me, I knew your father, we were friends!"

Chrisa can't focus at that distance, and the total darkness certainly didn't help her. She feels a sense of loss in hearing what the figure said, then tightens her hand firmly in her brother's, who is, to put it mildly, just terrified.

"Sis, what the hell is happening? I see that light over there in the corner on the right. And 'that thing' has spoken... did he really know dad? I am bloody scared; please take me away from here... I want to go to Marius and the others. Please, let us go away!"

The young *Annwyn* holds him by the hand, adding extra strength.

"Wait, he can't do anything to us, as long as he stays there," she whispers.

"Who are you and what do you want from us?" Chrisa demands, turning to the presence, "if you're not a coward, shows your true structure!"

From the apparition rises only a slight hiss as the light becomes more tenuous and less amber. It's pulsing, at the same rhythm of the human heart.

"Chrysalis, please don't fear my presence, I beg you. Your brother should not be afraid... I'm just here to deliver something very important to you. You are in great danger, all of you. Inhuman people know that you are in possession

228

of the *Vibratory Matrix*. Vamaran, this is the name of the guy, he was an *Annwyn*, but in circumstances unknown to me, he has now become something else, something back from the Legends of the past, Chrysalis, recalled from the myth of the darkness of the night of *Samhain*. He'll try to force you to go beyond the Projection... he has done it before, and this time he's not willing to return alone over *The Mists*. He'll keep you segregated on the Other Side, Chrysalis. His master, Lord Warden, wants to clean up the planet in his own way... using magnetic fields and who knows what other magical practices generated by the Cross of the Scriptures enabled with the *Vibratory Matrix*."

The voice became quiet, in the air remains only a faint echo of the threat just uttered. Chrisa tries to figure out who the presence may be.

"Show us who you are. Do you think we can trust what you say while you remain concealed? And who can confirm that your intentions are honest? I can't stand to confer with someone who I cannot even see..."

"I brought something that will explain a lot of things to you... of your past. I knew your father, Chrysalis; I worked for many years at his side. There would be many things I want to share with you, many of his discoveries that may be relevant... even if the Unified Power would do anything to hinder me. And it's for this reason that many times I've been looking for you during your astral travels, but unfortunately you escaped because you fear me... You know who I'm, you have me already seen. I'm the one who brought you to find the *Vibratory Matrix*, but I didn't think that my gesture would lead to this. I never imagined that someone could interfere."

The man's voice is a whisper full of pain and sadness, and Chrisa and her brother perceive the trustful tone in his voice.

"Ha... Hathor!" Chrisa stammers, full of terror. Joshua stiffens as he clings to his sister.

"Stay away from her, you bastard! Too many times you have tried to hurt my sister." The boy is visibly trembling, his voice hoarse and full of dismay, but defiant.

"You're wrong... I wish I could convince you of my honesty. You don't have to worry, but beware of those who will be presented as friends! Chrysalis, please, for the love which you bear to your deceased parents. I won't approach you, be calm. I leave here on the floor something that you will find interesting. I'll still be your ally and if... if you need me, you may summon me. For 23 hours I can still use the portal I activated in Paris. In the book you will find many answers... Chrysalis, trust me!"

In a slightly more intense gleam, Hathor disappears as he had appeared few minutes before. Chrisa remains rigid, clinging to her brother, out of breath and with the heart pounding loudly in her chest. Joshua is the first to speak.

"Damn... sister, I think tonight I have indigestion and it is causing hallucinatory events. Enough, with me, the story is closed but..." Joshua stops babbling in a confused way. She steps back a bit from her brother, and then stares at him straight in the eye.

"*But* what? Don't you think *I should* fear this man? Joshua, did you hear what he said? He was the person who made me find the *Vibratory Matrix* on the ground, *he...* you understand? We find ourselves in this story because of him. Damn!"

A strange sense of helplessness has taken possession of her mind; however, something in his voice had opened a tiny door in her heart. Hathor had spoken of her father, he said he had worked closely with him... and he had left something there that *would provide* tangible evidence. Moving slowly, in small steps, almost dragging her petrified brother, Chrisa arrives in the corner where Hathor had appeared.

On the ground there is a dark casing engraved with something that sparkles. In the dim candle light, the hands of the young woman gather from the stone floor an old leather-bound book. The characters look like golden runes, perhaps Celtic runes.

"What the hell is this? A book... no, it's a kind of diary; there are images, hand written stuff, clippings and pictures..."

Chrisa's voice is choked and full of emotion. On the first page, a beautiful photograph of her family with Hathor, alongside her father, who's holding the hand of little Chrysalis of perhaps six years old!

Chapter 35

Step into the Abyss

The young girl covers her brother with a thick Shetland wool blanket, Joshua is all sweaty, and obviously the effort was considerable for him.

"Here we are, with no answers but with an additional burden!"

Chrisa hopes that her brilliant idea doesn't have consequences for her brother. In her heart, she acknowledges being selfish in wanting to satisfy the desire to take him in a dreamlike journey. Outside its already late at night and the house is plunged into darkness; in the faint moonlight, the *Annwyn* thinks of Hathor's words and shudders.

Then she leads groping back to her bed, she hasn't the slightest desire to analyse the contents of the large book which Hathor had left her. Not now. She'll have to explain everything to Marius and Sibéal: considering how the circumstances have evolved, she can't just hide her reckless act.

A couple of hours later, she wakes up hearing whispers in the hallway. Cautiously approaching the room's door, she squints to take a peek outside. Standing, smiling and with a restored appearance, Marius looks at her, amused.

"What a face, girl! I thought a little sleep would do wonders for you too... instead look at you! You look like something out of a medieval witch-hunting book!" He chuckles. Smoothing his hair with his left hand, he continues, "my cousin is waiting for us with tea and biscuits, Martino went back down to the pub because he had promised Riordan he would, a kind of half-lie that he told him this morning to deflect any indiscreet questions or raise doubts. Certainly he will not be with us in Clonemacnoise, be sure. In a little time, Ualtar will arrive with another druid confrere. Are you two ready?"

*** In Voraginem Itinerarium ***

Chrisa noticeably blushes while trying to bring a little order to her hair, tying it back with a big clip. Then she mutters a few meaningless words before resuming her usual attitude.

"I, well... the two of us, maybe... damn... you're right, I feel like a monster among monsters. Oh Heavens, Marius there are problems! Big trouble in sight, wait, I wake up Joshua and then we'll tell you what happened."

Marius stiffens, his face suddenly becomes serious and a dark shadow covers his gaze, which was fixed on the girl's eyes.

"Don't say a word... Chrysalis, tell me that what I think didn't happen... you're a wretch! This is Ireland, the Holy Land, where there're invisible entities among us... you can't just use *the dream* to go around snooping and poking your pretty little nose left and right!"

'Good,' Chrisa thinks to herself, 'the pie is done, without having to explain everything word for word, and evidently Marius has the same powers of reading minds as Sibéal.'

Chrisa sighs and returns to the room to wake up her brother.

'Great,' Chrisa continues to think to herself, 'and to think that all these years he has always pretended everything was normal... and I've never been able to perceive anything that could make me uncover that he was endowed with extra sensory powers!'

A nice fire is crackling merrily in the living room; Marius' cousin has already served tea on the coffee table, accompanied with fragrant, freshly baked cookies. The old sailor is cautious and his mood is constantly darkened. Chrisa, followed by Joshua, now looks to the ground. Chrisa was clenching Hathor's large book in her hands. She put it on the low table in front of Marius.

"I did a foolish thing, I admit it... this was a terrible mistake; but maybe not entirely to our disadvantage, even if things could get ugly. Sorry Marius, you're absolutely right, these places are overflowing with anomalous energy, strange things are moving out there... entities which I perceive as disembodied presences that you can't explore or approach. But I would like you to have a look at this book and then I'll explain in detail what happened."

Apparently intrigued but always frowning, Marius takes the volume and puts it on his knees. Chrisa glances at Sibéal before suggesting:

"You look, too, please; there are several diagrams that I've never seen before. Drawings, photographs and records... it would seem to be a diary. I noticed that some references seem to be written in Gaelic... and there are also several inscriptions in runes!"

Intrigued, Sibéal sits next to Marius and with him she looks carefully, page by page. Then, as if stung by an insect, she gasps.

"Who gave you this book, Chrisa? This person is aware of the secrets that I thought were the prerogative of the *Tylwyth Teg*, the Fairy People of our Legend. Fortunately, these stories are considered Celtic mythology, and then deleted from the records by the Unified Power..."

Sibéal's face is ashy; she looks at the young who now is trembling with fear.

"It was Hathor. He gave it to us... The *Annwyn* whom has been chasing me for years in my *dream journeys*... why would he give me this manuscript? And what is this story of the Fairy People, Sibéal? What else is hidden from us? Who are you in reality? Look at the photograph on the front page, my family is portrayed! Hathor was a friend of dad and mom..."

The woman gets up; her figure now appears impressive within the silver dress attached at her waist, as always, with the strange belt from which she never separates.

"And where would he generously hand it over to you? If he were here, I would certainly have prevented his presence from coming into my home. This must not be given to those who transgress the secret that conceals the Legend... Marius and I belong to *Tylwyth Teg*, Chrysalis!"

Shocked by the revelation, Chrisa tries to explain succinctly their bravery of a few hours before, without neglecting any detail.

"In the end there was nothing to fear, I left the *Vibratory Matrix* here with you and I didn't think to encounter anything unpleasant. But if Hathor told us the truth, someone is looking for us... Hathor called this person Vamaran, he'll wait until we activate the *Cross of the Scriptures* and then... Hathor said that he would have forced me to follow him across the Projection and then held me captive!"

Chrisa starts to cry, gripped with fear that she is no longer able to manage.

"My little one," whispers Sibéal, "the Legend of which I speak is very old. It was passed down orally for centuries and fixed on some secret documents that are still kept in a sacred place, accessible only to the druid priests."

Then she sits down again by the fire.

"While we wait for the arrival of our friends, I will tell you the Legend..."

Chapter 36

The Legend of Gwynn

Sibéal begins to explain that in Welsh mythology, Gwynn ap Nudd, the White Son of the Night, is the king of the *Tylwyth Teg*. He rides in the darkness of the night of *Samhain* and his dwelling was Glastonbury Tor, identified with the sacred island of Avalon. Gwynn ap Nudd was described as a great warrior with his face blackened at the head of the *Wild Hunt*, capturing the souls of the dead to lead them into the *Annwn*, the realm of the dead, of which he was once king.

The woman fixes Chrisa with great intensity.

"From this definition the name given to you *Annwyn* was first coined... for they had made the association with the world of the Spirits, because of your extraordinary powers. The studies carried out by scientists had determined your longevity and the power to leave your bodies at will. The Legend tells us that in the wake of Gwynn ap Nudd, there was the *Cwm Annwn*, also called the *Hell's Hounds*. These presences had a white body and red ears, colours sacred to the Celts, indicating membership to the Otherworld, the realm of the Divine. Even the name of Gwynn, which means *white*, reveals his sacred and even lunar nature. He was definitely a God who shone in the darkness of the night of *Samhain*, to remember that even in the darkest period of the year there is a light to hold: a promise of rebirth. Gwynn ap Nudd has been a God connection, or rather a means which allows us to reach the Underworld. But Gwynn ap Nudd is also a God of incomparable supernatural force. In the Welsh myth, it's said that God gave him the strength of the *demons of Annwn* to make him invincible. In these ancient texts are also legends of King Arthur and the intrinsic connection which saw him befriended with the king of the Underworld. The figure of Gwynn ap Nudd was particularly powerful and fascinating. He possessed an impressive force, belonging both to the Underworld and to the Divine, perhaps because in the Celtic view, there isn't a clear separation between these two realms. In the White Son of the Night are two aspects of the Divine: the most frightening, symbolized by the physical aspect, from its nature of union between the world of the living and the dead as well as by his fury in battle, and the luminous meaning of his name, White Son of the Night. In fact, we find Gwynn ap Nudd present in both the major holidays of the Celtic tradition: *Samhain* and *Beltane*, which in the Cycle of the Year are located exactly at the opposite ends of the year, facing one another. However, Gwynn is a deity typically associated with the *Samhain's winter* and the torpor of death at that time of year when everything falls asleep and descends into the depths of the womb of the Mother. He's the one who, during the *Descent*, takes us into the deepest regions of our unconscious and ourselves, where frightening, hungry demons await us. He doesn't do it in a delicate or gentle manner, but he grabs us with violence by putting our deepest in front of us and forcing us to deal with them directly, without giving us the possibility of a second's thought or hesitation. However, his strength can become our own, helping in this way to overcome the fears that beset us and block us. Thus abandoning us to his grip and allowing him to carry us within ourselves with the right mindfulness, we can come out victorious; the winner is at the end Gwynn ap Nudd, a symbol of the balance between Light and Shadow that always follow each other but never overpowering the other, in eternal and cyclic harmony."

*** De Gwynn Fabula ***

Sibéal sighs, shaking her head slightly, her long hair, now loose on her shoulders, swaying and casting silver reflections. Both young siblings listened very carefully to the story, and Chrisa finds herself with a flurry of questions that suddenly overwhelm her mind. But there is something more that grows in her guts: the young woman is convinced that in Hathor's book, the intrinsic reasons for everything that is happening right now must necessarily be explained. The young girl hardly breathes.

"Do you think that what Hathor told us is the truth, Sibéal? But what is the connection between this book and the Legend?"

Chapter 37

Dark Visions

In the Experimental Team's offices in the small town on the shores of Lake Maggiore, chaos reigns. Commander Fenix is blaming several of his subordinates, perhaps venting his feelings of helplessness that gripped his bowels.

A couple of hours have passed quickly and Valery has worked hard, but the result? In the early afternoon, a call from the West Division ordered the Commander Fenix to abandon any kind of analysis and research on the lawyer Hathor Var Darquen de Aguilar; to confirm this imposition, all data relating to Var Darquen de Aguilar on the *Unynetweb* was now obscured.

"What's going on, Commander? We have serious problems with the connections to the central computer system," Valery's voice is agitated with a strong hint of frustration. "I contacted the Division, there is something wrong..."

But at the same time, a confidential call from the top clarifies to the commander the situation. Stunned, Fenix lets himself fall into his swivel chair, looking out the window, while letting out a string of unedifying epithets certainly inappropriate to his role as Chief of the Experimental Team.

His subordinates disappear in a stampede; only Valery remained, particularly displeased, sitting at a desk with her head between her hands. After turning off her terminal, the woman gets up and heads to Fenix's office.

"Can I do anything for you, Commander?"

The silence is eerie, the images of the remains of the two bodies found in the lake are always projected, witnesses on the wall as a warning to the viewer.

"Holy shit! And according to *those at the Summits* I should let it go? Look at that... those two poor bastards have been killed in a brutal way and the Unified Power demand me to give it up? The hell... holy shit, what lies beneath? What the hell are they trying to hide?"

*** Obscura Simulacra ***

Valery holds her breath for a moment, and then replied, trying to keep the tone of her voice as low as possible.

"Fenix look, I don't know what is happening, I think I understand that the video-call you had a little while ago is the reason for your discontent and opposition. If there are orders from above, I think it's wise to follow them without opposition... it's just a personal advice, believe me. This isn't the first time something like this has happened to me in the middle of an investigation. If I still can do something for you…"

Fenix raises his eyes to meet the penitent gaze of the woman, and then he turns off the LCD monitor on the wall.

"No, thank you, unless you want to walk Elvira, my wife's dog! I think I'm going home. I need some rest before I go over the edge."

The analyst smiles, thinking of the commander walking a dog, then again she becomes serious; she picks up her jacket and bag, and then she answers, "I don't like dogs, Fenix. I prefer cats, which are free souls."

She goes out of the office, leaving a slight hint of perfume in her wake. At the dispatch on the ground floor, she leaves her data for its registration and starts toward the exit.

After a quarter of an hour, also Commander Fenix leaves the Experimental Team's office. On his face, signs of the previous sleepless night and adversity caused by the day's events were visible. None of his employees spoke to him; all feel a sort of compassion for the poor wife who will have to bear with him for the rest of the day.

On the way back to his home, the commander chooses to take the path that follows the lake's shore. Arriving at the harbour, he sees the Avalon's Mist and the catamaran moored. He's grasped by a sense of anger, and then he notices that Alessandro is fumbling with the ropes:

"Hey kid, can I talk to you?"

His voice is peremptory, the young man, seeing the commander's uniform, approached immediately, thinking about the worst case scenario.

"Everything is all right, Commander?"

His tone of voice reveals a strain: he's not yet fully recovered from the events that occurred the day before.

"I would say that depends," Fenix responds with a grin, "on my way of seeing things!"

His gaze is fixed on Alessandro's eyes, causing Alessandro to blush up to the tips of his ears. Then the commander insisted:

"You know, I think you and I will take a stroll... like saying... as ordinary citizens. I was removed from the case of the murder of the two men. And that bothers me a lot, Alessandro... that's your real name, isn't it?"

"Well... yeah, Alessandro is my name, but my friends call me Al. I have nothing to add to what has already been reported during my interrogation by your agents, Commander. I didn't see anything strange, I'm always on the alert, believe me. The vessel owners pay me for this. But I still couldn't be of any help, unfortunately."

Fenix continues to stare, as if to pass him with the x-rays to find something the young man could hide.

"Fine boats! Especially that one, the Avalon's Mist... must be a fast sailboat. Too bad the race was cancelled because of the storm which should occur... it would surely have a good chance of winning. Don't you think, Al?"

Alessandro looks around, and then lowers his eyes, staring at the tips of his shoes; however he remains silent, not knowing what to say.

"Well? Don't you think that Joshua could have won the race, Al?"

The boy looks very embarrassed and, in spite of everything he feels, promptly replies. "Of course he may, the Avalon's Mist is the fastest boat on Lake Verbano, Commander!"

Fenix keeps talking, using a more friendly tone, almost whispering the words slowly and distinctly.

"I think the two youngsters and the old Irish man are in a big mess, Al. I have reason to believe they're in grave danger. As I said initially, I was removed from the investigation, and that means very big trouble directly with the leaders of the Unified Power. If you have some way of contacting them, try to tell them, you're their friend... as far as I know they spread a rumour to make us believe they're in the mountains. But I didn't drink that story, I'm not naïve, and I think if Chrysalis is somehow mixed-up in this, there is some *Annwyn* devilry. Now, do you want to take a walk with me?"

Alessandro throws a gaze around as if trying to find an excuse, then he shrugs and replies, "I would agree to a walk, but I can't leave the dock unattended, sir. I don't want to abandon my obligations, I'm sure you understand, Commander. I don't want to seem rude, but believe me, I have duties that I take very seriously!"

He tries to smile, but fear of the Experimental Team officer turns it to a grimace.

Fenix smiles back, then he pull out a magnet business card and wrote his private cell phone number on the back.

"If you remember something else, or if you happen to hear from the three '*fugitives*', tell them that I've been looking for them, you know... privately. This time it's the citizen Fenix that speaks to you... I wouldn't want anything bad to happen to those three. The story of the two guys that made you empty your bowels is enough. Good work, Alessandro. I'll see you one of these days!"

The Commander strode away, while the young man continued to watch him until he disappeared down the lane. Dismayed, Alessandro was initially tempted to pick up the phone and call Joshua on the unregistered number. But he's caught by a glimmer of wisdom, he realises that's exactly what Fenix wants him to do.

The Commander found himself, not just randomly, near the villa Var Darquen de Aguilar. Sure he is being watched by someone, he pulls right whispering to himself.

"Gee, I'd give a month's salary to find out what is behind this story. The fact that it can't go deeper annoys me and makes me even more in a bad mood. But Valery is right, better to let the waters calm down, in a few days I'll do some investigating. For now, let's get ready to deal with my pissed off wife, considering my tardiness... and at the annoying Elvira barking at me, demanding her walk. Poor animal, I don't envy her, since she has to endure my wife all day."

Chapter 38

Past That Resurfaces

Vamaran comes out of the bathroom, leaving behind him a scent of amber, somewhat oriental and troubling. He received his clothes, ironed to perfection by the woman in the hotel's laundry. Particular attention has been paid to the starching of the beige lace tunic, while the velvet damask brown suit was resting on the large bed. A light coat of soft camel hair a couple of shades lighter completed his attire. In the background, the *Annwyn* is listening to Orff's Carmina Burana, which gives to the scene a moulded atmosphere of mystery and seduction.

Pleased, Vamaran looks at his reflection in the wardrobe's mirror: his naked body is perfect in the ambiguity of his provocative beauty. He feels a deep sense of omnipotence, but for him, virility isn't important but rather his keen intellect, quite above the average.

'Now I'm just missing the more valuable particular: my better half... the complement that will allow me to return to be the King of the *Tylwyth Teg*. In fact Chrysalis is worthy of being *my* wife, in spite of that hybridist and despicable Hathor...'

A faint knock on the door distracts Vamaran from the contemplation of his own reflection. He turns down the music's volume, and putting on a silk robe, he goes to the apartment's door.

"Please, come in Lord Warden. I'm almost ready!"

The door opens and the old man enters, smiling smugly.

"I appreciate your taste, Vamaran, my friend. How could she refuse to follow you, our little Chrysalis? She will be captivated by your presence... she will melt in your embrace, about this I'm willing to bet."

The *Annwyn* looks grimly at the old Lord, and then he begins to dress, indifferent to the Lord's eyes that seemingly pierce his flesh in a way not chaste at all. The elder read his thought.

"Ahh, is that what you believe of me? Maybe I'd be tempted to abandon my good intentions, because of the fascination of what my eyes are seeing, but I'm not a person to be seduced so easily. If I wanted to, believe me, you wouldn't in any way been able to stop me, but I'm above the impulses of the flesh."

After turning his back to look out the immense windows overlooking the park below the hotel, Lord Warden continues, "you better hurry up, there are more than 900 miles between Lugano and Clonemacnoise. Considering that you want to go there, you know, physically... ah ah ah."

The evil laugh echoes through the room, accompanied by Orff's music that makes it sound cruel and terrible. Vamaran smiles, while wrapping a silk scarf carefully around his neck. Then he puts on the brown suede boots, pulls the jacket over his shoulders and takes the mantle on his forearm.

"I have already asked the driver to load the carry-on luggage onto the taxi, Lord Warden; I'd rather drive to

Lugano's airport alone. I need a little time to meditate on my... uhm, about our plan. I'll contact you as soon as I'm in Ireland. If everything goes as I hope, I'll have Chrysalis in my arms before midnight!"

Vamaran held the old Lord's gaze for a long time, as if trying to find something that the old friend had concealed. Then his face lights up with an angelic smile that has in fact changed his dark and frightening look.

"It is one stormy night, here and as well in Ireland. The strong winds of the Atlantic are sweeping across the continent with extreme virulence. I hope that this doesn't hinder my flight..."

Then when leaving the room, followed by the Lord, he adds, "a perfect time for a *prima nocte*… with a Virgin!"

Throughout the flight Vamaran looks eagerly at the photos of the young *Annwyn*, downloaded from the anthropomorphic tabs taken illegally out of the Unified Power's files.

*** Restituta Memoria ***

In the depths of his being, he's convinced that he's entitled to act this way. After all, wasn't it for this purpose that 120 years ago Lord Warden had evoked him through the Celtic magic ritual associated with *Samhain*? Gwynn ap Nudd doesn't have to remain segregated to ride into the realm of the dead, between the souls of his *Annwn*. It's not what you would expect from him, in fact, the Order of Othalan knows about his existence. When he met Fintan a century earlier, he had learned that the time would soon be ripe. The destruction wrought by humans on the planet, had only stressed the importance of worshiping ISA and LAGUZ, until they could supervene the same emanation for both runes. *Isa*, the female deity: lunar event like that one of Gwynn ap Nudd, while *Laguz* was none other than the initiation of the magical medium. And he, Vamaran, has become the strongest of them all... a *sorcerer* without equal, which no human would dare hinder. Passing through the gate of *Al-Hillah*, the ancient Sumerian Gate of God, he recognised the *codes* enclosed wisely in the *Pandora* as in the Legend that was revealed to men who wanted to hear! It was necessary, however, to exit the Projection to reach the Sacred Mirror, breaking it and then achieving what was described as Eden, the everlasting Paradise, with no need to return to the physical dimension by reincarnating into a new body.

But to activate the *Vibratory Matrix* and finally exit the Projection, he needed the presence of his other half, the female part of his being, the *yin*, the Light, his opposite. He needs to mate with Chrysalis, the new incarnation of the enactment of Isa and Laguz! After all, the fate of Humanity and the planet matters little to him, he doesn't care if the civilizations will raise their vibrations or not... For Vamaran, the land could be permanently destroyed once and for all. Of course, Lord Warden's idea was excellent: a civilization without aberration, a few chosen survivors who could control not only this dimension, but every other dimension.

He finds himself caressing the image on the photo; at this time he feels so much sweetness for the woman who would restore his true freedom. Is perhaps this love, which blinds men with its power? How pleasant it is to use the imagination... paint those moments of total abandonment, which would bind the woman to him. Certainly, the purposes of Lord Warden couldn't interest him less; the ideas of confining all the humans which he thinks don't deserve to live, to the other side of the mirror. If this will really happen, certainly another catastrophe will come true, much more serious than the one that occurred in 2022.

A strong jolt of the airplane brings the *Annwyn* back to the present, while the hoarse voice of the captain comes from the speakers.

"Ladies and Gentlemen, we are going through an area with strong turbulence. Please remain seated with your seat belt fastened. We'll try to rise higher above sea level; this should lead us out of the storm."

Vamaran puts away the photos, together with the map scrolls, inside his leather bag. Then, with both hands, loosens the knot of his scarf that wraps around his neck. He began to feel a warm numbness which is deceiving his bowels; he knows that feeling well, and he absolutely must not give in to its impulse. He can't be caught by the *astral travel*; this is certainly not the right time, nor the most appropriate place. He needs only to relax and enjoy a short rest; a night full of tension is waiting him, and certainly he should have required all his energies.

Chapter 39

Footprints from Ancient Times

Dark shadow hovers near Riordan's Inn, and the smell of burning wood is strong, carried by the wind that now blows from the west with extreme virulence. In the distance, you can see the glow of the first thunderbolts and the roar of thunder makes the skin crawl. A couple of cats roam along the side of the cold and soggy road, certainly looking for something to put in their empty bellies.

Martino pulls up the collar of his jacket, hurrying along the street, staying close against the massive walls of the neighbourhood's old houses.

"Gee, in a little while this place will turn into a swamp. I have the vague feeling that the other heroes of the gang will find themselves soaked before they even get to the ruins of Clonmacnoise!" The words, whispered through his teeth, emphasised his concern. "Maybe I shouldn't let them go alone! Well, not that I can change the meteorology. Gosh, they're in good hands with Marius, come on old Red Baron, don't give up your sense of positivity."

With a strong push, the pilot enters the Pub, pressing the solid wooden door inwards. His friend, Riordan welcomes him with a big smile, but Martino loses the desire to laugh when he realises that the strange guy with reddish hair and beard he met in the morning was still sitting at the counter.

"Hmm, my friend, it's time for wolves out there. In a little while the mayhem will strike down on Shannonbridge and on all Ireland with great intensity!"

Riordan looks at his friend sitting at a table not too far from the door, but near the big fire where stumps of pine burn, giving off a pleasant smell of resin.

"Come here and sit with me," Martino whispers to the Innkeeper, rubbing his hands. He mentions the shady looking man and says, "I have a few things to discuss, away from prying ears…"

Riordan nods, then turns behind the counter and goes into the kitchen. After a couple of minutes, he comes out, followed by an employee.

"I'll leave William to serve the customers, I told him to bring us two pints of *stout*, and I hope that's okay with you."

The voice of the Irish man is happy again; maybe the possibility of making some extra money with the sale of smuggled whiskey had put him in a good mood.

Martino begins by commending the goodness of the ambrosia he enjoyed in the morning, and then he lies boldly, reporting that his customers on the continent wanted to buy two dozen bottles.

"Of course, it's a big risk for me, Riordan. See for example the guy sitting there at the counter, the same I saw this morning, I wouldn't want someone like him getting me into trouble. You know what I mean…"

Riordan slowly turns a little to get a nice peek in direction of the big guy.

"Quiet Máirtín, that's Fintan, also called White Fire, he belongs to a strange Brotherhood guarding an eccentric *'I-don't-know-what.'* He just looks like a brute, but when he gulps down a bottle of whiskey, he becomes like a lamb and he wouldn't hurt a fly."

*** Veteris Temporis Vestigia ***

Martino doesn't trust his friend's words; a strange feeling in the pit of his stomach makes him uncomfortable. He thinks of Marius and the young people who are perhaps already on their way to Clonemacnoise.

Well, if he's here, at least he can't be a threat to them, Martino thinks to himself, you old fool, now relax.

Mentally repeating the phrase a couple of times, Martino ends up forgetting about it. He's happy to accept the food that his friend gives him; the fish in sour sauce cooked by Sibéal was delicious, but Riordan's lamb stew is far tastier. Whilst he was finishing eating, the door suddenly opens and a person enters who was completely misplaced in that place of old Irish drunkards in the mood to tell stories and legends of the past. With him, a gust of wind also carries inside the pub several leaves and water as a flash of lightning sends down a stony silence inside the Inn.

The man is smartly dressed and has an aristocratic look, and approaches Fintan, though with evident reluctance, he sits next to him on the high stool. Riordan immediately notices the intrigued and apprehensive gaze of Martino

"And that guy? Where does he come from?" Riordan whispers, "It seems to me a poor time to go to a date, did he come into the wrong place?" His voice lowers as he adds, "I already said that Ireland has become a meeting place for strange characters, who is that one? I never had seen him before today. Yet it seems that he's familiar with Fintan;

who knows, maybe they are conspiring to smuggle whiskey. Máirtín, maybe you have a rival!"

Martino pretend not to notice; he continues to eat, chatting with his Irish friend, but occasionally he peeks in the direction of the two strange men sitting at the bar who, after about twenty minutes, quietly leave.

Martino can't imagine, even in the most remote part of his mind, that these men are both linked to the fate of Marius and the boys. As if Destiny's archer, who likes to affect human lives, has placed the arrow in his bow and shot it in their direction. But now the new Red Baron's impulse is to follow them, heedless of the danger. Perhaps if Martino had heard the legend told by Sibéal and knew of Chrisa's transgression and her meeting with Hathor, he wouldn't have dared so much. But maybe the pilot is involuntarily an intrinsic part in the affair, and one can never know what Fate has in store for each of us.

Martino takes his leave of Riordan, paying in advance for the two cases of whiskey that he would collect the next day, before returning to the mainland. Riordan doesn't protest; something inside tells him that his friend knows his own Fate, and if he wants to stalk those two, surely it's for an important reason.

"Be careful, Máirtín, Fintan, deep down, never inspired much confidence in me, in reality. According to me, there is something really big at stake: I've always seen him either alone or in the company of other guys who dress like him. There are rumours they could be *Druids*, tough guys... you know about our old Legends, right? Believe me, my friend, there are several strange things, even plants that come to life and talk to you during the solstices or equinoxes."

Martino wrinkles his nose and stared his friend.

"Hey, look, brrr... don't you start with that stuff, too. Please, I ask you... please!"

The pilot slaps Riordan's shoulder, then starts quickly toward the door.

Outside it had begun to rain: it's really a spooky time. Martino, pulling up the collar of his jacket, looks to the right and then to the left, catching a glimpse of the two dark shadows as they turn the corner down the street.

"Well, you old fool! Now what? You turn out to be a detective, full of courage? I hope that some of the past's old Gods can give me a sleight of hand so I don't end up in some big trouble."

The phrase is whispered through his teeth, lightning brightens up the darkness and a few seconds later a loud roar makes his skin crawl.

Chapter 40

Secular Yew

In Sibéal's big house, Marius measures the perimeter of the room with small steps; he tries to stay calm, but anxiety is painted on his face: deep wrinkles mark grooves on the sides of his mouth, while others, smaller, are like a spider webs around the eyes. The sound of the wind brings squeaks mixed with the rumble of thunder:

"But why has Ualtar been so long delayed? He should have been here quite a long time ago. Maybe he changed his mind because of the heavy rain, but he could have contacted us..."

His cousin smiles, reaches Marius and puts her arm around his waist.

"I really think that this storm has changed the *Guardian of the Holy Door's* mind, or something serious happened!"

Chrisa moves away from the roaring fireplace. Her face appears darkened, and stubbornly she looked out of the window at the landscape illuminated intermittently by the lightning. The storm is long gone, but there is something in the air, a strange feeling and the young understood the interaction of dark and mysterious forces. At times, the memory returns her the ancestral visions of the past and of her previous lives. Had she already been in these places before? Like the ivy that wraps around the trunk of the trees in the undergrowth, a feeling of sadness and pain hurt her heart. She feels like a dry leaf when, in late autumn, the wind admonishes it to fulfil its last trip. Suddenly, the music and the chants that accompanied pagan rites resurface in Chrisa's mind. She sees again the crowns of gorse and bracken in which the women wove wild flowers gathered in the vast emerald green meadows. She see again the great fires of *Beltane* and *Samhain*, where the flocks and the people crossed the flames to purify themselves; at that very moment Chrisa perceives the intensity of the heat on her skin, while breathing the acrid smell of smoke. As in the throes of trance, the girl hears the call, instinctively, in the intimate voice of the wind and the passing of shining memories. At first she tries to resist, pushing away the perceptions with anger, but then, overcome by curiosity inherent in her being, she accepted the invitation.

"I know it sounds a stupid idea, but I want to take a walk down to the Great Yew. The storm is almost gone over to the east, and if Ualtar and his buddy don't show up, they might as well put it off till tomorrow... it's already very late."

Saying this, Chrisa looks at the clock that marks 11:00 PM; Sibéal glances in Marius' direction, but she remains silent.

"Well, little sister, I think I'm going to brush my teeth and then go under the blankets. I have already crossed all my limits today. Honestly, it's not that I'm going to cry if the second episode of this adventure is postponed until tomorrow... even if it means staying for at least another 24 hours here in Ireland. The place is nice, really," he says winking in the direction of the Irish woman, "and tomorrow we can take a walk around here. Until then, you please try to stay out of trouble, okay?"

Chrisa reaches him as he approaches the door which leads to the hallway to give him a hug and a kiss on the forehead.

"I promise you, I'm just taking a walk down to the Great Yew and then I'll be going to sleep too."

Marius avoids contradicting her, there isn't reason to fear and by then the thunderstorm is almost over.

The giant tree looks like a big blur in the darkness, broken occasionally by the lightning. In truth, Chrisa had already noticed the tree when they arrived in the early afternoon. Sibéal had revealed that the yew had been planted by the Druid priests at *Samhain's* feast some 3,500 years ago. Undoubtedly it would have been a really special, magical event of power and beauty; Chrisa still thinks of the legend of Gwynn ap Nudd, while from behind thick, dark clouds the moonlight suddenly appears. The atmosphere is enchanting, and the young woman finds herself disturbingly attracted to the secular presence.

*** Taxus Saecularis ***

Chrisa finds herself alone, wrapped in a large shawl lent to her by Sibéal, in the presence of the immense yew, which suddenly seems to embrace her with its gnarled arms. Almost as if by magic, the girl hears again the strange melody gliding in the air and filling her head with a haunting sweetness. Her breathing becomes faint while she caresses the hard and rough bark of the immense, secular tree. A breath of wind ruffles her hair, obscuring the eyes for a few seconds, and the young woman sweeps back the rebel lock with her left hand. Unexpectedly, Chrisa puts her hand on something soft and warm, something alive, because her hand a second later is, albeit gently, imprisoned and detained. The presence speaks to her, and Chrisa recognizes the French language.

"Ma chère, ça fait longtemps, désormais le temps a passé si vite!"

Chrisa feels a profound shock to hear that phrase, fearful of not being able to remove her hand, thinks at the possible presence of a faun. Then repented, she smiles to herself.

"Who or what the hell are you? I don't think this wonderful tree has hands that can hold mine, and I don't think it can speak French!"

Then Chrisa perceives the very pleasant scent of the mysterious presence, she seems to recognize this oriental scent with a background of amber. Strangely, she isn't afraid: she's in an unknown place in the company of something she can't see, but her senses are calm.

'Maybe it's the yew,' she thinks, 'I feel it so powerful... it was it who called me... and never would allow someone to inflict pain in its presence.'

The thoughts of the young are swirling fast in her mind.

"Chrysalis, it isn't the *Bhile*, this sacred tree, who is holding you. Your fate binds you to me; you feel it inside of you, because you have always known! And perhaps the *dryad* of the yew recognizes you... my Princess!"

Suddenly Chrisa finds herself between arms that firmly hold her, her head sank into the soft tissue while her mouth feels the fineness of silk. She's breathing heavily, without resisting, the male's voice continues to whisper in her hair in French. Moments later the embrace descends down from her shoulders, it melts, and his hands stroked down her spine. Chrisa finds herself experiencing sensations she had never felt before, inwardly feeling a strong emotion, a strange desire. She wants to say something, but her voice doesn't come out, instead only a faint gasp comes from her mouth... while a shiver of pleasure left her without air. The

259

man's hands move back to her head, and began to caress her hair, then her cheeks. These are light touches of incomparable sweetness, caresses which are vaguely reminiscent of those of her parents.

"Chrysalis, I've been waiting for so long. Devoutly I have spent years, centuries, waiting for your return. I knew I'd find you, I just had to wait until your soul would discover the way... You're beautiful, my Princess, I didn't dare to imagine your splendour."

His hands wrap around the face of the young woman, and the man leans down, bringing his soft lips to her forehead, then slipping down over her eyes to finally unfolding in a sensual kiss on her mouth.

Suddenly Chrisa realizes that the presence has full power, while her mind begins to unfold to him. She can't reject or detach, she feels completely at his mercy and abducted while she reciprocates the kiss with the same passion. When stronger gusts of wind collect her, she comes off and tries to look to see who he is. In her eyes is the vision of a man of exceptional beauty, the pale complexion highlights the darkness of the long hair, hanging down to his shoulders, and with eyes that shine with a mysterious light. Chrisa is fascinated and smiles in response to a new caress.

"Who are you? Are you a male *dryad* who lives in the old yew? And even if you are, I didn't know that *dryads* dressed with lace and silk fabrics so soft and fine..."

The man doesn't answer right away, he reaches for her a new kiss, while his lips redraw the contours of her face and then he moves down the neck to sink his head into Chrisa's shoulder. Chrisa laugh with fun, with crystalline notes.

"I feel so strange in your sight, you can read my mind, so then you're an *Annwyn*... You said you were waiting me for ages, but I don't remember you in my previous lives. My ancestral memory would know!"

Chrisa pulls a strong breath, filling her lungs with fresh air.

"I'm not in a *dream journey*, I think; we're both here with our material bodies..."

"Yes, Chrysalis. I can touch and feel you... and I can tell you're divine! Even your kiss and the way in which you hold me... confirm that you are *my other half*. You're the part that I have long awaited... My name doesn't tell you much, perhaps, unless you know the Legend of *Samhain*: I'm the White Son of the Night."

The phrase captures the young woman by surprise. Stammering, she answers, "Gwynn ap Nudd? The king of the *Annwn*... But, but I thought..."

The man smiles gently, taking both hands of the young girl.

"My beloved one, sometimes Legends allow us to remember what would otherwise get lost with the passing of the centuries. My love, you're the queen of the *Annwn*, your rebirth in a mortal body has been willed by the Gods, who wished you could reach the highest aim of every *Annwyn*, to help human evolution. If you've repeatedly returned to a mortal body, it is because you have not broken the *Sacred Mirror* to exit from the cycle of life and rebirth, Chrysalis. If you're ready, if you want to finally get out of the Projection... you can do it with me. I'll bring you into our world, where you can finally reign as the legitimate sovereign. It's the immortal life, I'm offering you."

Chrisa is stunned: she finds herself in Ireland, in the arms of a fascinating and disturbing unknown who claims to be nothing less than the God of the Otherworld, and, for the Celts, the ruler of the kingdom of the Divine. Kidnapped by his scent and touch, the young *Annwyn* begins to feel truly attracted to him; she hadn't known someone who could bring out these feelings, that she considered absurd, before. At twenty three years old, Chrisa hadn't known love!

"I'm afraid. I admit that I'm not prepared for all this, Gwynn ap Nudd... that is your Celtic name, isn't it?"

The man is still holding her, and passes his right hand through Chrisa's hair.

"Oui, Chrysalis, que est mon nom. Mais tu ne dois pas avoir peur, you don't have to fear me. Come, let me bring you to the most appropriate place, where we can be together..."

The young girl for a moment forgets the reason why she's in that place; she forgets Joshua, Marius, and the *Vibratory Matrix*. Everything becomes irrelevant: she feels protected by those strong arms, and the man's kisses are full of passion and so sweet. Then, suddenly she remembers her parents, the pain, the regret and fear. Something inside her snaps as a spring subjected to pressure.

"I can't follow you! I'm not alone here and... I don't find any sense in what's happening to us. I have to think, Gwynn, please, if you really love me as you claim... I don't think a few hours of waiting can change the course of our stories. If, as you say, it is a *Legend* that has been passed down for centuries, I can't rush my choice. Then maybe, tomorrow morning, in the light of the sun I will realise that it was only a dream! It is of course an unusual and beautiful dream... very beautiful, as I've never had until now. Let me go, I beg you!"

Chrisa's faculties came back to being those of an *Annwyn*; she tries to wriggle her mind and detach it from the feeling that Gwynn had created, holding her in front of the strange man. She thinks that maybe he's acting exactly as herself, obscuring his thoughts to those who try to read them. Evidently, he's aware: kissing softly Chrisa on the mouth, then he caresses her shoulders, afterward he bends down to pick the shawl up from the ground where it had slipped during their embrace. With reverence, he covers up her shoulders before taking both her hands and bringing them to his lips.

"Princess, it has never been my idea to hold you against your wish. You can go; you're free to make your own choices... Tomorrow morning, down by the River Shannon, over that hill, I'll be waiting! I hope you sleep softly…"

With these words, the provocative presence moves away slowly. In the moonlight, the surrounding meadows glow, covered by drops of dew; the air always sparkling brings the scent of Oriental amber back to Chrisa, making her shiver. Only when the man was gone down the street does Chrisa decide to return to the big house.

Chapter 41

Insuperable Problems

Elvira puts a strain on Fenix's nerves, who is already very tired. He wouldn't get into a fight with his wife, who was angry because of his late return. Armed with removable leash and bags to collect the dog's poop, Fenix heads towards the lake.

'Well, at least with the excuse of the dog I can retrace my steps and have a look at the villa Var Darquen de Aguilar... I'm convinced that this is about something big, very big.'

"Come on, Elvira! Give me a break; stop sniffing at every pole or plant. That sucks! How can you find the smell of piss attractive?"

Fenix looks around to check that no one is on the street. 'What do I have to do to keep the peace in this family? Holy patience, Gianna knew my job before we married!'

Thoughts are swirling in the head of the poor man, still pissed off about being relieved from the investigation of the murder on the lake. Arriving at the villa's entrance, he can't hold Elvira, who slips right between the legs of a distinguished gentleman who comes out.

"Excuse me; the dog just doesn't know good manners."

Fenix tries to apologise, but the man loses his balance and ends up on the ground, cursing.

"For God's sake, give it a little attention!"

Fenix forget the leash and Elvira to help the man to his feet.

"I'm so sorry, believe me. Is everything alright? I hope you aren't injured by falling..."

As a good police officer, Fenix makes sure that the man has nothing broken, and then leaves him his business card. Evidently Fenix doesn't expect the unpredicted reaction of the man in reading it.

"Head-Commander... of the Experimental Team... ahh, I have several very influential friends in high places," then the man's voice becomes mellow and trying to smile, he extends his hand, "Lord Warden, I'm very pleased to meet you. Why are you strolling here around? Is it a walk with the dog, or you're looking for the lawyer? I was told that Var Darquen de Aguilar left for Paris. Madame Rosengarden, his housekeeper, a woman without scruples, is efficient and competent, but she hates visits... and she's quiet as a mouse... if you know what I mean. I found out his destination from your superior in Turicum. Ahh, yes, he loves chess, a passion we share."

*** Invicta Impedimenta ***

Fenix had already deduced the character of the man before him: compulsive liar with a marked misogynist inclination, deceitful and full of money.

"Lord Warden, I'm certainly not here for the lawyer. As you can see, I'm taking my wife's dog for a walk! However, if you experience any problems as a result of the fall, please contact me. I'm terribly embarrassed, believe me."

Then taking the excuse of having to chase Elvira, Fenix leave, but not without having turned just enough to observe the old man from behind a column. One thing is certain: he isn't friendly, and it's strange that such a character is there in the villa's park.

'So let's do the math and let's fill this crossword,' thinks Fenix as he tries to gran Elvira from under a thick bush, where she was hiding.

"Damn, Elvira! Come out from under there, if I bring you home dirty, Gianna will be angry with me... before I shove you in the bathtub!"

Obviously, the word '*bathtub*' is sobering and the dog, beating her tail, finally comes out of her precarious hiding place. Fenix rewinds the leash in the box, and then sits on the first bench he comes to. He extracts his networked *unycell* and calls Sergio on his home phone number. A pre-recorded message, informing the caller that the number is not available at the moment, responds.

'He'll be asleep, lucky him, I'd rather trade Gianna and Elvira with Solaris and Selene... damn it. Well, come on, old boy, try to stay calm. Now let's turn around and go back home, I'm going to take a shower and then I'm going to get some sleep, too. When I'm rested, my brain will work at full capacity, Sergio will see that I called and definitely he will call me back later.'

From behind the thick curtains on the second floor of the villa Var Darquen de Aguilar, a shadow is watching the scene with marked curiosity. Afterward the shadow descends down the large staircase into the library where he starts to look carefully among the very old volumes. What he seeks is a large book bound in black leather on which is etched in fire and then covered with gold, a title in characters similar to the Nordic runes...

At 10:30 PM Fenix wakes up in a panic, caused by a bad nightmare. Trying to make as little noise as possible to avoid waking Gianna and the dog, he goes down to the kitchen.

"'Gosh, I planned to return to the Headquarter at 10:00 PM, if I arrive at midnight, I'll very lucky. Golly! I should have put on the alarm clock!'

He searches for his *unycell* and finds it in the bathroom, still in his trousers, where he had wildly abandoned them on the ground before taking the shower.

'But I say, damn it… she could at least pick up my clothes from the floor. I wonder what Gianna does in the house all day, besides gossiping with her friends or watching those idiotic programs on *worldvideo.com*. Even if I say it again in many different ways, it's useless, she believes all that crap… these programs are made especially to brainwash people. But nooo, Gianna thinks I'm a paranoid, so she became a perfect fool day after day.'

Still cursing about the many bad choices he has made in his life, Fenix goes toward the Headquarters. When he arrives, he first meets Sergio, who, evidently having forgotten to call the chief, feels abashed.

"Commander, I saw too late that you had tried to reach me in the late afternoon," he explains, "I was asleep and didn't wake up till I was due to resume service, well it was too late. But I thought you would be here by 10:00 PM…"

A little annoyed by the observation that brings bad light on his lack of punctuality, Fenix paints a smile and tries to change the subject.

"It doesn't matter, Sergio. It was nothing urgent; I just wanted to ask you about the morning's shift… you know, down at the Villa Var Darquen!"

For a moment even just pronouncing that name gave the Commander a strange foaming sensation at the bottom of his stomach. Of one thing he's sure, damn sure, he knows he has a very good nose for trouble, gift for a policeman!

Sergio pauses by the entrance of the building before answering. He looks around and makes sure they are not overheard.

"Nooo-good, Boss," Sergio says in a low voice, "but I think it isn't the *right place* to discuss it."

He moves his index finger to his mouth and nods his head to the office of the secretary, then using a difficult to understand mime, he try to explain Fenix something.

The commander is angry, perhaps because of his lack of imagination, which doesn't allow him to read his officer's visual message.

"Damn, I understand! Let's go outside..."

After turning the corner at the end of the building's avenue, Sergio finally opens his mouth.

"There is very big trouble; it seems that during our absence someone on the other side of the Alps has raided here. I've been told by the receptionist who was on duty that they took away several documents from our offices. If I understand correctly, even the metal box with digital lock in which you would have put those magnetic cards that refer to the double-murder case."

The commander feels the pressure grow over the limit; he required about ten seconds to process what his subordinate told him.

"Where is that bastard Sella?"

The question was unexpected and Sergio mutters:

"he was released, there wasn't sufficient evidence to hold him longer. And I dare to believe that it was providential to release him because if Turicum officers had found him in his cell, I think there would be further problems for us!"

"Why was not I informed? Nah, apparently the Commander of Ascona's Experimental Team, that idiot who walks Elvira and then collects her faeces, doesn't need to be warned! Damn it... but they can all go to hell..."

In the unmatched throes of rage, Fenix retraces his steps and like a sandstorm in the Mojave Desert, dashes into the building. They hear him yelling two blocks away. Sergio, followed him, thinking that if he doesn't compose himself, he would definitely suffer a heart attack.

Chapter 42

Masters of the Temple

Paris is shrouded in the darkness of a night of torrential downpour, water coming down from the sky like a waterfall. It feels wet inside, a feeling of sticky reality that affects every gesture. Hathor runs along the banks of the Seine, holding in his hand the handle of the umbrella that barely rejects the rain.

The storm's scent is something that the lawyer catalogues: the smell of water's downpour in the city is very different than in the countryside; these are atypical fragrances that are accentuated depending on the place where you are located. Sometimes it can smell of flowers or smoke, others can be the stench of filth. Unfortunately, that day, Paris suffocates even the best memories of the man. The scent he now perceives isn't the fragrance of the countryside, with notes of hay and grass, but rather the sad reality of the smelly, old crumbling, great metropolis.

The heart of Hathor Var Arquen de Aguilar is swollen, and the man feels pain beyond description. Once again, he wasn't able to talk in peace with Chrisa and couldn't convince her that he wasn't a threat. He knows that Lord Warden and Vamaran are very dangerous, that the power of the old aristocrat is immeasurable, as is the power of his circle of friends on which he could rely.

More than once in the last fifty years, the Lord had used any kind of influence to achieve his not always commendable objectives. Lord Warden is elusive, powerful and fearsome, a cocktail of pitfalls that is wise to avoid. One thing is certain, he isn't the kind of individual you would like to have as your enemy!

Hathor had not yet been able to evaluate in a coherent way: after all, he only saw him once and clearly at a moment of disparity. For him, at that time, Vamaran was just a love rival, a threat that could steal the sweet Chrysalis from under his nose. That being, so sensual and attractive, made him feel inferior and, that in some way, is a too 'human' feeling.

A whirlwind of thoughts dominates every idea of reconciliation. Hathor feels it isn't the mind or brain, to guide his thoughts, but rather the heart. In certain situations, the heart is impulsive, arrogant and selfish and it tries to overpower everything. Frustrated by this real condition Hathor tries to bring his thoughts to deliberateness. He wishes he could find a wise and favourable way to get the desired outcome: to have Chrysalis by his side.

*** Doctores Templi ***

After 10:00 PM, the hours elapsed quickly; he believes he made the right choice, to have act consistently, give his complete willingness to help the two siblings, if it were necessary and if they had decided to do so.

The portal may only remain open for twenty-four hours... and time is running out, this is a fact. The thing that annoys him is that feeling, a peculiar sensation that something is out of place. Being in some way connected with Chrysalis' fate, even if he was in Paris, Hathor perceived that she was in serious danger. The threat dominates in space-time and the man's vibrational level feels that something isn't going the right way.

Upon returning to the hotel at the end of rue Lagrange, Hathor called his housekeeper.

"Forgive me for calling you at this late hour, but I'm very uneasy, Madame Rosengarden. I'm in Paris, I am staying in the usual hotel. I was able to get through some of the work that I set myself, but I shall remain perhaps another 24 hours. Is there any news?"

"Ah, Monsieur, don't worry," the woman, responds kindly with a surprised and sleepy voice, "it was a quiet evening here, no calls. Only your friend, Lord Warden wanted to leave a package, perhaps some books, I gather from the weight. He left word that you had already agreed so."

Then she stays silent, in the background Hathor hears a sweet melody, most likely a Rachmaninoff piano concerto, Madame Rosengarden's favourite composer. She has the habit of listening to some very old piece of classical music, when she retreats to her quarters.

"Ah, I had totally forgotten about Lord Warden, damn my memory! You may leave the package in the library; I'll look tomorrow when I get back. I won't hold you any longer, Madame Rosengarden, good night and see you tomorrow. I'll let you know the exact time of my arrival in Lugano so you can send me the driver. I'll have to do a couple of things in the city, and don't want to run about with a taxi…"

Suddenly, however, Hathor realises that he can no longer rely on Adam. His heart jumped up and his voice cracked.

"Well, I'll tell you... forget it; I'll take care of everything. I'll arrange everything before my departure from Paris, I'll call the secretary. I'll see you tomorrow, Madame Rosengarden... good-night."

While disconnecting the communication, Hathor feels a strong sense of nausea wind up his stomach. Unwittingly, images from the past morning return with horror. He sees the lifeless body of his trusted butler and once again he feels a violent rage like no other.

To distract himself, he reviews a pair of recorded infrared images of both Waterhouse's paintings.

Despite the Lord's untrue indiscretions, he does not find the Codes in the *Pandora*, or in the other painting, *The Magic Circle*. That greatly annoyed the lawyer: he was duped, but by whom and exactly, for what reason? That bastard Sella got him both originals, paying their weight in gold.

The expert who had helped him to *'manipulate'* the canvas was the best available on the planet. The equipment and methods used by him are proven... there was absolutely nothing left out! And yet... and yet something had certainly escaped him. Vamaran had alluded to a hermetic vision to decipher the Codes. He, however, confirmed that they were hidden in the *Pandora*! But how and where had he been able to proceed with these tests? It was impossible, since he owned the originals of both paintings; certainly this was the hand of Lord Warden... and of Sella.

One thing was clear in his mind was the certitude that that crook Sella had something to do with it! But he also knows that the *'flatterer'* had immediately gone running to Commander Fenix, following Hathor's advice, to try to avoid further harassment. Without evidence, the Commander could not hold Sella in custody for long. And if he was released, where would Sella go into hiding? This was a simple task to be assigned to a couple of people he trusted, and the next day he would do so.

The thoughts continue to pester him while he showers; the hot water runs from the shower head with extreme intensity, massaging his neck and shoulders. Then, with a little reluctance, Hathor turn the mixer to *froid*: the cold stream first paralyzes him, and then inflicts on his flesh a sort of exhilarating pleasure.

After the shower, Hathor wrapped himself in a soft terry robe and lies down on the bed with the idea of reading for a while.

In his leather briefcase, he had placed the notes made with Dr. Bartók fifteen years earlier. These are bizarre notes of botany, in which it speaks of the value that certain plants had for ancient populations. Before the coming of Christianity, *Death* was not perceived as something definitive, but as a passage to another life. For the ancients, the boundary between the world of the dead and that of the living was not real, because the dead continued to be invisibly present for all important occasions. Dr. Bartók repeatedly observed that during the sacred ceremonies, to invite the dead, the living went to the burial mounds, believed to be the meeting point of the Worlds. In the *sacred circle*, death and life were one, because death was just a part of everlasting life. Bartók and Hathor were in agreement in defining the Yew as the tree of life and death, transcending this illusory duality. The Yew is therefore perceived as a *Gate* to the *afterlife* and its rune *eivaz*, slightly resembling a reversed *Z*, is a magical sign.

"*The Magic circle...* Damn it, what was the combination?" Hathor whispers, putting his head in his hands.

"What has Waterhouse's painting to do with the ancient Celts? Is there a connection, a sort of holistic link? May that be the *Holy Door* that he sought for so long? This very rune is represented with original drawings on various files and records belonging to the professor. But why had he nourished sort of obsession for this tree? What were the motivations that led the researcher to share his mystical knowledge of druidic origins with me?"

Hathor had from the beginning learned about the *presence* of Chrysalis, an *Annwyn*, whom Professor Bartók and his wife had genetically generated. But apparently, not all of Bartók's designs had been exposed. Hathor smiles to himself, thinking of his murdered friend; perhaps if he had lived longer, the basic findings reached by his studies would actually open men's knowledge so far they could not even imagine. Bartók was a genius, a great mind which may have catapulted the Unified Power's hegemony!

At the bottom of his heart Hathor is convinced that Bartók knew of his bond, in previous lives, to the mind/soul of his daughter, Chrysalis. On a couple of occasions, the professor had revealed that his wife had long meditated and recited prayers to invoke the specific presence *of this Annwyn*. Bartók had then somehow also discovered that his wife was a *'diviner'* and tried to take advantage of the possibility to evoke a presence that could directly impact on the studies carried out by both.

Hathor feels a shiver while a strong doubt assails him. Somewhere between the personal notes of the professor, there must be a key to understand... something that was similar to the *eivaz...* or a link with the yew tree worshiped by the Celts.

Chapter 43

Mystic Rites

At sunrise, Chrisa wakes up. With no little difficulty, she tries to make up her mind: she feels strange, very strange, and when she realises the reason, her memory is projected to the previous night and the meeting with Gwynn ap Nudd. Dazed, the young girl tries to dispel any doubts. It really happened: it's not a trivial dream, that man embraced and kissed her... and she went along with it!

Throughout her life, she had never been kissed by a man, she had always kept well away from entanglements. Joshua occasionally teased her by saying that she would become a spinster, sour like a lemon, but she never paid attention and didn't accept his challenge by arguing. She found a couple of her brother's friends *nice and kind* but nothing more than that. Some occasional timewaster had the misfortune to get in her way, but Chrisa had prepared the arguments in order to make them quickly change their mind.

She feels her cheeks burn erratically, then her stomach tightens and in her most intimate thoughts she curse herself for the damned desire to see him again. Gwynn is certainly a person out of the norm; otherwise he wouldn't have aroused in her these strange emotions. In addition, he's an *Annwyn* and this might greatly facilitate things.

Joshua is still sleeping, evidently exhausted by the events of the previous day; he let himself go into a restful sleep. 'That way he'll be back being my favourite brother,' Chrisa smiles, 'and he'll want to play and take everything with great joy.'

Chrisa slips to the shower on tiptoe to prevent waking her brother. After that, she got dressed again and goes out into the hallway where she finds, on the ground, the shawl that had fallen from her shoulders. As if by magic, the Oriental amber smell of her mysterious suitor lingers on the shawl. The ambiguity of that perfume makes her dizzy, the memory becomes even more vivid and she thinks back at Gwynn's last sentence: *"Tomorrow morning, down to the River Shannon over that hill, I'll be waiting!"*

*** Mystica Sacra ***

The young woman feels a strange apprehension: she suspects that something is going wrong. Inside, there was a kind of war between heart and mind taking place: on the one hand, she would like to hear Marius and Sibéal's opinion, but on the other hand, she's convinced of being able to manage all these problems by herself. Arriving in the room, she finds Hathor's book on the table beside the chair where Marius had been sitting.

Chrisa decides to give it a more accurate look, besieged by the curiosity of Hathor's explicit warning, which had been clear: a person named Vamaran waits for the activation of the Cross of the Scriptures and then would force her to follow him across the Projection and take her prisoner! But who is this Vamaran? It seems so strange and unusual that it was the same Hathor, who she so feared, to give her this information in order to protect her.

The big book weighs on her lap, the pages are yellowed and many phrases, written with a fountain pen, were faded and difficult to read. Here and there are pencilled notes in a tiny writing, making the whole thing difficult to read. To the eye of an historian, this looks almost like a topographical map of those used a couple of centuries ago. What intrigued Chrisa is the name of his father noted several times: *prof. Dr. Bartók* followed by places scattered throughout every continent and dates going back to when she was a little girl of 4 or 5 years old.

Some photos are of her father with Hathor, but the most beautiful picture is that one of her family in the garden of the villa Var Darquen de Aguilar. No doubt the photo was taken with a wide-angle lens because you could see the entire villa, up to the tower. Many notes, however, had some strange dates, dating back to three or four centuries before: there are notes in Latin, dated 1657, others written in languages that Chrisa don't even recognise.

'I should seek Marius's advice, maybe he can help me.'

She looks out the window with a little uneasiness, contemplating the green countryside around Sibéal's house. It is natural that her eyes look for the enormous yew, under whose branches she had kissed Gywnn the night before. The rays of the sun already caress its branches, lapping the entire surface; the tree is of a dark tourmaline green with brown central spots to confirm the magnitude of the branches attached to the trunk. It sinks, majestic and imperious, into the earth. The small hill markedly emerges from nature, a particular which initially escaped Chrisa.

The sudden arrival of Sibéal from behind makes her wince. The blush on her cheeks is even more marked, and the young woman immediately tries to close her mind to the woman to avoid her reading what had happened the night before.

"It's wonderful, isn't it? That yew had been planted by the Druid priests during the commemorative feast of *Samhain* 3,500 years ago. Not by chance it is on top of a hill, Chrisa, around here there are many burial mounds, located in a circle around the plant. To the ancients, death and life are one, and the yew is the tree that combines both, a kind of Door to the afterlife. When the *Vibratory Matrix* is activated, this should help all those people who have reached an appropriate vibrational level to connect with their place in the Universe. For this reason, your work is very important, my child!"

Chrisa looks at the woman with a confused glaze; she manages with great difficulty to hide her thoughts, haunted by the appearance of the previous night. Maybe Sibéal realised that something had happened during the night, but since she's a very wise woman, prefers not to ask questions.

The young woman takes courage in both hands and asks: "could you look closer at what is written in the book?"

She indicates the large volume left on the low table.

"Sibéal, there are several pictures of my father! And many of his notes, I recognise his handwriting, although I admit that I don't have many of his writings to be taken for comparison. It's a kind of *deep feeling*... almost a certainty that this is tangible and real evidence. For years I shunned Hathor during my astral travels, now I realise that he lived and perhaps is still living in the same town where Joshua, Marius and I have spent the last seventeen years. What intrigues me most is that he had to be a close friend of my father! But I was so small, and the memories are blurred, and after the death of our parents, I don't think that Hathor ever contacted us."

Sibéal approached in silence and after a reflective pause, she replied.

"Nothing is left to chance, baby. I almost dare say that if this presence is finally revealed in a different way, not through *the dream*, but rather he reached you through a portal, he'll have his reasons. Don't rush your thoughts and don't try to look for answers where you may find only other questions. The Magic in which we live is very great..."

Sibéal leaves adding softly, "in a little while Marius and Joshua will arrive, you have to plan your day and something tells me that we'll also receive news from Ualtar."

Chrisa, still staring at the big yew, is overcome by a sense of sadness, but tries to dampen the emotions whispering:

"I don't want to disappoint him, he's waiting for me..."

But her fleeting thought oscillates between uncertainty and perplexity. A thousand questions are looming in her mind like dark clouds on the horizon of a new day. The omens are like stains that creep in her heart, into her instinct, trying to bring wisdom to prevail over her impulses. It feels like a very old, absorbing paper which was used in ancient times to blot excess ink. She's assimilating emotions and feelings in an indistinct way, and this isn't good.

Chrisa remains in the room, with the old manuscript tight in her hands, contested between two shores: below her, the hypothetical darkest abyss in which her fears emerge under the form of certainty. Then over the abyss, a possible bridge that connects the proposals of Hathor and those of Gwynn; Chrisa, perhaps for the first time in her life, realises her hesitation before a categorical choice. But perhaps she *shouldn't choose*, but rather simply wait for the fate to trace the path? She never wanted to be a tightrope walker, unprepared, because the wire which stretches over the abyss appears to be invisible!

It isn't me who is in a hurry, the voice of her conscience knocks gently on the door of memories, *it is Time that struts... swift and terrible, that with bites, tearing apart my heart, looking for a gap.*

"Hey, sister, did you sleep well? I struggled for a bit, but then I fell asleep... and I didn't have nightmares! This is beautiful! When will you do another *run about...* maybe in the Caribbean or the Pacific Ocean? Would it be possible to project ourselves on to a sailboat?"

Joshua is approaching from behind and then eagerly embraces his sister, almost causing her to lose balance. The girl gets bored, not so much because of his way of appearing, but rather for his brother's speculations about the dream journeys.

"Damn you! But don't you want to learn some manners?" Then Chrisa gives him a big smile with a kiss on the forehead.

"I heard noises from Marius' room," Joshua smiles, "I think he's awake, too. Did Sibéal hear something from Ualtar? I'm afraid something really serious may have happened to him..."

Chapter 44

The Power of Fear

After he vented a little, railing against everything and everyone, Commander Fenix forces Sergio to follow him outside, down the driveway from the building used as headquarters of the Experimental Team.

For a while, the commander remains silent but then turns to his subordinate:

"Sergio, I know that you don't hold much sympathy for me... and I don't blame you, believe me. I'm in an abnormal and very annoying situation: I was relieved of the murder and as if that wasn't enough, they also confiscated a large amount of material directly from my office! This is a takeover, Sergio, a demonstration of arrogance and recklessness. There is certainly something very big going on... Look Sergio, I don't want you to end up in trouble because of me, please believe me. But well, I would be very grateful if you could give me a hand. Let's say in a *confidential* manner. Maybe we could go somewhere without prying ears and put the puzzle together. When I was walking my wife's dog near the mansion... something strange happened to me."

The commander looks sideways at his officer and then makes the gesture of returning to the building. Sergio thinks he can earn some credit by willingly helping his boss; he never got high regard from Fenix, and this is an opportunity served on a silver platter.

"Okay, all right. When I'm out for my patrol round, I'll let you know where I am... I'll use the phrase *there is a little wind* and then add my location. You can come to me, Commander, and try not to be followed!"

"Thanks," Fenix says, turning to look into Sergio's eyes. "Thanks, I was sure that I can trust you. You're the best! I'll try to disperse any nosy watchers, but I don't think they come up to do that."

Then he quickly strides away, towards the head-quarters. Sergio remains there for a while, giving the commander time to get to his office to avoid arousing suspicion. From the old clock tower's bell, he can hear the twelve strokes of midnight.

"Brrr... it's time for werewolves or vampires," Sergio mutters, shuddering. "Not that I have a great desire to end up in a horror movie, but luckily I'll be with Solaris and Selene."

*** Timoris Vis ***

Up in his office on the top floor, Commander Fenix tries to remain calm. Even with shortness of breath and a twitch in his right eye that shows no sign of wanting to stop, the man begins to scribble several notes on a sheet with a pencil. A couple of centuries earlier this technique was called *brainstorming*, fixing ideas and concepts on paper. These were then elaborated on, adding or removing anything that was not the case. After half an hour of work, the potpourri is almost perfect. How many things can happen in 48 hours, and everything is there clear in its details. Obviously they were missing the photos and the rest, but this brainstorming bears no resemblance to the data and pictures he had seen projected on the wall of his office. He did it in spite of his superiors, a clear sign of the man's itchy curiosity to know what was going on.

'Great, now I'm just waiting to hear from Sergio. Then I will try with him to make sense of this whole story. Too bad I can't use the support of Valery, but I think it would be a too big a risk. No, no, I can trust Sergio. Maybe he's really the only worthwhile person here.'

Fenix pulls out a drawer of his desk and places his feet on it, looking for the most comfortable position. Now he only has to wait for the call of his man. He's taken by surprise when the secretary suddenly passes him the long-awaited call.

"Sergio must ask you something about tomorrow's round, Commander," the woman's shrill voice informs him.

"Commander Fenix, Sergio speaking. There's a *bit of wind here* in the Grand Hotel's parking square, and it's a little chilly. Sorry if the reception is not good... as I have a broken turn, I wanted to ask permission to take 24 hours leave starting tomorrow morning at 6:00, if you'd allow me? I think I have some kind of fever and I think it's wise if I take care of myself..."

At first, Commander Fenix smiles at the cleverness of his employee, since he's aware that all calls are recorded. Sergio obviously wants something in return for the risks he's running for privately helping his chief. Trying to push back these thoughts, Fenix responds with an authoritative voice.

"Well, actually in the last two days you have been under a lot of stress. I think health is important and should not be overlooked. Your request is accepted, the secretary can resume this communication to make a note of your leave. See you in two days, good-healing, Sergio."

Fenix closes the communication with a grin painted on his face: this time he'll wind all of them around his little finger. A sort of revenge, a miserable one, but at least they didn't completely outwit him; Fenix has always defined himself as a clever and cunning person. Pretending nothing is amiss, the commander is quietly sitting at his desk. A couple of employees walk in front of his office's window, peering inside with evident curiosity. After a quarter of an hour, he goes to leave, taking with him his jacket and his briefcase:

"I'm going back home. Since the *problem* of the murder was closed early, there is no reason that I need stay here to spend another sleepless night. Oh, and don't have a second thought about writing it down clearly in the Protocol, as I have just described," Fenix smiles good-naturedly at the secretary. "Between my wife's dog and the trouble here in the office, I don't know which one is the less wicked! I'll see you tomorrow at noon, good work... or good night, as you prefer."

The secretary looks at him funnily; maybe it's the first time since she was assigned to the Ascona division that her Chief, too loyal to the job, is compromising his rigid ethics.

"Thanks Commander Fenix, I wish you a good rest!"

As usual, she records the data and times, then disconnects the commander's *earth-frame* and puts away his device.

"All right, so let's see those bastards track me down now! I bet that chauvinist Xernon is behind this mess. Ah, but they think they know how to handle things better on the other side of the Alps! They're the ones that send most deviants to the hospitals in the statistics. To hear them, here in the south, the rest of the scum are having a great time. And that's just because we take life with a pinch of philosophy here. I never liked that Xernon, not really, and I think it's a mutual feeling."

Meanwhile, he thinks and plots about the possible conjectures of the Unified Power; Fenix follows the first part of the journey in the direction of his home. Just the thought of having to take Elvira for a stroll makes the man irritated. Then, after checking that no one was following him, he takes a short cut by jumping over a private railing, quickly entering a long driveway heading to a couple of houses.

After about ten minutes, a bit out of breath, he arrives on the forecourt of the Grand Hotel. Even before he sees his man, Fenix finds himself in the presence of the two *jaglynx*. A shiver down his spine paralyzed him for a few seconds.

"Be good! Solaris, Selene come here; don't you see that you have frightened my big boss?"

From the mocking tone of voice, the commander is fully aware that Sergio is taking some kind of revenge on him. But he restrains the impulse to immediately scold him, as he used to do with his subordinates, which of course they absolutely don't appreciate.

"So, is there a place we can go to discuss matters in peace, without busybodies around?" Fenix demands explicitly.

"Well, as long as my *earth-frame* is connected we are tracked with every step that I and my animals take," Sergio replies. "The last half hour I have walked around while waiting for you to come, so I wouldn't arouse suspicion. May I propose two solutions: to take a stroll, remaining well away from popular trails, although at this time of night I have serious doubts that there's a living soul around... or we wait until I finish my round and then meet at my place. I saw that you are disconnected; don't tell me that you got fired!"

Sergio's voice is a little worried; meanwhile he peers at his superior inquisitively.

286

"No, for now they haven't kicked me out. I was just relieved of the case, as I told you, although for me it's almost the same thing. Let's say that I have taken, following your advice, a day of leisure!"

Fenix smiles and taps his temple, "we'll try to work the brain without all the electronic data. I won't rest until I see the whole story clearly. It isn't just a matter of throwing someone in prison, if those two young siblings are in danger; I want to ensure that they don't end up like their parents. Sergio, are you with me?"

The man caresses Selene before asking, "and you, Commander, do you have children?"

A silence falls on the two men while icy, invisible fingers are gripping Fenix's heart…

"No. I didn't have children with Gianna. Let's say that my wife didn't feel strong enough to manage with the interference of the Unified Power, which finds itself always mixed up with every parent who wants to have kids... Why this question, if I may ask?"

Sergio looks at him straight in the eye, and then he whistles to call Solaris.

"Just curiosity, Fenix, mere curiosity. You see, these are my children," Sergio strokes both beasts, "I don't hide the fact that I would do anything to protect a child. Even at the cost of my life."

Fenix doesn't need to hear any more, his man has clearly expressed that since Chrysalis and Joshua are concerned, he's willing to risk even death. What the two men may not know is that at that precise moment Chrysalis is between the arms of the creature that is trying to change the course of events for the whole humanity on planet Earth.

Chapter 45

Guardian of the Threshold

Marius isn't in a good mood: he has obviously spent hours waiting for a sign from Ualtar, sign which didn't arrive. The old sailor is sure that something strange must have happened to the last *Guardian of the Threshold.*

'Maybe he changed his mind, finding it absurd to activate the *Vibratory Matrix.* And why, after all, should they help people to reconnect with their place in the Universe? It won't be an access gate to other dimensions, to help and lead humans to conceive the real reason for their presence on this Planet! Would it perhaps generate tangible changes in evolution? Certainly, it could be something more radical, considering that the terrible catastrophe of 2022 had taught the peremptory lesson only a few!'

With these thoughts in his heart, Marius feels depressed. Just 24 hours earlier he had thought he could change the course of events, validated by the presence of the *Matrix.* Since then things have fallen, the feeling of inadequacy has become a constant that haunts his mind. Now the old man looked at Chrisa with apprehension, somehow he perceives from her aura that something had altered during the night: something has changed irreversibly.

"Chrisa is there something that you don't want to reveal? In my veins flows the blood of a noble race with sacred rank... my people are over *The Mists*, the *Tylwyth Teg*, Chrisa. And among them I might now be in peace... but not before I have fulfilled the purpose here!"

The young *Annwyn* tries to avoid his gaze, blushing visibly. This motion doesn't escape Sibéal: she reaches and then embraces the girl.

"Tell us what happened last night by the side of the Great Yew. That secular tree hides from human vision many mysteries; but since it's a *Bridge* between the two worlds, maybe you can uncover something which is darkened from our eyes!"

Joshua plays with a fork, bouncing it on the large table where everything is already prepared for breakfast.

"Hocus pocus! Yes, yes, these are the concepts that fascinate my little sister!"

The girl's eyes caress the memories, while looking beyond the window. The woman, looking at her, is now certain that something serious had happened, and squints in an effort to penetrate the mind of the girl.

Chrisa, who still held Hathor's book tight in her hands, feels the anguish contract in her stomach, which feels to her like a malaise, an abnormal sensation that entirely prevents her from filling her lungs with air.

'What's happening to me?' Chrisa thinks to herself, 'is that possible that within a few hours all my paradigms can break like twigs under the whips of a strong wind?'

"I met the man from the story that you told us last night, Sibéal. Gwynn ap Nudd, the king of the Annwn," Chrisa blurted out in a trembling voice. "But maybe I imagined everything and it was only a dream, even if his presence went straight into me and uncertainty was made tangible. I'm scared. I am unsure that I am able to perceive the truth: shall I believe his flattering words or give credence to what Hathor told me? My father's scribbles and notes, photos and everything else... prove without a shadow of doubt that Hathor tells the truth! I'm confused, terribly caught up in misleading feelings. It's all so irrational. On one hand, a man who I don't really know, but who certainly spent countless hours with my father, and on the other hand a being of unique charm that promises me a sort of immortality."

*** Custos Liminis ***

Marius slowly turns to first lay his gaze on the girl, then on the bound book.

"Chrisa... what this book contains... are great secrets, in relation to the studies of your father and Hathor, I checked various data. I have no doubt it's an original which contains years of study and research. But I can't find a reason for the appearance of last night near the sacred Yew. If he's really a metaphysical being... why did he fool you? I believe that the *Forces* involved are multiple and perhaps the situation is now more complicated, with the appearance of this Gwynn. My dear, if Hathor gave you this book, it is because he trusts you and your wisdom. There are several alchemical formulas, very old, which go far beyond the limited knowledge that I have mastered. It may be of interest to scholars of Ishtar, for example. I wish I could understand what is the connection existing between the book and the *Vibratory Matrix*. I wonder why didn't Hathor give you both, explaining what he wants you to do!"

Chrisa is troubled by Marius' words, and with appealing eyes the young woman look towards Sibéal, hoping that the woman will give her a tailor-made solution.

290

But Mauris' cousin remains silent, staring at her cousin, without intruding or giving an opinion which will change the course of destiny. No. It must be Chrisa to ponder for the right choice; unless it can be defined *choice* the implication *take it or leave it*.

"Did you hear from Ualtar?" The girl asks Marius, "I'm afraid that something bad did happen... Have any of you seen Martino? I thought he was staying here!"

Chrisa turns her gaze to the Irish woman, her face is milky and with a slightly furrowed brow.

"I didn't hear him come back last night," Sibéal says laconically, "but they are now too many things I'm missing... maybe it's my time to cross *The Mists*."

In fact, none of them could imagine that the brave Martino had stalked two people out of Riordan's Pub the night before. This wasn't the first time that he, during his existence, had played games of chance with his life. But once again, he got away, although at that moment he was lying unconscious in a dark basement of a crumbling Shannonbridge building.

Almost as if evoked by their thoughts, Ualtar suddenly burst into the house. He first apologises, talking excitedly in Gaelic with Marius, and then his gaze falls on Chrisa. He bows before the young woman, bringing his hands to chest level.

"I apologise, I had no idea... I couldn't be aware of what, in the end, my job would be. Late last night, Fintan came to my house. He wasn't alone; the man who had dared to cross the threshold of Al-Hillah was with him! The same man who had long ago shown me the *Vibratory Matrix*. At one point I had serious doubts and I didn't think it was wise to go along with you to Clonemacnoise. Where is the *Matrix*? For the Strength of the Great Mother, keep it hidden and treasure it, even at the cost of life. The potential of that object isn't only to allow an *Annwyn*, accompanied by his other half, to pass through the projection and destroy the Sacred Mirror. The man who was with Fintan can connect the worlds of the living and the Underworld. That man is the rightful king of the Annwn, he is Gwynn ap Nudd!"

Chrisa feels faint; the room begins to swirl and she collapses to the ground like a sail in a flat wind. Ualtar's words spin in her head as she tries to pull herself together; she can still feel the Oriental amber smell of last night's meeting. Sibéal is the first to help her: she runs a hand over her forehead, realising that she's hot, her face is flushed and she's breathing heavily.

"She has a fever, she is losing energy, and I begin to believe that the young woman is *connected* to something or someone that can change her vital functions at will."

She turns angrily to Ualtar. "Infidel! You should know what the punishments are for those who betray ISA!"

Sibéal helps Chrisa to her feet and to the couch. Ualtar looks perplexed, almost shocked. His eyes move from the young woman to Marius, then looks questioningly the Irish woman.

"I don't understand what you mean, lady! I haven't perpetrated any sacrilegious or blasphemous act... The King of the *Tylwyth Teg* has the power to use the *Matrix*, what he wants is simply to link the two worlds, as it says in our legends. Avalon will be reached again by the Chosen... I don't think Gwynn ap Nudd has malicious intentions."

"Ualtar, where is Fintan?" Marius asks, a little apprehensively. "I think he's the other druid that should help us to celebrate the activation of the *Vibratory Matrix*."

The runes on Ulatar's tunic seem to glow for a few seconds. "He remained outside..." Ualtar answers.

Marius feels a deep sense of fear: until then they believed that Hathor was the one who made sure that

Chrisa would find the Vibratory Matrix. But maybe there are others still manipulating events in the background?

"Tell him to come in, please; I have to ask him something."

At Marius' peremptory order, Ualtar retraced his steps down the hall. After few minutes, a man in his fifties with reddish hair and beard enters the room behind the *Guardian of the Holly Gate*. Without asking permission, he sits in the chair; in his right hand he's holding a coin that he rolls above the knuckles with dexterity. His tunic is worn below the elbows and dirty all around the slit pockets. Marius feels that he's armed.

"Welcome. I think this isn't the first time I've seen you, is it?"

Marius's voice is authoritative and hard, Fintan tries to smile, but the attempt failed in less than five seconds. With marked discomfort, he replies:

"I don't remember. I don't usually memorise the faces of ordinary mortals, unless they are on my path by mistake."

If this was a threat, Fintan obviously used the wrong tone of voice. Marius runs around the chair before reiterating, "So it should be you to help Ualtar so that the sacred rite can be celebrated properly?"

The eyes of the newcomer glows with a strange malicious light.

"Maybe. Or maybe not," he responds with a touch of arrogance in the tone. "You don't play with the legends of the Druids, this should be clear to you."

The coin flashed before missing the support and ends up on the ground. Marius, in a fraction of a second, gathers it, but doesn't give it back to its owner. The elder mocks him.

"Ahhh, but every ritual has its *price*, doesn't it? And what's the price of activating the *Vibratory Matirx*, Fintan? Is it the life of the young woman? And where is this cowardly Gwynn? Something tells me that he can't be very far away, like a poisonous spider weaving its web, then remaining silently lurking in a corner."

Chrisa, who had recovered a bit from her illness, turns her gaze towards the emerald green of the fields that could be seen through the window. Her face is full of sadness and resignation. She felt the fluttering of butterfly wings within her heart. No, that can't be the language of love; something escapes her and, again, she has the impression that her head is elsewhere, beyond the emerald fields, further down where the Shannon flows idle and silent. Her Dark Prince, the King of Darkness who rules over life and death, is waiting for her.

Fintan doesn't reply; without saying a word, he looks at the young woman, then, when she turns around, he stares straight into her eyes. The silence became unfriendly and even Joshua hasn't the shamelessness to come out with some sarcastic joke. Marius's voice rings out hard in the air.

"So? Have you swallowed your tongue? Or have you considered it wiser to remain silent rather than betray the true intentions of Gwynn ap Nudd? Then I can bet that you are the guy that Martino told us about. Lo and behold, something tells me that if Martino didn't return here last night, almost certainly, you can say where he is."

Marius is acidic and approaches the man with an attitude that doesn't bode well.

Chapter 46

Life and Death: Together

The sun shines high in the sky when Hathor finally decides to get up. He had been lying in bed to reflect; he had reconsidered the last 100 years and all the ups and downs with which he was compared against his will. Perhaps, for an *Annwyn*, longevity is the most insidious problem. It seems paradoxical: all mortals seem to want immortality and seek for the *Philosopher's Stone* or some other devilry conceived in the illusory myths of the past. Being imprisoned in a material body can become a sort of obstacle, but the problem is only one relating to the concept of *death*. But everything should be clear, at least for those who have penetrated certain laws: life and death are one, inseparable, because in fact it's a deceptive dualism.

*** Vita et Mors Unum sunt ***

The sun's rays penetrate through small crevices between the threads of the heavy curtain. The man watches the dust that creates bizarre bright blades, beams that are rapidly dwindling approaching the fabric. Flares of the indistinct shapes are reflected on the wall covered with outdated wallpaper.

'What is behind the tapestry? What is beyond the wall and then even further out of the room, outside the building? Away from any barrier or frontier designed by man?'

The *Annwyn's* thoughts are like the leaves of a tree in autumn: colourful visions that swirl endlessly and then lean slightly on his heart.

Hathor's mind runs fast, retracing the rue Lagrange to the Seine: the Notre Dame is there, in its unbridled greatness, unchanged over the centuries. Those walls built on sacred places where they worshiped a very ancient cult, and have seen civilizations rise and fall. There are vestiges of people who have testified in poverty or in luxury, burning martyrs for religious or social ideals alongside with those who had the courage to point the finger towards tyranny.

With a strong apprehension, Hathor thinks of the *Portal* concealed in the Cathedral. It will remain open for another few hours. Unfortunately, or fortunately, the two young siblings have not called, even if the man is convinced that they both need his help. It would have been sufficient a call on a subliminal level, he could perceive it. But Hathor is convinced that even if Chrisa's life was in danger, her pride would prevent her from summoning him!

In the end he gave her totally trust, leaving to her the most precious thing he owned: the *Book*. But it's also possible that Chrisa doesn't understand the deep meaning of that gesture. Fortunately the old sailor and the old Irish lady were with her. Hathor knew that both belong to the *Tylwyth Teg*, the Fairy People.

The *Annwyn* is aware of many details, rumours that professor Bartók had revealed to him during one of their travels in the Americas. But for Hathor, the concern was Vamaran: who is really this man, and why he was in the company of Lord Warden? Hathor always had a kind of deep suspicion for the man, even if sometimes he had the resources to be able to attain some of his far-reaching goals. But Hathor's only real friend was Professor Bartók, father of the two siblings. Perhaps for this reason, the *Annwyn* felt compelled to protect them at all costs.

The studies of the famous researcher are very popular, especially overseas. Several times his friend had gone to attend important meetings as a speaker where the greatest men of science gathered to discuss; the same luminaries who stubbornly stood every time to quibble about everything. They were engulfed in such disputes, able to create a lot of negative energy, which was even able to change the structure of the air they breathed. Hathor knows that many of these great men hated Bartók with marked wickedness, not precluding the idea that right one of them had been able to get to the point of killing him just to silence him.

Of course, it was the *Force of Fear,* by which means the Unified Power was able to achieve hegemony, forcing people into submission in the 23rd Century. But with his friend Bartók, they had found a way to analyse what existed in the Planet Earth. Both scientists had repeatedly used the *Portal* for noble purposes: to preserve nature and the animals that had been saved from the catastrophe. This event, which had left anywhere terrible scars, should be a pragmatic lesson for every sentient being. It should have... but this wasn't the case because of the greed of a few.

Hathor remembers Lord Warden with a sense of deep anger. What actually are his shady schemes? And why did he use Vamaran, a creature as subtle as he was attractive? The man continues to think about the possible reason why Adam was assassinated; within 24 hours, three deaths for which he couldn't determine the exact reason: two of Sella's henchmen and Hathor's own trusty butler. Who's the culprit and what is the reason? They will surely be discovered by the Commander of the Experimental Team; at least that is what Hathor Var Darquen de Aguilar thinks. But he still doesn't know if there is a much larger game of power going on, and the stakes are of immeasurable value.

Hathor gets up and approaches the large window, obscured by a heavy curtain; his hand caresses the fabric, rough to the touch, which reminds him of the texture of the bark of trees. With a slight movement, he pulls the fabric open to let in the sun. Outside, Paris had awakened; everywhere you look, life flickers like fish in a pond, while the blue sky looks like a Picasso's painting in his Blue Period. Hathor smiles: on the garden down there, the parasols are whitish spots scattered around like big mushrooms or the fluorescence of some strange plant.

The ringing of the phone suddenly tears him from his thoughts. Who could it be? He coughs a few times to make his voice clear and then, with a sharp tone, he answers the call by pressing the appropriate button.

"Var Darquen, I'm listening."

On the other side of the phone comes only a sound, as if the communication isn't established correctly. After a few seconds, irritated for not knowing who the interlocutor was, Hathor presses the button again to stop the contact.

'Who can it be? Is it my office or Madame Rosengarden? There is no one else who knows of my presence here in Paris... or simply a wrong number.'

Assailed by a thousand of doubts, Hathor can't find peace. A little confused, the man enters the hotel's switchboard number.

"Excuse me; I'm calling from room 307, Var Darquen. I think the call to which you connected me has been cut off. Can you please tell me from where it originated?"

"It was a call from Ireland, Monsieur," the receptionist replies, after a pause while she checked. "But it wasn't a registered number... I don't understand. Maybe you left your contact to some Irish acquaintance..."

Hathor is even more upset and answers:

"Thanks, yes, I think it's just as you say. Maybe they will try again, it's nothing urgent. Have a nice day."

With a lump in the pit of his stomach, the man sits on the edge of the bed, his glassy eyes fixed on the wallpaper.

'Behind, further back, beyond the concept of size and space; someone is trying to find out where I am... Well! It will be a game; apparently this person doesn't know that I can move between dimensions. And it certainly wasn't the two young siblings, or their friends. That person is in Ireland, and without a doubt it must be Vamaran!'

Hathor analyses every possible conjecture and his doubt becomes certainty: Lord Warden is the author of all the events that occurred in these 48 hours for sure, and in Hathor's mind begins to take shape the gloomy doubt that Vamaran is plotting against him, at that precise moment.

Chapter 47

Power of Flattery

Madame Rosengarden slowly descends the stairs of the large villa; she becomes vexed, thinking that one of the other young maids could have opened the door. And yet, another ring of the bell strikes her eardrums, making her feel a sense of an insidious rage.

'Damn these young girls, I bet that they are gossiping in the kitchen or in the laundry room.'

"I'm coming!" She screams when finally reaching a few feet from the front door.

'But tell me if these are the times to come and disturb respectful Christians.'

Sunlight was close to reaching the lawn, where weeds have invaded even the large Florentine earthenware jars decorated with the mouths of lions, purple poppies and white lilies. For too long, her master, the lawyer Var Darquen de Aguilar, has overlooked the garden. He stubbornly claimed that the gardeners were ruining the beauty of Nature, and that everything must grow spontaneously, without the interference of the human hand.

This change happened progressively with the altering of his mood. Madame Rosengarden had noticed the obstinacy which had installed itself as a pernicious disease in his habits. It didn't help trying to convince him that carelessness would only end up making this immense garden a sort of jungle in which only wild animals would take refuge. But apparently the man didn't care, in fact, he had clapped his hands like a joyful kid, saying that at least there would be one place in town where one could return to the feeling of purity and love. And the old woman knows in her deepest heart, that her master was right.

She had heard the old stories told by her ancestors, those same stories that would end up becoming legends and then myths. The world in which they live had suffered devastating changes, for the human race but basically for all life form. But what's sad, and despite thousands of years of teaching, is that inherent in man is the habit of *forgetting too fast*!

*** Adulations Vis ***

Always gathered in her thoughts, the housekeeper opens the door and even before the man can open his mouth, the woman accosts him.

"I regret to inform you that the lawyer is not present. If you have something to deliver, you can leave it with me, otherwise you'll have to call in a couple of days! Excuse me, but don't have time…"

The man is standing on the mat, smiling benevolently at her.

"Excuse me, madam. To tell the truth I wouldn't disturb you or your master... but unfortunately my dog has entered your property, and despite having called her several times, she has not returned. It's a small dog, something like this size," and he estimates Elvira's length with both hands.

"She's a coward by nature but sometimes barks beyond belief. You see, I don't want her to enter the villa through some open window, poor thing. I thought it was best to ask permission before taking a look around. My God, if I go back to my wife without the dog, she'll ask for divorce!"

Mrs. Rosengarden looks at the man, holding the dog's leash tightly in his hands, and then moved by a sense of sympathy, she kindly smiles.

"Ah, these dogs. I know something, many years ago my family had a couple, and they continued to run away. It was a real nuisance to go search for them or, worse, to go and get them from the dog catcher. I give you permission to look for her in the garden; perhaps she'll be pleased to chase some rabbit. Have you seen what a mess this garden is? There will be hundreds of rabbits or who knows what other animals; hopefully they didn't eat your little dog... Ohh, I'm sorry... don't worry, you'll find her. Do you need some help? Do you want me to send the boy to look into the bushes? What did you say her name was... the dog's name?"

Giving her his most radiant smile, Commander Fenix squeezes her hand firmly.

"Her name is Elvira, that little monster. But for Heaven's sake, don't send anyone; Elvira is so fearful that if she sees a person that she doesn't know, she would hide so we don't find her! Then she bites... a way to defend herself, you see..."

Completely satisfied with the outcome, Fenix trotted down the villa's stairs. Once in the garden, the man makes his way through all sorts of grass, trying not to end up in some hole or stumble on the ground.

"By golly, I'm lucky I don't suffer from allergies, with all this pollen there is the danger of being put out of action, or worse, end up in the hospital to be given an antihistamine."

Reaching the back of the house, near the wall covered by a thick hedge of jasmine, he called quietly to his co-conspirator.

"Pssst, hey, Sergio! I'm here."

After a few seconds, out of the hedge emerges the amused face of his subordinate.

"Ah ah, Boss what are you doing with that leash? Do you want to use it as handcuffs to immobilize some alleged scoundrel?"

Fenix frowning, with a quick gesture thrusts the leash in his pocket, and trying not to be too bluntly says, "No, I thought it would make the whole story more credible. The housekeeper is alone in the house with the rest of the staff. The lawyer is not at home, and from what I have heard, he will return only in a couple of days. I received permission to patrol the garden... in search of my dog, Elvira!"

He holds a chuckle, while motioning with his left hand to cross the fence.

"We must hurry, the housekeeper has given me permission to look for the dog, but I don't know how much time we have, and I don't want to attract attention."

Sergio's idea was brilliant! Fenix had locked the dog inside his employee's apartment with some succulent biscuits. He hopes she won't make too much noise, with the risk of disturbing the public peace. Gosh, it would be a real mess if the whole thing would be discovered and Fenix absolutely didn't want to jeopardize his and Sergio's career!

"Okay, I'll step in from the back, I'll try to find out from where you can access to the basement. You stay away from the windows to the west and south, please, although, on the ground floor they'll probably have all the blinds closed, but I don't want some maid seeing us. We must try to get inside. If I remember correctly from the images reworked by Valery, you could see a doorway under the tower. Unfortunately, there is apparently no opening visible from the outside, maybe it's some old-fashioned gimmick. There used to be very strange mechanisms used to conceal the openings, which are operated by well-hidden levers."

Sergio shakes his head in denial. "Well, Boss, if there is a way to get in, the safest is to *force* windows. After all, we may try not to do much damage, with a little lever into the right place..."

Fenix smiles at his subordinate. A sense of pride pervades him in realising that his employee is awake and aware that sometimes you have to use unorthodox ways to get a quick response. This time, though not in service, the motive was still that of safeguarding the citizens! If the leaders have decided to *cut it short*, it was certainly to protect some big shot, and he, the honest Commander Fenix, would discover the murderer. The man, in his heart, gloated about having so much courage.

After having repeatedly flayed his fingers in the search of a possible opening mechanism, Sergio lets out a curse.

"Boss, if you had been a man who lived in the nineteenth century, how would you have concealed a release device?"

A little embarrassed, Fenix scratches above his right ear before answering: "well, I would put it in a place clearly visible and certainly not hidden; the obvious things always go unnoticed, today as well as centuries ago!"

Both men take two steps backwards, observing the brick wall. About six feet above the ground, there is one slightly lighter than the others with a bas-relief dark spot.

"Look up there," whispers Sergio, "something is engraved. Chief, you mount on my back, I'll hold you up."

The commander comes over and rises above the arched back of his officer. A bit teetering, he manages to hoist himself and reach for the tile.

"What does it mean?" Sergio asks with a curious and at the same time worried voice.

"It looks like a tool that was used by the geometricians a couple of centuries ago, you know, that thing... I think it was called compass... and below is another geometrical tool. But of course! I've seen it represented on various *Unynetweb* boards, these are things of the Unified Power in Ishtar, I believe."

The commander first tries to remove the tile, with a gesture a bit rushed, but without success. Then, caught by one rabid click, Fenix presses strongly inward. A strange hissing sound could be heard as something at ground level moves from under a mass of brambles and jasmine. Puzzled, Fenix jumps from Sergio's back, he lands badly on the ground, crouching down for a moment. The two men glance around the garden to make sure there are no unwanted spectators, and then they try to free the opening of the door from the tangle of vegetation.

A terrible stench leaves both men without the courage to breathe again for several seconds.

"Holy God, what a stench! Or is it the smell has concentrated over the centuries, or I would be tempted to believe that we are entering a burial vault. Gives me the creeps... Boss, you have seen the images analysed by Valery. Do you think we may enter this way, without even a warrant?" Sergio pauses, obviously repenting that they were both there unofficially.

"Okay, no warrant. This is a patrol of the private type, which has nothing to do with the Experimental Team. Fenix, you go first or I shall first take a look? We're looking for the dog, after all. However, we hope not to find a corpse in an advanced state of decomposition to welcome us, in its own way, to the underground!"

Fenix shakes his head vigorously, the assertion of his officer and now his 'accomplice in business' just made him even more nervous. They were both really digging their own graves, nothing more than decomposed corpses or yellowed bones with the passing of time! The man tries to dispel the morbid visions that leer before his eyes; in the depths of his long career as a police officer, he already had seen that sort of thing and certainly wouldn't let a dead man scare him.

Once they penetrate inside, they maybe take four or five steps from the trapdoor, when suddenly some mechanism concealed in the earth returns to the initial position with a thud. Now, in the complete darkness, both are seized by a feeling of nausea and fear.

"Holy-bloody hell! Sergio, where are you? The hatch... We certainly hit something, some gimmick or other in the floor. Well, these masons were intelligent, if the architect of this house wanted to catch mice, he succeeded, and I would say that he has taken two big ones."

The officer is silent for a moment, and Fenix thinks the worst, to be precise that his subordinate is already dead, possibly hit by some poisoned sting.

"Boss, wait, I have a lighter with me. Yeah, I have the bad habit of smoking... at least this time it'll serve some useful purpose."

After about ten seconds, a slight glow emanates from Sergio's hands, bringing gloomy and shaky shadows to the narrow space. Without wasting time talking, both start to scout around, maybe hoping to find a light switch, or rather, a way out. How could they explain their presence under there to the housekeeper or the servants? They would think about it when needed.

With no small wonder, Fenix lays his hands on something soft about four feet in height.

"Come here with the lighter, Sergio, I found something."

In front of their eyes was flattened shape of a very old table, covered with velvet full of dust and cobwebs.

"Well, it looks like a dining table with a tablecloth for special occasions... but I lost my appetite, believe me."

Fenix knits his eyebrows, perhaps surprised that his companion in misfortune could still find the situation funny and make sarcastic jokes.

"Let's see what is hidden under the velvet..."

Chapter 48

The Voice of Legends

There is still much time before the *Fleadh Nan Mairbh's Celebration* and Gwinn ap Nudd doesn't want to wait for it because he believes he could no longer live without the presence of the young Chrysalis. No matter, then, that the *Great Shield of Sketch* shall be lowered: he's now able to remove the barriers between the worlds and allow the natural *Forces of Chaos* to invade the *Realms of Order*, for the world of the dead to come into contact with the world of the living.

While the young woman looks in the direction of the secular Great Yew, Gwyann ap Nudd appears in Sibéal's living room, passing through the walls in front of all those present.

"Voices from the meadows
Lost in the torpor of Summer
Memories of experienced illusions
Caresses and songs
Samhain

Too many regrets!
In his hands dance
The embrace of the World
And the sleep in the Mists!"

The man affably smiles as his eyes settles like a caress upon Chrisa. But the air is so markedly electrified; they clearly perceive that *the presence* has dominion over the elements!

"I waited for you, down near the banks of the Shannon River. When I sensed your discomfort, I realised that something is happening here..." Looking a little puzzled the King of the Annwn looks curiously first at Fintan and then at Ualtar.

"This wasn't the agreement; I haven't asked you to come here to terrorise these people. I first have to explain everything to my Queen before involving her family, why haven't you done what I asked for?"

Now his eyes are full of anger and severity. Fintan gets up and backs away, as if fearing that the presence endangers his life. Chrisa recovers from the initial amazement and moves near Gwynn ap Nudd.

"I can't... follow you! I think I understand the reason of your presence... and I believe it was you who let me find the *Vibratory Matrix*. But I can't help you in your task, Gwynn. It's true that the deep sorrow for the loss of mom and dad have repeatedly urged me to be reckless, to want to go beyond the projection and then break the *Sacred Mirror*. But this is only related to my fears... and my anger... and too much resentment. I can't involve those whom I love in my anguish and rage... and in any case, I couldn't leave without Joshua."

The woman's eyes fill with tears as her cheeks blushes; sobs are choking her voice in the throat.

"I'm so scared! I have never had the feeling of love before, but I doubt even that you are sincere. You are akin to us *Annwyn*, but at the same time I feel you are so different and distant."

Gwynn approaches her; he takes her in his arms as the silence falls over everyone present. Marius and Sibéal don't want to intrude themselves, they know the young woman has to decide; the old sailor glances at Joshua, whose face was bleached.

"Hey, Chrisa..." Joshua murmurs, his voice shaky and insecure. "I don't understand what's happening... the hocus pocus isn't my favourite, do you remember?"

At this point, the Annwn's King speaks again addressing to those present: "I don't want to hurt you. Although things may seem very strange, I would need a long time to explain every little detail; maybe I can start by telling you that in this earthly world I have taken the name of Vamaran."

*** Fabulae Voces ***

His gaze comes to rest over the leather book with the engraved golden runes.

"And I think you have well met Hathor Var Darquen de Aguilar, if this manuscript is in your possession. I'm sure he'll have warned you about me, right Chrysalis? It is perhaps for this reason that you now feel strong suspicions, and you can't decide what your heart tells you? I might even offer to all of you the chance to enter *The Mists* and to reach the *Tylwyth Teg* people. I'm able to do all that... Marius, Sibéal, are these your names? The *Fairy People* are your own people; you have done the task that was assigned to you in the past. Now you are free to choose... With regards to Hathor, my beloved Chrysalis, I tried to contact him, but then feared that the call could be intercepted and I gave up. He's mentally connected with you, and if you want him here, you just call him at a *subliminal level*. He's located in Paris; we could get things clarified once and for all. I'm aware of Professor Bartók and Hathor's works; I met your father at a conference in the Americas... I couldn't really tell him who I was, I just wanted to know him because I knew that he was the genetic father of... my Queen. Then I went again back to my people, where I regenerated. I used the influence of a person who pulls the strings at the top of the Unified Power, a being vile and despicable, greedy for power that would destroy most of the humans. He aspires to the Eden of the Holy Scriptures, but he isn't a simple fool, unfortunately. The man has acquired enormous power over the Elements, over the Mind, but can be stopped... and that is what I set out to do. Lord Warden, this is his name, may be called the New Era's Lucifer."

Gwynn is visibly upset, he gently detaches himself from the young woman and adds, "what I've discovered only last night is that Hathor had been romantically linked to you, several hundred years ago, Chrysalis... in one of your previous incarnations, in the Middle Ages."

The breath froze in Chrisa's lungs; the young woman feels like a fly caught in a subtle web in the silence. She seemed to be quite shaken, she moves away from Gwynn with certain coldness. Then, thinking hard of Hathor, she evokes him by means of the power of thought, hoping that the presence of an old friend of her father's, who she had so feared, might bring some clarity to the situation, which is becoming increasingly confused and tangled.

Gwynn perceives it, but he only adds in a calm tone of voice, "It's a wise decision, Chrysalis. Only Hathor can explain some details, and perhaps when we both are telling you the same thing, without considering the merits of the choice that you have to make, everything will be clear to those present."

Marius's face relaxes a little, while his cousin remains detached, observing the scene as if it was something that doesn't belong entirely to her. Maybe the old woman had decided to stay there in Ireland just to fulfil the circumstances that were linked to the *Great Legend*... or maybe not. Sibéal actually had crossed *The Mists* as a child, but this was a fact known only to Marius and very few friends with whom they still found themselves with for the celebration of the mystical *Beltane* and *Samhain*. But why wouldn't Sibéal want to express her opinion on everything that was happening? In truth, she now finds herself in the presence of the king of the *Tylwyth Teg*, her sovereign, the maximum power that can bring together both worlds: that of the living and the dead. But it's also certain that the realm beyond *The Mist* isn't only what humans consider the kingdom of the underworld. Everything is tied a double knot to the *Great Legend*!

Energy crackles in the air, like during a storm in which lightning is released with extreme force, generated by colliding currents of air at high altitude.

Chrisa felt in every cell that what is going to happen is beyond her influence; she can't escape, even if she used the *Dream,* but anyhow she doesn't want to leave her brother. She isn't a coward! Joshua looks at her with some respect, perhaps intimidated by the presence of Gwynn, and again his tongue had lost his wit and sarcasm. The young man is perhaps sceptical since he notes that neither Marius nor Sibéal, or even the two druids, speak.

What's at the end of this strange and unusual circumstance? Something that is perpetrated over the centuries: in the 'raison d'être', there always coexist ancestral fears and terror of the unknown. Yet everything is there at hand for those who want to understand, the luminaries, as indeed had been Chrisa's father, saw that in other worlds, in other dimensions, in a sort of metaphysical challenge, there is a collaboration of Energy waving free.

In his Paris hotel room, Hathor appears discouraged. Recurring in his mind was the same questions, the same doubts that at that precise moment are absorbing the mind of his beloved.

Then, clearly, the man perceives that strange pop behind his head. A feeling permeates the stale air full of dust of that hotel room, the *Annwyn* is certain that the young woman is calling him. But there is neither urgency nor threat in the invocation, this is certain, and then the two young people aren't in danger of death.

Hathor feels the rhythm of his heart increasing, growing his blood pressure. After a few minutes, he puts on his jacket, shoes and a silk scarf turned several times around his neck. He can't waste time: he takes the black leather folder, throwing it over his left shoulder and then puts his possessions in a bag and leaves some money on the pillow as a reward for those who would tidy up the room.

He doesn't wait for the lift but goes down the stairs, two steps at a time, wanting to earn every possible second. At the Reception he's received by the employee's smiling face, he pays the bill and takes his leave; he would no longer return to Paris, this is certain.

He strode down the long avenue leading to the Seine, the same path that he had observed from the hotel room where he was until recently.

The coolness inside the immense church takes him a little off guard, and then the strong smell of incense and burnt wax pulls him toward memories now hidden, but always full of charm and seduction. In the side hurdle is a big dog that rummages within, perhaps to spend the night or looking for something to eat. Pigeons flutter everywhere, lurking on the pillars, or between the shards of broken glass neglect by the elapsed time. Through the portal and using the power of the transcendental mind, Hathor projects himself in the dimension of space-time to reach the place where Chrisa is at that time.

Inside the great Irish cottage, Chrisa, Joshua and the rest of the group wait for the summoned person to appear. The only one to perceive the magical event as an abnormal situation is Joshua, for the other magic is something inherent and harmonized in the human soul... everything is quite magic, Life itself is the most appropriate form of Magic!

A very bright blur appears in the left side of the fireplace. Chrisa holds her breath and closes her eyes. How can she accept Hathor's presence after years of fear and hatred stirred in her soul? Had she really incorrectly believed that the murderer of her parents was Hathor? Was she solely guided by misleading prejudices as dictated only by resentment?

Hathor's appearance generates a further bustle among those present. Joshua is growing visibly uncomfortable, he remains on the side-lines, while a myriad of ideas are swaying in his head. Marius and Sibéal welcome the *Annwyn* with a nod, but they remain silent.

The two druids, Ualtar and Fintan, sit on the couch, carefully avoiding meeting Chrisa's stern and angry gaze, the woman is slightly trembling.

"Thank you... for answering my call, Hathor. I think it's the desire of all present here to finally get to the bottom of this story. I'm not Theseus, but although there is no Minotaur, the labyrinth in which I find myself is distressing. I have spent a lifetime trying to figure out the boundary between right and wrong... I pursued dreams, *dreaming* thanks to the faculty that are given to us *Annwyn*, of a better world... and perhaps I only wanted to receive back my dead parents. Yet now, in this moment, when I'm able to choose and finally exit the Projection and the

314

reincarnation linked to Samsara, at this moment, I sway! Should I opt for a choice that I can't do, unable to accept that *a man* is to establish my future? Maybe I realised that everything I have concluded in earlier lives, has led to this new life, beyond my will, although I had consciously chose the family that hosted me."

The girl looks with inquisitive eye the two men in front of her: Gwynn and Hathor. Maybe this is free will? Must she consider what her heart says, or what wisdom suggests?

Chapter 49

Archetypes of Apparent Reality

Lord Warden beats both fists furiously on the top of his desk, inlaid with malachite, lapis lazuli and carnelian. Before him, the background of the attic's window which gives a beautiful view over the Lake Verbano makes him even more aware of his inability to act.

"I don't care about your government's transgressions; they couldn't leave me more indifferent. You're to be considered guilty for losing control and letting things get out of hand! For many years, we together have tried to restore order on the planet Earth. For many years, I have equivocated, trusting the wrong person. I'm certainly not allowing the decisions to be made by the head of the Unified Power or the Experimental Team in Turicum or Ishtar, thinking they pursue the most rational decisions. However, they didn't receive the appropriate consideration from me. Enough! This time I think you should opt for a categorical solution; when Vamaran activates the *Vibratory Matrix*, it will generate such a mess on the planet that self-destruction will be evident and spontaneous. What happened in 2022 is just a fragmentary idea, ridiculous. Respect to you, Sir! Remember to the members of the

Power that there will be no chance of survival, not if it conforms to the parameters dictated by the wisdom of the ancients; well... ashes to ashes. Gentlemen, I take leave!"

With a nervous snap, the Lord disconnects the audio-visual communication and leans back on his big chair, rocking slightly. His party has already ceased to exist in its abstraction of apparent reality.

Lord Warden put his total trust in Vamaran, the rightful King of the Afterlife; he'll know what to do with the hundreds of thousands of souls who'll flood his world like a tsunami. The hounds of hell, the Annwn, will feed on the reminiscences accumulated of those silly lives, or they would have had to train new recruits.

"At last it'll become a world without corruption, without prevarication and insubordination! It'll be the return to Adam and Eve's Eden, and I'll be the promoter of the Armageddon as predicted almost three millennia ago in the Apocalypse of St. John."

The old man let out an intense guffaw which fills the great hall with its fury. His thoughts become the boastful perceptions of a madman! But how many like him, in the past centuries, have marked the history of the planet Earth, coming so close to the annihilation of nations?

*** Per Speciem Veritatis Archetypa ***

The air vibrates, time sits silent, while the rays of the midday sun are like as sharp swords, hungry for vengeance, reflecting on the various metal objects contained in a glass showcase. Dozens of pieces of *Vibratory Matrix* are aligned, equipped with a digital mark on which data of the discovery, location, and the person with whom the object has come in physical contact is recorded. For over one hundred years, the old Lord had gone through every exhibit secretly guarded by the Unified Power. With great patience,

317

he was finally able to go back to specific data that had allowed him to draw a map of the finds, on the basis of the *Hermes' Emerald Table*; all had therefore been retraced as in the stars and planets. The importance of those objects was such that nothing on earth could be equalled! Although Lord Warden was aware that the lawyer Hathor Var Darquen de Aguilar possessed three Matrices, he doesn't feel much disturbed. One day, very soon, these will become his own.

In the darkness, Sergio's voice is a little comforting:

"Boss, look what I've found!"

The dim light, there is a kind of flare, which fragments, and seconds later flickers in the fetid and damp air of the cellar.

Commander Fenix's voice is mollified and a little hopeful.

"And where does that thing comes from? And what kind of devilry is it... it doesn't burn, it looks like a molecular torch of quartz crystals!"

Bringing the light closer to the centre, Sergio first responds with a nod of the head towards the long table.

"It was under the heavy cloth... There is a lot of weird stuff concealed beneath it. I almost scorched something with the lighter's flame..."

Fenix looks very suspicious, he glances at the device with a grim eye, but didn't dare to touch it. Evidently there are several things down there that deserve a particular and thorough examination. His brain begins to project some kind of devices, perhaps extra-terrestrial gadgets, strictly prohibited. But for now his priority is to quickly find an exit, and he doesn't care to find out if the relics are leftovers of a few centuries ago rather than artefacts from some other dimension, stolen in spite of the Unified Power's prohibitions.

"Forget the secrets hidden under the tablecloth, Sergio. Rather, try to find the mechanism that drives the opening to the outside... or look if there is a door that opens on the inside. We have to get out without being seen. That strange little voice that you sometimes feel inside is suggesting that the housekeeper wouldn't tolerate our slipping illegally *inside* the private property! The permission to seek Elvira was limited to the garden, certainly not into the cellars."

Suddenly a strange noise silences them. Without thinking too much, Sergio hides the light device under his shirt, then realises his foolishness: that thing isn't a human artefact! The two men are close to the source of footsteps that comes just from the other side of the wall.

"Psss, I don't think that we are alone down here..." Fenix whispers, "without considering the mice and disgusting insects. If these are rats, they must be enormous, considering the noise they are making."

Sergio at the idea of rodents as big as a dog or worse lets out a mournful sigh.

"I wish I had brought Selene and Solaris with us; they give me a sense of security."

"This time we'll have to do without rat catching *jaglynx*, my dear," Fenix replies, "but perhaps we may be able to find a way out..."

Groping, trying not to make noise, the two men begin to inspect the west wall with their hands. When they hear the voices on the other side, they stop, holding their breaths.

Sergio withdraws the light from under his shirt and directs it towards the part of the wall in front of them.

"Just here... someone is on the other side of the wall." His whisper is barely audible, while the voice on the other side comes clear and sharp. It had a strange accent that distinguished it from the other one which responds with a resolute and arrogant tone.

"Of course! If Var Darquen has gone away, he'll have it well hidden. Maybe there is a safe in the villa... I tell you that I checked everywhere in the library, and also on the first floor using the detector, but there is no trace of the manuscript."

"We can't hold back here much longer," the other voice responds with a mellifluous tone. "I fear that if the staff discover us here, the situation could get complicated. I have already expressed *His* disagreement to use violence, *and He* has been unequivocal. What happened in the lawyer's office in the town centre must not happen again, do I make myself clear?"

The murmur is moving away, until it becomes a muffled tic-tac of something that closes, then there was absolute silence. Regardless, Sergio points the beam of light in the face of his superior.

"Gee, maybe we should ask for help? Now what?"

"Now we uncork a couple of nice bottles, we remove the dust from the table, we set the table and we look around," Fenix huffs.

"Maybe there is also some old cheese or some other product banned by the Unified Power. At this point, I'm waiting for a spectre of some Middle Age' knight..."

The man's voice shudders and becomes a gasp as his whole body stiffens. Sergio continues to illuminate him with the light beam and suddenly he notices the strange behaviour of his superior.

"Hey Commander, is everything okay?"

Chapter 50

Towards Death

Before starting to expose the facts, Hathor stares at the audience with a strange look.

"In my long life, I have never been in a similar situation. Attempting to restore Order to avoid Chaos to fall with his strength soaked in terror."

Hathor observes the seductive Vamaran with envious eyes, a slight tremor of his hand betraying him when he extends it to greet his rival.

The first to notice is Chrisa, who deliberately keeps at a distance with her eyes apparently absent. Inside her an atavistic struggle brings back to her the experiences she had in her previous lives, a ferment of very strong emotions, sometimes destabilizing. But this isn't the first time that this has happened. The young woman eventually learned to manage these emotions, characteristic for an *Annwyn*, and to take from them the specific teaching.

Flashes of visions from the past flicker before her eyes, as events from centuries ago were viewed like videos in slow motion. Here and there resurface the faces of people who were very important to her in her previous lives. But now she can't relate each image to its proper context: the *shell* a Mind needs to get to be reincarnated changes with every new rebirth.

Except Joshua, those present perceive the painful fragmentation that is taking place within Chrisa's consciousness.

Finally, as to remedying the concealed agony, Hathor speaks.

"I have come as requested. But I don't want to reach a hasty choice, please believe me. I'm here in complete good faith and I would like to clarify a couple of shady issues that obviously have, over the years, created against me an unjustified hatred."

Hathor observes Chrisa with a pained look and then he smiles to her.

Sibéal sits on the couch, leaning her head on her left arm. She appears even more diaphanous and her figure exudes an unusual light. After a moment, Marius moves to sit next to her, placing an arm around her shoulders.

Hathor indicates the armchair to Vamaran:

"Sit down, what I'm about to tell you will take some time and I don't think, at this point of the story, that some of you may be in a hurry..."

Then he throws a grimy look at Ualtar and Fintan who, reassured, take their place on the other sofa.

"Do you want to remain standing, Chrysalis?"

The man's gaze is now appealing, and the young woman feels like she is dying inside. Once again, the balance between heart and mind is in big trouble.

"It doesn't matter, Hathor. I prefer to stand... if it doesn't bother you."

The man breathes briefly, and then he goes on to explain the exactly reason for his presence on Earth. Some of those present are stunned, and they listen to the man with great concern.

"There are deeper mysteries than those found and catalogued over the centuries by men: some are found due to chance alone, or revealed by studies taken with perseverance and courage! Much has been faithfully reported in the book by Dr. Bartók by means of alchemical formulas, but not all. I had the great fortune to study at his side, Chrysalis. The book contains the ultimate truth, the reason that binds humanity to this planet, in this specific dimension."

Hathor Var Darquen de Aguilar turns to look straight into Vamaran's eyes.

*** In Cospectum Mortis ***

"*As below, so above*. These were, thousands of years ago, the words of a great philosopher, who, with his research, changed the course of human existence. And it's not surprising then that the realms above and below, or rather the *'higher realms of soul and spirit'* and the *'lower realms of the elementals-fire-air-water-earth'*, are in reality structured in the same way. Hermes revealed to us a key, handed down from generation to generation, always well hidden from the eyes of the infidels. Everything is Vibration, then. Frequencies different from those normally known in this third dimension; when there was the great cataclysm two centuries ago, the *Vibration* of the human's race had been raised within the energy field. The entry in the New Era was long anticipated by *'Channelling'* that had brought further clarification to those people who already were preparing for *quantum mutation*. Some were able to raise their knowledge above the concept of 'good or bad', causing and activating the process of rising of the Human Consciousness. Already since the beginning of acceptance of the *Law of Attraction*, this gradually brought the Humans to attend an intensified frequency..."

The man shakes his hands in front of him, immediately the dust becomes more visible and a pulsating light appears around them.

"Well, this is 'Vibration' tuned with the innate power within each of us. By means of the *Vibratory Matrix,* this vibration might involve levels of awareness even bigger... It could, I'm almost sure, generate real 'passages' between the Spheres and the Dimensions."

Hathor looks in Vamaran's direction, and then he adds in a low voice: "I don't know what you want to achieve, Vamaran, I'm led to believe that Lord Warden is only using you... as he did with me and many other people within the Unified Power."

Vamaran smiles, then folds his hands on his chest before detaching them, a myriad of sparkling particles self-generating between his hands. The light becomes more and more intense, as if the sun with its rays had penetrated through the walls of the room.

"I agree, my dear Hathor. Every word of yours is true as it is true that we are both *Annwyn*... although I'm able to 'control' my Essence. I feel a little ridiculous being here to negotiate... for *her*."

Slowly, the man turns to face Chrisa, while the young woman has become even more hesitant and nervous.

"Indeed, the activation of the *Matrix* means allowing a quantum leap, but what that poor Lord Warden hopes to achieve is the annihilation of all the people who have not yet reached the appropriate vibrational level. And there are many... Warden didn't actually manipulate me; I may say it's quite the opposite. To enter into this dimension, I needed a little help, and I admit that Lord Warden gave it to me. I do have a great power over the realm of *Annwn*, but on this side, outside *Avalon's Mists*, it is completely different. Maybe it's fair that you know who I really am: my name is Gwynn ap Nudd, the rightful King of the Afterlife."

Hathor shudders and for a moment his face becomes vitreous.

"Now I understand..." he responds in an authoritative voice. "Everything is clearer; I should have come to understand by myself!"

Gwynn doesn't respond, remaining silent for a long moment, without taking his eyes away from Chrisa. He then continues, pointing with his head towards Sibéal, Marius and the two young people.

"Why you don't allow them the opportunity to choose, Hathor?" Then, turning to Chrisa, Gwynn followed, "my beloved, you can bring your brother with you, even Marius and Sibéal have completed their task among mortals. Beyond *The Mist* awaits a realm other than this, and I think you'll find it stunningly beautiful. You, too, Hathor Var Darquen de Aguilar is there anything that keeps you here? I'll give you free will to choose..."

Meanwhile, on the continent, in the lakeside town of Ascona, Lord Warden doesn't see that he could become the victim of his own conjectures!

The old aristocratic sips his favourite tea from a cup of fine Chinese porcelain dating from the seventeenth century. Sitting in front of his desk, laboriously inlaid with semi-precious stones, he reflects on the content of the conversation he had with someone of the utmost importance at the top of the Unified Power. Through this influential friendship, cleverly cultivated over time, he was allowed to build his empire over firm foundations.

But what is happening at that moment in Ireland, of course, is not part of his diabolical plan of hegemony and spiritual cleaning.

A more mighty and arcane force is setting new ethical and moral paradigms: Love is putting its conclusive seal and no one can hinder those involved. Once again in the history of mankind, the Woman is playing the key role in the legend of *her Eden*.

Chapter 51

The Randomness doesn't exist

Commander Fenix holds his breath for a moment.

"It can't be... Sergio, where are you? Do you see what I see? Sergio, for God's sake, answer me..."

The man's voice becomes soft, a gasp seasoned with terror and awe while, from behind, his subordinate pulls his jacket.

"Yeeess, he-re... I'm here, Boss, and I assure you that I don't like it at all. What is that thing? What have you touched?"

Both try in vain to hold on to what is at hand, as they are swallowed up from the strange apparition. For a long moment everything becomes dark, and then the particular molecular consistency gives them full power of perception.

Sergio finds himself with his face pressed against the back of the commander, out of breath as if he had been running for a couple of miles without stopping. The smell in the air is a particular mixture of wet wood and earth, the same scent that you smell when you walk in a forest of old trees... Fenix coughs, perhaps to reconcile his voice to the apparent reality of those moments in which, in all honesty, he wonders if he was already dead! Then, feeling the push from behind and the soggy substance under his buttocks, he got up to his feet like a coiled spring; he collides with his head against a rough surface tree feet above.

"But what the heck... damn, where are we now? Maybe it's a trap and we have fallen in... Perhaps. But I can't give a correct description of what happened."

Sergio lets out a groan before trying to get up, first using his stretched arms to better understand the situation in which both were.

"Boss, I think it was something else. We haven't fallen down, but something has sucked or pushed us... somewhere... wait, we can use the flashlight to see!"

Sergio pulled the device he found from his waistband and turns it on. The slight glow spreads around, and after their eyes become accustomed to the new light intensity, both men manage to see details of that place.

"Looks like a basement or closet, rather well ordered. Look over there, there are shelves with stuff on, fully assembled and well ordered."

When they followed the narrow passage for few feet, the two men find themselves in a larger room where countless wooden shelves full of paper documentation are lined up. The smell is due to the moist earth floor, where time had damaged the wooden slats that had been laid directly on the ground.

"It must be a very old archive! I believe it's been several centuries since there has been printed material. And look here, they are marked in alpha-numeric codes, or perhaps they represent dates. Let us see if there is some other light system. Sergio, try to check the walls over there."

Fenix regains his composure and tries to rearrange his thoughts; he does it loudly, perhaps to convince himself that he has everything under control.

"Good. Then we're somewhere else, in effect, but without even having moved a step! Some strange device in the basement of the Var Darquen de Aguilar villa's tower made this happen. Ahhh, I had heard, of course! Now that I think, something like this has been made possible, and allows you to move in this dimension without using the motion. But I thought that is possible only to the *Annwyn*; obviously I'm missing some detail. Sergio did you found something?"

His subordinate mumbles an unintelligible phrase before answering: "I think so..."

Meanwhile a halogen light shines all around, and the reverb is so strong that Fenix for a moment close his eyes.

"All right, now let's find how to get out of here and then let's look at this documentation to find out to who it belongs to."

For twenty minutes the two men are looking for a door or a passage but without success.

"Boss, what if there is a gimmick like the one that allowed us to access the tower from the garden? Remember, behind the hedge, the tile that you had manipulated? Do you remember exactly what it looked like? I think you mentioned the Masons... Perhaps the builders used here the same system."

Trying to stay calm and not be caught by anguish, both men inspect minutely every tile, every stone and even the lime that holds the entire structure.

"It looks like architecture of the nineteenth century, my dear Sergio. It has centuries since lime has been used as a fixative! It means that this building is located in a very old area... Well, I dare to hope that we are still in our beautiful Europe... I've been thinking for a while, but I can't explain in concrete terms what happened earlier, this is a subject studied by quantum physics, well yes sir! Those are the damn things which those at the top of the Unified Power are plotting for... obviously. And who pulls the strings, my dear; those who hold power are also those people who have removed me from my duty. Let us see if this is about something really huge, because otherwise all of this has been nonsense! After all, we were just trying to find out the murderers of the two criminals."

The commander shut up, something flashed in his mind, he had maybe read it somewhere... but it was not a simple coincidence. He loudly cheers out.

"Nothing is left to chance, every situation is closely connected and everything turns out to be like a canvas, woven plot after plot... in fact there is no randomness!"

*** Casus non existit ***

His voice echoed in the room, while Sergio stops pointing the light directly into his superior's eyes before asking: "so what? You want to say that being here now has something to do with the reason why you were removed from your case? Excuse me, Commander, but I'm not very good with this reasoning."

Fenix sighs and rolls his eyes, then he shakes his head and as courteously as possible, he answers the man with a startled face.

"Listen Sergio, I mean that we followed a track lead by the instinct, mine perhaps, or even your own, but this is relative. If our chief in Turicum believed it was necessary that we stop the investigation, it's obviously because this story involves those at the top of the Unified Power, or some other character who apparently has a great influence! But what those idiots haven't realised is that I'm damn stubborn and even consider myself a citizen of unparalleled ethics and honesty... or nearly so."

Fenix has a toothy smile on his lips; he's obviously pleased with his clarifying soliloquy. Sergio, even more confused than before, shrugs his shoulders without replying; clearly his boss knows a lot of things that he doesn't and at that moment, in fact, he's just happy it's like that. He has heard about certain things, but never tried to find out more. He feels a strange feeling of tightness in the belief that a so called *'law of Attraction'* can really end up influencing the existence of a human being. Perhaps it's precisely what Fenix has just explained, however it was, he has to hurry to find a way out.

Thinking about the urgency, Sergio slapped his forehead.

"Wow, but we can breathe, that means that there is air!"

Fenix turns to him and mockingly responds: "wow... that's insight; fortunately you got it to understand!"

Then he breathes a strong sigh and continues: "of course there is air, and it seems to be stale and foul, but at least we can breathe. If there is air, it means it comes from somewhere within a duct or from some fissure that we can't find because we have scoured all four walls from top to bottom, Sergio! I'll bet that when we find the gap, we also find a way to get out of here."

He turns and begins to feel every stone, checking the corners and even using a piece of lime that detached from below. After another twenty minutes and when his fingers already aching, Sergio let himself drop heavily to the ground.

"Enough, I'm tired. My fingers are almost bleeding. I would like to have a look at this archive and who knows; maybe we'll even find a map that will show us how to get out of this place!"

Fenix, who was examining the bottom, sits up on his legs and pulls a strong breath before answering.

"Okay, we will take a break and look at what's in these files. I admit that I'm curious about them, maybe there are secrets related to the Unified Power, who knows, it would be advantageous to have some proof, if we were to be arrested for insubordination!"

Both men, preceded by a beam of light, move to the shelves, which contained cataloguing boxes, coded by Roman numerals and strange letters that look like curious drawings. Fenix studies them for a moment.

"These are runes, I believe, a kind of calligraphy used a few thousand years ago." He motions to another file, "and these are Greek letters."

Fenix pulls out a box covered with dust from the shelf, and in doing so, dislodges tiny particles of dust that start to swirl in the air. Carefully, to avoid things getting out of hand, the commander opens the container, putting to light other files labelled with a lot of names and dates. The files are order forms, filled in by hand, in handwriting very difficult to decipher and in an idiom that was not in the Latin language. More and more astonished, Fenix shakes his head, annoyed by his inability to find an answer to his initial question.

"But what the hell are these? As a rough guess, there are thousands of them... but I don't understand the cataloguing system, and the writing is hermetic... Maybe we should let it go, for now. I'm sure the lawyer Var Darquen de Aguilar will give us the answers to our many questions!"

Suddenly, as happened a few hours earlier in the basement of the villa, before their eyes the wall of stones is dematerialised. The astonished eyes of the two men pass beyond, and finally lay over several stones arranged in a complex two-colour design. Finely chiselled sand in a concentric arabesque motive, is placed over a perimeter of a few square yards; as well a stone basin, is full of water in which grow pink water lilies.

"What a damn thing, Sergio! Now, where the hell are we?"

Chapter 52

The Choice

On top of the hill, the Great Yew shakes vigorously, moved by the fury of the northern wind. Dense clouds cover the sky and suddenly it seems as the sun has turned off.

"It's the force of the elements, which I can manage and govern, in this world as well in the other, I don't want to cause you harm, but I only want to show you my power."

The voice of Gwynn ap Nudd is a sweet whisper, unlikely to be the voice of someone who had power over Nature. Abruptly, in front of the window of the porch, a dark shadow appears. A magnificent deer with majestic antlers bows his head, almost with deference, standing still as the sky opens, spilling on the earth cascades of water with a crash.

"Can you believe what your eyes show you? Will this demonstration affect your choice?"

Gwynn looks at Chrisa with languid and passionate eyes; with difficulty he is able to hold a certain emotion, while with a gesture of his hand he gets rid of the wall that divides the interior of the cottage from the external nature.

Those present find themselves in the rain, or rather, around them the whole landscape has changed and the rain continues to fall heavily, but never hits them. They feel like outsiders, in a kind of unreal but still tangible dimension.

"Here, behind *the Eternal Mists*, beyond the cascades of water, there is Avalon. In your dimension, it exists in myth, craved by those who worshiped our Fathers, who even to this day continue to perpetuate the ancient sacred rites."

The voice of Gwynn ap Nudd, King of the Annwn, press on softly: "look around, you can move with complete freedom... What I offer you is a vision of what you can achieve if you choose to do so, if you want to go beyond the *Projection* that binds you to the material world. Everything is relative, in the everyday of your planet Earth, as indeed in millions of other Spheres, in billions of other dimensions. Everything is negligible, but only related to the reason why you're sitting in this very place as a result of a cosmic law. The law of *cause and effect* produces the impact of life and death and rebirth as long as you don't choose otherwise. For an *Annwyn*, from which I descend, the choice was conditioned by our enormous potential to drive changes in Minds of others. For this we are born, our screening and selecting a *'diviner' genetic Mother*. But there are other secrets hidden in the scenes of your pasts, by mortal men or whatever is your nature. Do you understand, my beloved Chrysalis? You have always pursued your purpose, which is to go beyond the *Projection* and break the *Sacred Mirror*. In setting this goal in your mind, you did nothing more than accentuate the process and from vibration into vibration, the rest of your world is aligned and the facts have happened and still continue to happen..."

Gywnn turns to Hathor. "Hathor Var Darquen de Aguilar. You have collected the *Vibratory Matrix* in the belief that it was the only way to achieve what you desire! On the one hand, Hermes left it to understand, he repeated

335

and transcribed it. But the hermetic reading obviously has many visions, often twisted. The tasks of the Brotherhood came to an end: with my *return* there is now no need to protect the *Codes* and therefore Ualtar and Fintan's duty has ended. If they want to follow the deer over *The Mists*, they are free to do so; their journey was very perilous and long."

The King of the Annwn remains silent for a moment as his eyes fill with the presence of Chrysalis. Hathor is watching him, trying not to show his wrath; he must at all costs achieve superiority of mind and, therefore, accept the obvious challenge of his rival. Hathor is sure that the two youngsters could be safe, after all he would give to both his unconditional protection. Although the deep love he feels for the young woman could play some trick, he's still an *Annwyn* and then he's beyond mere instincts. The girl is the daughter of his former best friend, and the lawyer worships the deep sense of friendship; Hathor knows that the Mind of Chrisa's father should be somewhere. All the studies that they had done together brought him to another vibration's level and it isn't just believable that his opponents could erase his extracorporeal presence. It's something that he hasn't yet externalized to the young woman and it isn't even written in the manuscript he had donated her, but apparently the occasion to discuss this matter with both siblings will arrive soon. This isn't to instil illusions, but rather to explain a part of science that isn't touched, seen as a potential threat by the Unified Power.

Gwynn ap Nudd is wrapped in a strong radiation that pierces from his inside to spread around. He appears as a being of light, as if it was composed of particles of pure energy. He smiles benevolently and his gaze is like a gentle caress on the hearts of those present. Even Hathor feels shaken in his innermost soul, looking down to the ground he asks who, he thinks, is only merely an opponent:

"But, then, what is the meaning of Life? If, after several times in a material body, I could reach the spiritual density to take shape as an *Annwyn*, what's the reason for which I want to pursue the illusion of materiality, when I'm convinced of being able to refrain from the concept of attachment?"

The man appears afflicted; a slight tremor strikes his body, made heavy by the long years. Chrisa is watching him curiously; her eyes now seeing in him what before she didn't want to see. He's a man full of charm, a very wise and learned man who had shared the same passion as her father. She is not afraid of him anymore; all was forgotten, washed like the rain washes away a drawing made with sand, as in the ancient Tibetan mandala. That is an ephemeral design, an ephemeral life.

The man's words are like feathers, blending into the mind of Chrysalis tickling her arcane memories! And the wings of the young woman, clipped from the everyday fears in life, are now flying around in the ether as fragile mementos of her childhood dreams. But Mother is no longer there, among them…

*** Electio ***

The big deer which just stood at the window appears again in front of their eyes. Chrisa approaches him with a hesitant step; she reaches out to caress him. The animal approaches, spontaneously, going to rub his nose against the side of the young woman. Within herself, Chrisa hears a clear voice:

"My little one, you have to follow your spiritual heart! Trust your perception; it never will let you down."

Chrisa feels a strong urge to climb on the back of the deer but her eyes seek those of her brother. Joshua is shocked, realising that the hocus pocus is tangible... he's in

337

it, he's experiencing it first-hand and, worse, he can't do anything to escape it. Dazed, he looks at those present, almost fearing that the strange presence may implode like a supernova, destroying each one of them.

"I understand that this is what I was waiting for." Marius is lightened, his voice is determined and his arm strongly encircles Sibéal. The woman smiles, and then gently caresses his face; white hands that ply the wrinkles of his face proven by the events of life.

"I'm ready, cousin. Chrisa?"

The question remains suspended in the air, while the large animal approached the two beings that belong to the *Tylwyth Teg*. The old woman doesn't wait for an answer and, clinging to the long hair on the deer's neck, she added without looking at the young woman: "you'll know what to do in our absence. We'll prepare your home for when you reach us... goodbye. May love always be in your heart and lead you to us!"

Chrisa feels like she is dying inside. She wants to run to embrace Marius and his cousin... but she respects the separation, she shouldn't feel any attachment, that had been taught to her. Chrisa suddenly felt a strange vibration in the air, something imperceptible at a sensory level because you have to use the brain-wave Theta to identify the origin of the oscillation. Initially, she thinks it's a widespread electromagnetism created by the confluence of energy produced by Gwynn ap Nudd and the other *Annwyn* present. But then the young woman realises that it's something quite different! The language is clear and as Chrisa mentally focuses her attention, she realizes that the entity of the speaker is the *Earth* itself. The language belongs to a very archaic form of transposition of thought. Chrisa feels a sense of apprehension since it's the first time that this is done under so peculiar circumstances.

As a child, her mother had explained that the Great Mother communicated with mortals by means of specific vibrations, sometimes associated with meditative states, a language in its disarming simplicity allowed the Earth to involve those who lived on it eating her gifts. Mom had learned that it was necessary to bring to the Earth great reverence for all that was needed for humans to survive; she gave to it without asking for anything in return except respect. The Nordic rites, deemed as 'pagan' with the prevalence of Christianity, rightly brought the veneration and gratitude to the great Mother... but it had already been centuries; these had been considered mere practices in use by the inner circle of followers.

Unfortunately, all the natural disasters that had occurred over the millennia had been wrongly attributed to the Great Mother as a measure of punishment against the humans. In the end, and this was the lack of wisdom of this inferior breed, humans were always self-punished and destroyed each other. The Earth had only been a witness, although sometimes involved with deep wounds caused by war or natural disasters created by incorrect use of the technology of the 20th Century and onwards.

Her father, more rarely, had marginally explained some small detail about his studies. But the girl was too young to grasp every teaching. Chrisa is now aware that the Life Force is no longer a secret and that in the laboratory the scientists had discovered even too much. In genetics, the progress had been astonishing and disturbing, to decompose and recompose the desired atoms and molecules, generating forms of life chosen, but few were aware of these technological breakthroughs. Evidently the Unified Power has its reasons for not letting information that may upset the theological and philosophical level of the world population be leaked.

Now the vibration became so intense that Chrisa's body feels numb, she looks for her brother, as if to reassure

339

herself with his presence. But first she crosses Hathor's eyes, who smiles sweetly.

"Have no fear, I feel it too, *she's* transferring us messages that we'll have to decode, Chrysalis."

Then he turns to Gwynn ap Nudd, the smile disappeared from his face, that now looks very old.

"Well, I think you perceive *Her Voice*, that of the Great Mother, you can then decide whether to accompany Marius and Sibéal or if..." For a moment, a strange light flashes in Hathor's eyes before he continuing, "or if you want to stay on this side of the *Mists* to contend with *her*!"

With a steady hand, Hathor indicates Chrisa, who appears surrounded by a bright light, while the vibration of the body of the young *Annwyn* is in perfect harmony with that of the Great Mother. Gwynn accepts the challenge, pursing his lips slightly, two tiny dimples outlined on the sides of the mouth giving him a touch of childish bliss.

He is all smiles: the eyes have wised up just like a baby caught stealing cookies in the kitchen, only the full brown two pieces damask suit make him look like an elegant and damn sexy gentleman.

Stroking a lock of black hair, the large ring embedded with the dark stone casts a sinister glow. Gwynn waits a moment that felt like an eternity before answering defiantly.

"Of course, my dear. She is the *'price of the tribute'* and I'm sure it will be an interesting battle, from every point of view. I love her, in an absolute manner, as only the King of Annwn can do; there is nothing that can wreck what was written on pillars of stone, even before her arrival on this planet. No, believe me, Hathor Var Darquen de Aguilar... only I own the key to *her Soul*!"

Gwynn ap Nudd approaches Chrisa, with a sweeping gesture with both hands, he raised the light emanating from the astral field of the young woman; Chrisa notices the interference and slowly turns her gaze to sink deep into Gwynn's eyes. He approaches her until his lips are almost touching her face; the young woman perceives the inebriating and destabilising fragrance, while something invisible begins to tighten her stomach.

She remembers the passionate and provocative kiss of the night before, she remembers the impression of vanishing into darkness, transported across dimensions and an immense desire clings to her flesh. With flushed face and dry mouth, as if it were a magic spell, she's waiting for the man to kiss her, she closes her eyes.

Chapter 53

Dimension of the Living and the Dead

The officer, a little mentally lost because of the sequence of events, remains silent while he looks around in shock.

"Boss, perhaps we have entered a magnetic field where the projection is different from the concept of the mind. I have heard of such things when I was in Turicum for a training course with Selene and Solaris. It's a kind of an apparent reality, how to explain..."

"Yes, I understand," Fenix interrupts him angrily. "But it's the first time that *I'm in it*: it is one thing to be told and another to live it. So we may believe that in the Var Darquen de Aguilar's villa are devices so sophisticated that they allow the movement of the matter apparently at different levels of visual and physical perception? But what then produces the vision?"

A little more agitated than before, Fenix kneels to touch the sand and stones with both hands. When the man gets up he realises that an area of the visual field to the right is slightly blurred. With a firm step, but not without dragging along his subordinate, the man reaches that point in a couple of strides.

Suddenly a voice with very gentle and cheerful tone catches them by surprise.

"Welcome, I hope you have a search warrant, Commander Fenix! Otherwise, this would be considered a burglary..." The lawyer smiles, and extends his hand to Fenix. "What circumstance leads you to my private garden? Let me guess, you followed your dog so far and then 'puff' the animal has vanished into thin air?"

Hathor Var Darquen de Aguilar's face gets serious, but the molecules around him stir and his aura vibrates and expands.

"Your private garden? I'm sorry, lawyer... obviously there're several things that should be clarified. Let me explain," Fenix shakes the man's hand, a little hesitantly, "I'm not here as an officer of the Experimental Team. I may have poked around a bit too much... but where are we, exactly?"

The lawyer blurts out a laugh that makes both men uncomfortable.

"We're in my studio in the centre of Ascona! But lo and behold! And having poked around more than you should have in the Unified Power's affairs, did you find anything better than putting your nose in my businesses? I'm listening to you, Commander Fenix, and I hope that your story is true and detailed; I hate liars... and don't tell me that you were blindfolded and lead into the basement of my house!"

The man turns, showing the way to the two poor souls who increasingly felt the weight of the situation as a rock above the shoulders. They entered the office on the ground floor, the private one usually used only by the lawyer, and the three sit around a round mahogany table, with a helical section of the planet earth, before the catastrophe of 2022 built into the table's surface. The light is soft, a bit muffled by the heavy curtains that prevent sunlight from getting inside the room; large bunches of cut flowers are well placed in the corners, lying in huge crystal vases. The scent wafting in the air reminds Fenix of his youth, when he used to have lunch on Sundays in the English garden of his parents' house, where a myriad of flowering plants and fruits grew.

The music lingers in the air: a perfect combination with the soft scent of the cut flowers. Fenix blurts out an observation in a low voice: "it is certainly a very old song..."

Then he thinks that everything is too perfect! Hathor smiles, a delighted and pleased expression is on his face, however, he looks tired.

"Seventeenth Century. Bach... a great composer, my favourite, in all honesty... These are the Cello Suites from one to six... It's the Prelude of each of them that defines the character, the fifth is the most stormy and dark and it's the one I love the most..."

Then the man darkens again, contemplating the two humans just rescued from the *Space-Time trap*. The ancestral memory leads him to a special occasion where he had heard the Suites at a concert with the Lamoureux Orchestra in Paris. It was December 17th, 1899, and the solo cellist was Pau Casals... the same man who had for years studied the Suites in a particular and absolute manner, describing every detail.

The memory affects him, and for a fraction of a second, he felt his heart rhythms increase. How many lives ago was that? What was the name of his wife? The same incarnation that is now called Chrysalis?

"Can I get you something to drink?" Hathor says suddenly, shaking himself from his reverie. "Would you like some water? You appear rather shaken by your adventures."

After a few minutes, Hathor returned with a jug filled with water and ice; the two poor wretches drank with great pleasure, restoring their vital functions in a short time.

Fenix and Sergio confess in detail everything that happened since the lie they told to the governess about the disappearance of Elvira in the house next to the lake.

After a long moment of silence, during which the lawyer observes both men with severity, he pours water into a third glass, drinking a sip before speaking.

"What you reported is flawless; I think you were entirely sincere. If your officer followed you into this, dear Commander Fenix, he's risking a lot. If Turicum were aware of these facts, both of you are in trouble just above the neck! You risk being eliminated... but in all honesty... Fenix you said that you did it to protect those two, Joshua and his sister. Why? Why jeopardize your lives for a cause that doesn't directly involve you?"

The commander shook his head; he doesn't even know why, maybe just for moral and ethical reasons. Perhaps because in his heart, he's tired of serving the oppressors, perhaps because he doesn't have total confidence in the Unified Power, especially after what happened just the night before?

Hathor Var Darquen de Aguilar sighs, and thinks of Chrisa, who has already left Ireland accompanied by her brother and Martino. The object that could change the events and the future of humanity, the *Vibratory Matrix*, was wisely hidden. Chrisa, as sensible woman, has been able to grasp the message that her father had left behind. In doing so, the Unified Power's astrophysics would have another big headache! The lawyer doesn't know what to say, and considers whether perhaps it's best to keep everything secret and let events evolve on their own. For now, he just wants to discover how much the Experimental Team knew, and if it was wise for the two siblings to return to Ascona... and remain under his protection.

Suddenly the lawyer thinks of the old Lord. He doesn't believe that Lord Warden, after the setback received by Chrisa, would soon succeed to implement his strategies, while remaining the greatest danger at that precise moment. For too long, the power in the hands of that being, blinded by the thirst for hegemony, has been overlooked. And to think that he had thought himself as a friend! Even those who hold higher places in the Unified Power must certainly fear the Lord.

"I'll be honest with you," Hathor sighs, standing, "up to the end. But this is not the right time... and I find it hard to just give you some detail that will explain everything. You need to trust me and let events take their course! For me too, the lives of the two youngsters are important... I owe it to their father! He was a dear friend, a fellow researcher... As you have understood rightly, in my house there is a generator that allows for dimensional shifts: a device that connects matter in *space-time* that anyone can use. The displacement, however, is limited to a few hundred feet, in fact. There are other, much more ingenious, portals that allow the teleportation to any other place on the planet Earth... and beyond..."

Sergio looks wide-eyed at the lawyer while Fenix starts playing with Elvira's leash.

"Look lawyer," Fenix dares to ask, "mired as we are in this awkward situation, I just wonder what exactly is going on. I don't know what your involvement is; I admit that it's no accident that we are 'interested' in your villa and property. Following the double murder of... yesterday... or is it already the day before yesterday? Obviously the facts are overlapping. Therefore it is possible that the notes we made on your property before I was dismissed are already in the hands of Turicum. Honestly, I tell you that I suspected that the siblings were kidnapped and maybe hidden on your properties. I realise that I acted rashly, driven by emotions at seeing the images dating from the murder of their parents…"

Fenix puts his head in his hands and for a moment was silent, as if to convey his real anguish. Then, perhaps awakened by the fragrance of flowers and memories, he continues his soliloquy.

"I have reason to believe that you know where Chrisa and Joshua are because you didn't show any reaction when I mentioned their possible involvement. I just want to know if they are alright, and that you'll take care about them, so they don't have to fear anything."

*** Viventium et Mortuorum Sphaerae ***

Hathor smiles at him, friendly, in his heart thinking that he would soon see Chrisa again; the orders given to Martino were clear; they must wait for night to fall before landing in the small airfield in Ascona before sunrise. He wonders if the Experimental Team would question the two young people to find out where they had been and why the old Marius hadn't returned with them. He doesn't know how to reveal that other part of the story to the commander, perhaps it's wise to wait and evaluate what Lord Warden would do first, now he knows that Gwynn Ap Nudd is an opponent? Scary stuff, indeed, it would have ended up being a bad story for all of them… for the entire planet!

"Fenix, don't worry about Chrysalis and Joshua, they're fine. Unfortunately, their old Irish friend died… a sudden heart attack, but he died in peace. His remains lie where he was born: in Ireland, Clonemacnoise, to be exact." The face of the lawyer becomes serious as he continues. "All will return nearly to normal. The murder case was closed, unsolved, like so many others. I don't think that those at the top will give you a hard time; maybe they will put you in retirement, so you can take your wife's dog on more walks!"

The lawyer barely stifles a laugh, nodding towards the leash that hangs in the hands of the man, apparently humiliated.

"Your subordinate has nothing to fear, after all you've gone for a ride and nothing more, the story ends here, and nothing will be revealed from my part. I only ask you that you keep your visit to the Archives secret... In due time, those documents will serve to restore order, but the time is not yet ripe. I can recommend a good reading?"

Hathor Var Darquen de Aguilar rises and reaches a shelf and extract a book, not very old but quite dusty.

"Here it says something more about your... uhhh... search. It's an old dissertation, written with Professor Bartók thirty years ago. It will bring some clarity and information about the *Annwyn*... but the Unified Power has seen fit to censor and prohibit its disclosure. Many centuries ago, the great philosopher called Seneca said: *Navigant et quidam labores peregrinationis longissimae a wage perputiuntur cognoscendi aliquid abditum remotumque...* Or, some people navigate and endure the hardships of a long journey only for the reward of knowing something hidden and remote. But in wanting to be spectators, we forget to be mainly actors! Take care of it, and keep it hidden, Commander Fenix! We will see each other very soon, I think. Gentlemen: I will accompany you to the exit, if would please follow me..."